A WORLD ON THE VERGE OF RUIN

LIN SHAW

Copyright © 2024 LIN SHAW

All rights reserved.

ISBN:

TO K, WHO WILL EVENTUALLY GROW
INTO HIS ADULTHOOD.

CONTENTS

	Preface	i
	Prologue	Pg 1
1	New Year	Pg 7
2	Dream	Pg 21
3	Ring	Pg 29
4	Remembrance	Pg 38
5	Visitors	Pg 51
6	Lady of Oblivion	Pg 61
7	Mysteries	Pg 70
8	Truth	Pg 82
9	Souvenir	Pg 92
10	Hometown	Pg 99
11	La Retrouvaille	Pg 107
12	Avalon	Pg 115
13	Priestess	Pg 122
14	Mia	Pg 130
15	Trap	Pg 137

16	Castle	Pg 146
17	Doctor	Pg 154
18	Foundation	Pg 161
19	Confession	Pg 169
	Epilogue	Pg 176
	Postscript	Pg 191

PREFACE

In 2016, K, who was not yet two years old, saw an inflatable dragon in the Children's Discovery Museum of San Jose. Most of the time, it lay limp inside a plastic castle. However, when a curious and patient child started fiddling with the switches nearby, the dragon would unexpectedly inflate, accompanied by a loud marching tune, and wobble out of the castle. The first time K witnessed this scene, it left him stunned. In that moment, I couldn't help but feel an impulse to write a story—a grand tale as if crafted by Tolkien.

I imagined the protagonist, now a starship commander, leading a human fleet beyond the solar system. Suddenly, he recalls the distant afternoon when his father first took him to see the inflatable dragon. It felt natural at that time. The radiant glow of the bygone era had not yet faded. People were discussing artificial intelligence in its early stages, transcending borders and stances. The Falcon Heavy's near-perfect launch could still awe humanity, and even struggling rock singers began humming "Interstellar Traveling." In such an atmosphere, one couldn't help but feel thrilled, thinking that in the not-so-distant future, technological and cultural progress would unite humanity, casting aside differences, and proudly bidding farewell to the old era—a theme essential for an epic story.

When I finally started writing, it was already 2019. After looking around, I realized the world had already undergone a radical transformation: Confrontation and hostility were on the rise, criticism and intimidation dominated the media, major military parades were underway, and social media was ablaze with excitement. Under the trending topic of "DF missiles," the alarming phrase "nuclear bombing" appeared, turning nationwide diplomacy into a norm. People lost their enthusiasm for discussing scientific details and instead immersed themselves in searching for what kind of national spirit lay beyond those details. Even old relics of the past like mobile phones could trigger a massive debate, culminating in a destructive onslaught.

Later, with the once-in-a-century pandemic outbreak, the plot took unexpected turns. Scientific issues such as viruses, drugs, and vaccines became entangled in nauseating political struggles. The public's anti-intellectual behavior, driven by populism, was despair-inducing, something people didn't want to face and dared not speak about. So, how can you make your protagonist proudly bid farewell to the old era amid applause and songs? Perhaps you would lean towards believing that this old era will be the best and the last, even if you sincerely hope that it's just your own illusion.

Lin Shaw
December   2020

PROLOGUE

"Oh, dear, what should I do? Ah... There must be a way..."

From early morning until now, Anya's heart-wrenching cries in the hut hadn't stopped. Each sob felt like a spear piercing through Um's heart, causing unbearable pain. Several times, he almost couldn't resist rushing into the hut, kneeling before Anya, and using a sharp knife to cut open his chest, letting the fresh blood slowly flow. He wanted to swear like a warrior in front of her, pledging that he, Um, the incredibly brave son of a highly recognized leader among the Dogon people, would bring Nina – Anya's beloved daughter and Um's future wife – back to her unharmed, come hell or high water.

"Oh, my dear, how could such a thing happen if Aci were still alive? How could the lion-like Aci fathered a son like a gazelle..."

Upon hearing this, Um's body trembled involuntarily, and the thought of entering immediately vanished. He turned around, sprinted, and in the blink of an eye, disappeared into the vast and endless jungle.

There, he dashed through the thick vegetation like a headless fly. After exhausting his strength, he finally stopped under an old tree, squatted down, and cried loudly.

Um, the coward.

Since his father's death, that's what the villagers called him. He never argued; every time he heard it, he just blushed and ran into the woods, escaping to a place where not even a trace of human sound could be heard, just like today.

The shade of the trees overhead shielded him from the scorching sun, and a faint floral scent wafted through the air. A few butterflies fluttered by, bringing a sense of coolness. Um finally calmed down, wiped away his tears, and breathed heavily as the unforgettable scene replayed in his memory:

"Gah gah—Gah, gah gah—Gah—"

This was the signal from the riverbank. Um's father and the most skilled hunters in the tribe were concealed along the shore, waiting for that thing to approach. The prearranged signal meant that the creature had sensed something and deviated from the planned route. The traps needed to be relocated.

Um, responsible for setting the traps, had practiced with his father more than ten times. But this time, it was the real deal. Several rows of sharp bone knives were already set and buried beneath the sand.

"Gah gah—Gah, gah, gah—Gah."

Um's father and the others signaled again, urging Um. Reluctantly, Um pulled out all the bone knives tied together with ropes, and after the struggle, he was drenched in sweat, unable to open his eyes. Wiping the sweat off his face, he cautiously peeked towards the riverbank and saw his father in the woods making a gesture. He dragged the bone knives in the direction his father indicated.

"Thump thump—Thump thump—Thump thump."

Another sound came from the riverbank, indicating, "yes, this is the right place." Um collected the bone knives and began to remake the traps. Halfway through, an urgent sound came from the shore: "Goo goo, goo goo, goo goo…"

Danger! Danger!

He was startled, stood up, glanced in that direction, and saw the enormous creature. Oh my! Since he was fifteen, he had never seen such a huge crocodile. Its body was as long as a python's, more robust than a hippopotamus, and it exuded a lion-like ferocity. Clearly, it was the monstrous beast guarding the gates of hell from his mother's stories!

"Goo goo goo goo goo…"

His father and the others were getting anxious, shouting

desperately.

At this critical moment, Um found himself frozen in place, the strength in his limbs disappearing inexplicably. His hands and feet were numb, and he couldn't even hold onto the bone knives.

He was terrified and began to scream towards the riverbank with all his strength.

"Dad... Dad..."

Suddenly, the giant crocodile sensed the commotion. It stopped, crouched down, and then rapidly accelerated, charging towards Um.

"Dad... Save me! Dad... Help me!"

"Run! Run! Run fast!"

The hidden hunters along the bank all stood up, shouting at him. However, Um stood there like he had lost his mind, continuously calling for his father.

The creature was just a few steps away! The bloodstains on its uneven giant teeth were clearly visible. Just as Um thought he was about to end up in its jaws, the crocodile abruptly halted and began to laboriously turn its massive body. It was only then that Um noticed a familiar figure agilely leaping behind the creature—his father. He swiftly thrust a spear at the crocodile from different directions, but the spear made of animal bones couldn't penetrate its thick skin. Instead, the crocodile got infuriated, now turning its attention to Um's father.

"Um, run! Can you hear me?"

Um's father asked calmly, his resolute expression jolting Um back to reality. Finally, Um pulled up his legs and fled.

"Um cannot be the chief; his cowardice killed his father. Allowing him to be the chief would bring punishment from the Great Star for the entire village!" Declared Nacza, the priest in the village.

As a result, the Aci Family lost its eligibility for the chieftaincy, and Nacza took control of the village's affairs, making decisions for both minor and major matters.

"Would you marry a coward?" On the riverbank, Um tossed pebbles into the water, watching Nina washing her long hair by the river, his unease evident.

Nina didn't answer. She casually twisted her wet hair and walked lightly to Um. She kissed his cheek, giggled, and ran away.

No one in the village was unaware of Nina's beauty. Her dark skin radiated a captivating glow, and her long eyelashes fluttered like butterflies in the forest. Her smile revealed impeccably white and orderly teeth, unseen among the villagers. Women would gossip, and men would be entranced.

"What a beautiful flower, gnawed by a timid rat. What a shame!" People would say privately, but there was nothing anyone could do. The marriage was arranged by Aci and Anya. However inadequate his son might be, Aci's prestige among the people wouldn't waver even a bit.

People recalled the days of devastating floods, and it was Aci who led everyone, crossing mountains, battling giant pythons, and hunting crocodiles. In the end, they discovered this peaceful valley along the Nile, where the village now stood.

But Priest Nacza persistently visited Anya, urging her to marry her daughter to his unmarried younger son. Anya was extremely unwilling, each time using Aci's name to turn him away. In her eyes, Um, despite his shortcomings, was a smart and robust young man, far superior to Nacza's son—a waste, in his twenties and still soiling himself.

So, Um felt that as long as Nina kept a soft spot for him, he had no reason to worry. Once he turned sixteen next year, he would have every right to bring Nina to his home.

However, fate took an unexpected turn. Nacza's younger son suddenly died.

"Oh Mother—Supreme Creator, give me a revelation!" Heartbroken, Priest Nacza set up an altar in his courtyard, crying out to the sky until dawn.

"A great disaster is upon us! My son is just the first—he sacrificed himself to warn us!" he announced the next day, after gathering all the villagers.

"The Mother is furious, and the gods of the Great Star are about to descend upon the Earth. They will suck blood and devour flesh, leaving no one alive!" Nacza continued.

Whispers and murmurs spread among the crowd.

"But is there a way to be saved?" someone asked in a hushed tone.

"My son... He sacrificed himself in exchange for the lives of everyone!" Nacza choked up, kneeling on the ground.

"Spread the message of the Mother. The tribe must offer its virgins as sacrifices. The most exceptional flower—"

Anya's heart tightened among the crowd.

"Anya—" Nacza suddenly stood up, his sharp gaze fixed on Anya.

"Last night, I heard the Mother's revelation…" His tone gradually became strange, unclear, but rhythmically repeating the same phrase, "the gods of the Great Star want Nina, sacrifice her! The gods of the Great Star want Nina, sacrifice her! The gods of the Great Star want Nina, sacrifice her!"

"Sacrifice her! Sacrifice her! Sacrifice her…" the crowd echoed as if under a spell. "Sacrifice her! Sacrifice her! Sacrifice her…"

Even now, that horrifying sound occasionally echoed in Um's ears, making him breathe rapidly, large drops of sweat beading on his forehead. He sighed, trembling as he stood up, aimlessly wandering through the woods. After some time, he found himself in front of a yard surrounded by vine fences.

Isn't this Priest Nacza's dwelling?

In an instant, he seemed to see Nina bound, and he heard her moans of torture. Not knowing where the courage came from, he tiptoed to the vine fence, using one hand to create a gap and gripping the bone knife he had carefully prepared in the morning—the relic of his father, crafted from crocodile teeth, the sharpest weapon anyone in the village had seen.

Through the gap, Um saw three thatched huts in the yard. The largest one was the residence of Nacza's family, while the other two were used for storing tools and hunting equipment. One hut had Nacza's robust eldest son guarding the entrance. Without guessing, Um knew that Nina must be locked inside.

It was already noon, and Nacza's oldest son squatted there, seemingly dozing off.

Um couldn't resist contemplating: "Could it be that the Mother was giving him a chance at redemption?" The expression of Um's father before his death flashed in front of Um's eyes. He suddenly felt a feverish sensation all over his body, and strength surged into his limbs. Summoning courage, Um slipped into the yard, approached the oldest son who was napping, reached the big man's side, drew out the bone knife, pressed it against the big man's neck, and with all his strength, made a swift cut. Blood spurted everywhere. This big man breathed his last without uttering a word.

Um wiped the blood splatter from his face, kicked open the wooden door, and yelled, "Nina!"

The scene before his eyes was unbearable. Nina lay naked on the ground, her hands and feet bound, unable to move. Her mouth was stuffed with animal hide, only allowing her to emit low groans. A short figure pressed on top of her, moving undulatingly.

Rage ignited within Um, as if his internal organs were about to be burned. He rushed forward in a single stride, grabbed the short man, and began stabbing him relentlessly in the chest with the knife. The man immediately lost consciousness, his head hanging down, revealing an increasingly grotesque face—It was Priest Nacza.

Nina tightly closed her lips, tears streaming down, refusing to utter a word. Um lifted her in his arms, unsteadily walking into the yard.

"Would you still marry a coward?"
"No!" Nina stared at him, responding firmly.

Just then, in broad daylight, a bright star suddenly flashed in the sky. The light rapidly expanded, quickly forming into a radiant moon, but it continued to slowly brighten and enlarge. In a moment, it almost seemed to engulf the entire sky, making the blazing sun gradually pale in comparison.

"The gods of the Great Star want Nina, sacrifice her! The gods of the Great Star want Nina, sacrifice her! The gods of the Great Star want Nina, sacrifice her!"

As the celestial display unfolded, whispers began echoing from all directions. Strange glimmers flickered before Um's eyes. He felt a wave of dizziness, swayed for a moment, and collapsed on the ground, never to stand again.

1. NEW YEAR

In the wintry December of 2058, the great Himalaya Spaceship shattered the tranquil routine of the spaceport with its unexpected return, following its mysterious departure months ago, just as the world prepared to welcome the New Year.

Ordinarily, the spaceport only handled dozens of missions a year, all meticulously planned. However, the abnormal operations of Himalaya cast a shadow of uncertainty, disrupting the carefully orchestrated rhythm. The whispers of speculation echoed through the corridors.

Rumors ignited like wildfire, spreading tales of clandestine boardings and shadowy figures lurking in the spaceship's gangways. Some swore they glimpsed armed militants with eyes as steely as the void of space, while others whispered of technical malfunctions and covert experiments gone awry. With each passing moment, the truth seemed to slip further from grasp, obscured by a fog of uncertainty and fear.

The tension in the air was palpable, a silent warning against prying too deeply into matters best left untouched. Even the bravest souls tread carefully, mindful of the consequences of probing too deeply into the mysteries surrounding the Himalaya Spaceship. For in a world governed by secrecy and uncertainty, curiosity could be a dangerous game indeed.

As the passengers emerged from their enforced quarantine, whispers swirled anew, carried on the icy breeze of anticipation. The official press release didn't offer much solace, its terse words doing little to quell the rising tide of speculation. "Yiming Lee, the Foundation's Commander-in-Chief, compelled by health issues, necessitates administrative leave and returns to Earth aboard the Himalaya Spaceship, rendering him unable to fulfill his duties." It was a statement that raised more questions than it answered, leaving the reality hidden behind a veil of half-truths and evasions.

Fortunately, it was New Year's Eve, a time when the airwaves buzzed with tales of triumph and promises amidst the uproar of celebrations, encapsulating the achievements of yet another remarkable year. In the expansive sea of information, the brief announcement regarding the Himalaya Spaceship and the Foundation would only make a fleeting appearance, lost in the overwhelming flood of uplifting stories, insufficient to cause widespread concern. Yet, no one would have expected such an inconspicuous piece of story would have been pushed to the top of Temur's feeds.

It was an early morning, and Temur, a skinny teenage boy with disheveled hair covering his head, lay curled up on a wooden bed in the basement. The cold tendrils of dawn seeped in from the road surface, dissuading him from rising. Several faint chimes prompted him to reach out for his electric card beside the pillow. With a flick of his index finger, the video of the Himalaya Spaceship docking to the spaceport began to play. By the time he attempted to sit up for a closer look, the camera had already switched to the scene of the crew disembarking from the landing capsule. It was then that he noticed a middle-aged man in the center, appearing exhausted and spiritless, surrounded by others and escorted into a flying car. The car spread its wings, lifted off, hovered for a moment, and soon vanished into the gloomy sky.

Temur had long grown accustomed to these bizarre stories. The intricate algorithms behind them remained beyond his comprehension, yet he couldn't shake the feeling that they were glimpse of omens, bestowed upon him by an unknown force. This belief stemmed from a peculiar connection he always found between the cryptic messages and his own experiences, regardless of what they exactly were. Here the *Foundation* he just heard from the news might be such a thing. To many, it was just another sterile term woven into the fabric of propaganda films, but to Temur, it resonated with a past he would rather forget.

Back to the time before he escaped Abandoned Harbor, whispers about the *Foundation* were pervasive. People there spoke of it as a promised land for all, as long as you were fortunate enough to secure passage. Yet Temur soon realized it was all a charade. Otherwise, why would anyone need to flee? Upon arriving in his current reality, he discovered people here had never heard about such a thing at all. The word *Foundation* echoed only in fleeting news fragments, and it became a hollow term devoid of substance, failing to trigger even a bit of the imagination promised by those tales he once believed.

Temur's mind drifted into a momentary haze, the worn image of the middle-aged man from the video still imprinted on his thoughts. However, the urgency of the present quickly snapped him back to reality. There was a more pressing matter at hand. Stretching his limbs to shake off the lingering fog of contemplation, he dressed himself and secured the electronic card in his pocket.

Throughout most of the day, Temur cloaked himself in an aged army-green raincoat, silently biding his time on a nondescript street corner in the Second District. Across the way, rows of condominiums fortified with high-security measures loomed, housing government officials and corporation elites from the adjacent Central Government District. As noon approached, a subtle hint of panic crept into Temur's gaze. The success of his meticulously crafted plan hinged on finding a suitable target, and failure loomed ominously.

"Godam it! " His disquiet mingled with a muttered lament about the capricious weather. In recent months, the sky had maintained crystal clarity, but as the year drew to a close, an unexpected shroud of clouds and rain enveloped the city. The inclement weather concealed the ebb and flow of pedestrians, adding a layer of complexity to Temur's task. Frustration gnawed at him, and Rat's counsel to relocate to the Eighth or Ninth District seemed increasingly sensible. With each passing moment, he questioned the wisdom of persisting in the Second District. Had he followed Rat's suggestion, success might have already been within his grasp. Those were civilian areas, yet opportunities abounded, and the spoils, perhaps not extraordinary, could still have accumulated to secure the cherished gift for his sister.

What Temur wanted to gift her was a handgun, which he believed would be a shield against the dangers that lurked on her daily commute.

At that moment, a lone figure caught Temur's attention: a man of medium stature standing alone on a street corner. He was dragging two suitcases, without a raincoat or umbrella, and was stiffly gazing up at the sky.

Temur scrutinized the scene, quickly realizing that this was the same man from the morning news.

"That's him!"

Excitement surged through Temur as he believed this was the hint he had received. Rubbing his hands together, he hastened forward, calling out, "Sir! Sir!"

When the man heard Temur's shout, he wiped rain from his face and turned toward Temur, eyes filled with wariness.

"Sir, you're back from the space station, aren't you? I saw you on the news this morning."

The man looked puzzled. He pushed his suitcase behind him, attempting to adjust his tone. "You... Do we know each other?

"No, no, we don't. Have you been enjoying the rain?" Temur redirected the conversation with a grin.

"Lovely rain, isn't it?" The man seemed to appreciate the change in topic, responding with a touch of excitement.

Temur seized the opportunity, almost blurting out, "it's my dream to be an astronaut. I never imagined I would see you in person today—a real astronaut. Space travel must be an incredible experience..."

The man immediately became alert and questioned sharply. "Where are you from, and what do you want?"

"No, no, it's not like that. I'm just a space enthusiast, dreaming of boarding a big starship one day—Don't mistake me for a spy seeking secrets, and I won't pry. Promise!" Temur defended himself with an innocent smile, though he felt a bit anxious. After a brief pause, he tentatively continued, "would it be okay to take a selfie with you?"

Observing the man's silence, Temur hastily added, "not now, of course. It's still raining. How about I help you move your things first, and then we can take a picture?"

The man hesitated for a moment, and Temur thought he had

secured an agreement. Without wasting time, Temur picked up a sizable box and stood obediently behind the man. The youthful sincerity on his face, an emotion difficult to conceal, seemed to play a role. The man finally nodded, and the two walked side by side, covering several hundred feet to the apartment entrance.

"Authentication in progress!" The mechanical voice inside the door said, "Yiming Lee—Verified. Welcome back home, Mr. Lee. Who is the other one?"

"I'm a friend of Mr. Lee!" Temur interjected.

Lee smiled helplessly. "He is with me."

The warning light turned green, and the door opened. Temur diligently dragged the large box, following Lee into the main gate.

After getting into his home, Lee asked, "okay, ready for your selfie?"

"Yes, yes." Temur scratched his head in embarrassment, retrieved his worn electronic card from his pocket, leaned in close to Lee, grinned, and said, "alright!"

Lee remained expressionless, not offering a smile. With a wave of his hand, he signaled for Temur to leave. Taking the cue, Temur obediently exited the room, thanked Lee, and hopped into the elevator.

Back then, Lee hadn't anticipated that this episode would usher in a series of troubles. His mind remained shrouded in the numbness brought about by a cascade of upheavals, still trying to touch, recognize, and accept every new reality around him. Some aspects left him feeling despondent, while others brought him joy—like this rain. How many years had it been since he last experienced that endless softness and wetness?

On his way home, instead of sticking to the usual route and letting the flying car land on the roof of the building, Lee asked the security guards who escorted him to touch down in the square a few hundred feet from his home. The guard was a large, silent black man with a somewhat old-fashioned demeanor, and Lee tried his hardest before persuading him with a bottle of aged Cognac. The booze was among those brought over a decade ago on his departure from Earth, and he had brought several back before boarding this time. Most of them were consumed during the trip, and the remainder was stashed in the suitcases.

When Lee stepped out of the cabin, onto the rain-soaked solid surface, and looked up to see the pink canopies of kapok trees, he felt that the decision to change the route was spot on. This was the true feeling of returning to the real world. Alternatively, had his first contact with the real world occurred in the same house he left, would it have offered the same genuine feeling?

"No, it wouldn't." He shook his head, gently closed the door, and walked into the living room, glancing around.

The furnishings were exactly as Lee had left them, with few items out of place. The large painting on the wall opposite the sofa, a piece he had purchased during his youth while traveling in Africa, still adorned the space. When he used to drift into a daze, he would nestle on the sofa, staring at the bound girl who kneeled in the center of the painting. A crystal vase on the coffee table cradled a handful of delicate flowers. The mess he had left—books, bottles, socks, belts, unwashed coffee cups—had vanished, indicating someone had taken care of it for him. Now, the windows sparkled, the tables were free of any dirt, and everything was impeccably clean.

Then, a sudden sense of loss enveloped Lee. He had expected the same disorder—books, bottles, socks, belts, coffee cups—all covered with thick dust, untouched since he left. He thought he would pick up a random item, tap the dust of it, and memories of how it was left would flood back. However, time was not a discarded object; once touched, it could never be the same. He sighed, returned to the entrance, dragged a smaller suitcase over, opened it, and the contents spilled onto the floor: bottles of aged Cognac, a few diaries, a Glock pistol, and countless small, unrecognizable objects.

Lee selected a small wooden painting among them—an image of a brown-haired, emerald-eyed woman in the white dress—and carefully embedded it in the wall. Contentedly opening a bottle of Cognac, he retrieved a brandy glass from the kitchen, settled onto the sofa, raised his glass, and whispered to the woman in the painting, "Happy New Year!"

Temur hadn't truly left for sure, and he remained standing quietly on the corner, watching and waiting until darkness descended, convinced that, at some point, Lee would emerge from the apartment, whether to dine or for some other reasons.

The misty rain and fog set the stage for the peculiar dance of oddly shaped flying cars overhead, their headlights flickering relentlessly. These aerial vehicles served as a symbol of prestige for the elites, a striking testament to their opulence. Most were the emerging folding-wing models, boasting a wide body, robust horsepower, bright high beams, and a subtle ionic mist. This new generation differed markedly from the old whirling models, standing out boldly in the night sky.

As the flying cars whizzed by, Temur cursed under his breath, determined to keep his eyes wide open, fearing he might miss the prey he had diligently spotted.

The hard work paid off—Lee finally stepped out, wrapped in a coat but without an umbrella, and briskly walked through the drizzle before slipping into an exclusive restaurant. Temur put on his rain hat and followed closely. Through the window, he spied Lee casually flipping through the menu, so he knocked on the glass. Lee, perplexed, noticed him, and Temur seized the opportunity to go around to the main entrance, barging in without alerting the waiter.

"Apologies, sir," Temur began, adopting a sheepish grin, "I'm afraid I have left my digital card at your place."

Lee raised an eyebrow. "Your card?"

"Yeah, the digital one. Must've forgotten it after snapping that selfie with you—Guess I got a bit too excited," Temur explained, scratching his head with a nervous chuckle.

"Really?" Lee frowned and turned to his intelligent assistant. "Gia, is it true that the boy left his card in my room? Can you check?"

A gentle female voice responded from nowhere, "please wait, dear Lee."

Startled, Temur took a step back in surprise, his eyes darting around to locate the source of the unexpected voice.

"Confirmed, an all-purpose electronic card has been dropped at the entrance."

"Hmm..." Lee looked embarrassed, not eager to deal with the situation.

"No worries, sir, let me just go and get it myself!" Temur suggested.

Lee agreed after a short pause and instructed, "then you can go. It is on the floor of the entrance."

"Thank you, sir!" Temur turned to leave and asked, "is there anything you would like me to bring to you?"

Lee waved him off but then called him back. "Help me get a bottle of drink—The one that was opened."

"At your command!" Temur saluted and rushed out the door.

"Request Authentication!"

"I'm a friend of Mr. Lee!"

"Please wait, confirming…"

After a few seconds, the verification passed, and Temur reached Lee's door unhindered.

"I'm here to help Mr. Lee pick up something!"

The door opened, and everything went smoothly.

Suppressing the excitement in his heart, Temur hurried to the living room and searched quietly, hoping to find something of value. In a rush, he identified the Cognac as a rare commodity, considering only the prominent figures had access to fine wines in recent years. Quickly picking out two unopened bottles, he stuffed them into his raincoat pockets and then retrieved his card.

It was at that moment when Temur noticed a small gray ring-like object laying on the floor. Swiftly, he picked it up and tucked it into his close-fitting pocket.

Entering the elevator, Temur breathed a sigh of relief—no alarms, no one in sight, perfect! A smug look instantly filled his childish face.

At the dining table Lee had been preoccupied with something else, oblivious until he finished his meal.

"Gia, what about the child?"

"Dear Lee, the surveillance indicates that the kid found his belongings and assisted you in bringing the liquor."

No—no, Lee's heart skipped a beat and he hastily got up.

Once home, he scrutinized the surroundings, quickly realizing that two bottles were missing.

"Dammit! Gia, check the child's information!"

"I'm sorry, dear Lee, this person's information doesn't exist in the system!"

"Scavengers… Too careless." Lee muttered.

He felt a twinge of displeasure, but it wasn't a significant concern, hard for him to take it to heart, especially considering more pressing matters at hand.

The authorities' tone regarding his return seemed positive so far. He contemplated the press release about his leave countless times, the reasons boiling down to *tired from work, unwell*. As for the accident, he couldn't even find a word. Although a lingering suspicion persisted, he began to feel relieved, understanding that the information released to the public was like poured water, extremely hard to retrieve even if they found something amiss afterward. One example was what happened to his former superior. When he was in his prime, everyone knew about all his legendary feats. Then something happened and the authorities had to clean it up, which proved to be an arduous and impossible task to complete. Now, seven or eight years passed, Lee still believed that if he walked into a neighborhood bar, casually grabbed someone and asked, "do you know the Titan Immigration Plan?" The response would likely echo: "Why not? If Chief Chen were still kickin', my friend would've been outta this lousy place ages ago!"

Night had fallen without Lee's notice, and he walked to the full-height glazing, gazing at the southern city he once knew so well.

Rain continued to cascade outside, adding to the city's mystique.

At the same time, Temur was traversing the streets with two bottles of liquor in his pocket. A prior message to Rat had set their rendezvous at a tattoo parlor near Snake Field Station. The establishment's owner, Coyote, had assured Temur that he could fulfill his request if the price was reasonable. Now the top priority was to locate the nearest metro station. While the aging transport network had been struggling to function for decades, it still served the purpose of preventing these undocumented homeless folks from being confined to the city's corners.

After a lengthy sprint through the city streets, Temur's breaths came in ragged gasps. As he glanced upward, the once-familiar sight of flying cars had disappeared from the overcast sky, and the streets transformed into narrow, bustling pathways. Vibrant crowds filled the space, illuminated by red and bright roadside lights, accompanied by a peculiar stench lingering in the air. The rain and sweat made it momentarily challenging for Temur to open his eyes. He stopped, wiped his face, glanced at the flickering metro sign nearby, and contemplated the approaching New Year, a smile gracing his face.

Upon reaching the Snake Field, Rat stood waiting on the platform. Seeing Temur jump out of the carriage, he rushed over, delivering a playful punch to Temur's shoulder. "You've got some skills, huh?"

Temur smirked.

"Listen up, I've arranged to meet Coyote at eight o'clock. Remember, be flexible when you're there. That guy's got a temper. Never mess with him. He might lose it and end up killing someone, and I won't be able to help you then."

"Yeah, yeah, let's go!" Temur replied nonchalantly.

When they arrived, Coyote was immersed in his work. He called Temur in, instructing him to sit and wait. "Kid, what treasures have you brought?"

Temur, observing Coyote tattoo a half-human, half-horse monster, couldn't resist asking, "what's that?"

"This—let me tell you, remember, this is Sandul, and it's very popular now!"

While continuing his work, Coyote returned to the previous topic. "Bring it out and let me take a look so I can make a solid bid!"

After a brief hesitation, Temur slowly pulled out one bottle of Brandy.

"Aaargh" the guest emitted a sudden cry of pain. Distracted by the bottles Temur had brought, Coyote inadvertently caused the discomfort. He quickly dimmed his gleaming eyes and offered a swift apology. "Sorry about that. Sorry about that."

Then, turning angrily to Temur, he commanded, "you, wait outside!"

Unhappily, Temur got up and left the room.

In less than ten minutes, Coyote ushered the guests out.

He cast a glance at Temur, who appeared a bit impatient by the door, then fetched a package from inside.

"It is yours now, give that to me. Ya got a really great deal!"

Temur took it and tore open the oil-soaked wrapping papers to reveal a small, dark green pistol inside.

"Such a tiny thing? Not worthy those bottles!"

"You know nothing!" Coyote cursed as he snatched the gun from Temur's hand, pulling the chamber with a decisive "click," as if to shoot Temur in the head.

Temur was frightened half to death. Instinctively, he jerked back, almost stumbling and finally steadied himself, covering his pockets with both hands.

"You think I don't know who you're giving this to? Let me tell you, boy, this is a North American product, CPX-2040, gun for babes—lightweight, hidden. Do you want passers-by to know your bitch sister has a gun?"

Despite the anger welling up inside him, Temur snatched the gun back with one hand, took one bottle of liquor from his pocket and tossed it to Coyote heavily. He then turned around and left.

"Wait, boy, where's the other one?"

"Let's talk about it next time!" Temur said coldly.

"Tsk! Kidding me?" Coyote snapped his fingers, calling two of his men out of the house. Temur desperately guarded the pocket containing the liquor. The hand holding the gun raised, its empty muzzle first pointed at Coyote, then at the two men. A rare fierce light gleamed in Temur's eyes, like a small beast cornered.

"Temur!" Rat, who had accompanied him, hurriedly patted Temur on the shoulder.

"Okay, okay, let it be," Coyote softened his tone. "How about taking two boxes of ammo as a little compensation? Empty guns can't scare anyone!"

After speaking, he glanced at the two men. "9 mm, two packs!"

One of the men nodded, entered the house, and returned with two packs of bullets, which he threw to Temur. Reluctantly, Temur accepted them, allowing one man to snatch the other bottle from his pocket, and under Rat's guidance, he left the dangerous place.

The workplace of Temur's sister was not far from Coyote's shop. Rat accompanied Temur to the door, patting him on the shoulder and whispering a farewell. "Bye, see you tomorrow!"

Tumer responded, "see you tomorrow!"

Rat took a few steps, then suddenly turned back. "By the way, Happy New Year!"

"Happy New Year!" Temur's eyes welled up, and he blinked hard, fighting back the tears.

"Waiting for your sister again? She's going to have a lot of work today; I'm afraid it will take a while!" The proprietress observed Temur through the glass window and pushed open the door to address him.

Temur nodded, silent.

It was a massage house, and on the day his sister picked him up, he realized this was where she worked. Although aware of the type of clientele it attracted, he never questioned her about it until a particular day. On that day, she pulled him aside and solemnly said, "I know you've always wondered about my work here, and perhaps you've been too embarrassed to ask. Let me assure you, regardless of what others do here, your sister only does clean work."

Temur hugged his sister, overcome with tears of joy.

He still remembered the year when he swam across the river. Those adults in Abandoned Harbor always said that those on the other side lived in abundance, but no sooner had he come ashore than he fell ill and lay dying on the side of the road, without food and medicine. As he awoke, he was greeted by the sight of a narrow wooden bed, sunlight streaming through a low window, and countless feet passing by outside. A thin figure approached, revealing a fair, bloodless face, and a warm hand gently pressed against his forehead. Struggling to sit up, he couldn't help but cry out, "sister!"

"Temur!" His sister stepped out, her expression displeased, drawing him back to reality. "Didn't I ask you to wait for me at home?"

"By chance—by chance!" Temur responded with a mischievous smile.

It was already late at night, and those still roaming the streets in search of illicit entertainment had dispersed. As the rain waned and the clouds cleared, a cold moon faintly illuminated the scene. Silently, Temur and his sister walked down the street together, descending stairs and passing through a dark underground passage. On either side of the wall, figures of various shapes lay in the grotesque shadows, emitting strange wails. They climbed the steps, one after the other, and traversed a narrow alley where a man smiled maliciously as Temur's sister cautiously squeezed through. Temur snorted at him, his hand clutching the gun in his pocket. They climbed down a ladder in the dark and returned to their dwelling—or rather, their home. Throughout the city's underground, such places provided shelter for those undocumented homeless people, referred to as "Scavengers" by the authorities.

After they returned home, Temur's sister began preparing food. She attempted to remain calm, but her joy was evident as she spoke, "it's New Year's, and I have a gift for you."

"Hmm." Temur responded indifferently.

His sister looked a bit surprised, and emphasized, "it's a pair of BioBoost Athletic Shoes, right under your bed. Don't you like them? I always worry you don't run fast enough!"

Intrigued, Temur bent down and groped. "Sister, are you afraid I'll get into trouble and get caught?"

"Better not be!"

Having retrieved the box, Temur eagerly opened it, put the shoes on, and stood up, lightly jumping on tiptoe. "Wow, these are going to fly!"

Despite having heard about the shoes for a long time, Temur was excited by the actual experience, bouncing around the cramped basement.

"Sister, I also have a New Year's gift for you."

After a pause, he sat back on the edge of the bed, reached for his pistol from his pocket, and with some hesitation, walked over to his sister, handing it over.

His sister's expression changed instantly, and she asked sharply, "where did you get it? Don't get into any more trouble!"

"Don't worry, I won't!" Temur assured with a casual tone.

"I don't want it! I won't have it unless you tell me where you got it. Or just send it back where it came from!"

"Yeah, all right, I'll spill it.—It was from Coyote; he gave it to me."

"Lie! Don't I know who exactly Coyote is?" His sister gave him a fierce look, "card, give me your card!"

Temur remained still as his sister grew more insistent. She pulled him closer and thoroughly rifled through his pockets. The first thing her fingers touched was the ring—it was unexpectedly heavy. Without intending to, she let it slip from her grasp, and to their surprise, it punched a shallow hole in the floor upon impact.

"What is this?"

Temur didn't answer but handed the electronic card to his sister in his clutched hand. She then scrutinized the message history.

"How could you break into someone else's house again?"

"A friend," Temur pleaded softly.

"Friend, what friend? What friend can we have?" His sister's voice choked, and her eye circles began to redden. In a hurry, Temur snatched his card, flipping out the selfie to show his sister.

The moment Temur's sister saw the photo, she froze, petrified. With her mouth slightly agape and her eyes distant, she seemed lost in a faraway gaze without focus.

"Sister, sister—Are you alright?" Frightened by his sister's unusual reaction, Temur grabbed her hand and shook it a few times. Slowly, she returned to the present, straightening the strands of hair that had fallen to her forehead.

"The friend you talked about turned out to be him?"

"You recognized him? But you don't usually watch the news!"

Without saying a word, his sister bent down, picked up the ring, held it in her hand, and reached for a small iron box beside her bed to place it inside.

"If you take other people's things, you have to return them to their owner!" She asserted.

At this time, a few muted sounds drifted in from outside, and through the small window, they glimpsed colorful lights. It was the scene of people celebrating New Year's with fireworks.

2. DREAM

These days, Lee had been haunted by the same dream continuously.

He finds himself entering—or perhaps being led by someone—a detail he never quite recalls—into a palace-like structure crowned with a towering dome. The dream bathes everything—walls, floor, and dome—in a peculiar milky tone, creating an ambiance that feels both ambiguous and hazy. There seems to be no visible window, yet a soft light seeps in gently from the outside.

At the center lies a hexagonal platform, seemingly modest in size, surrounded by evenly spaced stone pillars. Oddly, these pillars bear nothing on their tops, which isn't quite common. The platform and pillars share a uniform milky-white hue, with something in the center shimmering—a faint mist tinged in golden hues.

He wants to run over to check out what is going on, but it is obviously more distant than his senses have indicated; even after he is already out of breath, the platform that seems to be close in front of him remains untouchable.

But now, he can see more clearly, that there lies a naked person, a woman to be exact. Look, with her fair skin and long dark brown hair—she reclines in the middle of the platform. Consumed by great curiosity, he quickens his pace, striving to catch up with the platform that seems poised to elude him at any moment. As he advances, he hears singing, he hears drums. His hand extends towards the stone pillar, and that's when the woman stirs.

She sits up, gracefully concealing her undulating chest with the cascade of the long hair, then fixes her gaze on him with a profound intensity. Dark green eyes flash, as if transmitting a cryptic message, for he senses a silent plea for help. Advancing another step, enough to discern the woman's face clearly, he feels his pounding heart reaches the brink of escaping from his throat, "Sharmin?"

Upon hearing his voice, a subtle joy dances across the woman's face. Simultaneously, the previous song crescendos into a jagged chorus—a hymn or perhaps a prayer. He notices a group of uniformed people pouring into the hall, methodically forming a large circle around the platform, gradually closing in on the center.

They are the Pioneers!

"Stop!" He turns around and shouts loudly, opening his arms in a protective stance, as if warding off the crowd. But those people deviate from the norm, ignoring his instructions, and they even join hands and start a strange dance that he has never seen before, their voices rising in a haunting chant. "Sacrifice her! sacrifice her! sacrifice her…"

All of a sudden, a powerful beam of light descends from the dome, striking the woman's ivory body, and in an instant, she ignites, radiating an incomprehensibly brilliant light.

He freezes in place, eyes barely open, yet he keenly feels the woman's earnestness, expectation and anxiety. Thus, this complex emotion has planted a seed deeply into his heart.

As the radiance dissipates, the woman vanishes from sight. He leaps onto the platform, gazing upward in search of the light's source. All that remains is a symbolic pattern etched into the dome.

"Gia, turn on the lights. What time is it?"

"Dear Lee, it's 3:53 in the morning; your voice sounds a little tired, and you really need a good rest!"

The voice of the intelligent assistant Gia, soft and kind as ever, provided Lee with a slight sense of relief despite her artificial nature. Slowly, he sat up, and the soft glow of light revealed a half-empty bottle of Brandy at the head of the bed. Searching around, he found no glass, so he grabbed the bottle, uncorked it, and poured it straight down. The alcohol sliced through his throat like a sharp knife, prompting a violent, involuntary cough that sobered him instantly.

At this point, returning to bed was out of the question.

He got up and walked to the living room, selecting a diary from the scattered items on the floor. Settling onto the sofa, he quickly flipped through its pages, hoping to uncover fresh clues.

This ritual had become routine for Lee every time after he woke up from the dream, a practice he had repeated multiple times. Initially, he had faith in the diary's potential, believing those pages might hold the key to the recurring dream. While he remembered the entries from day to day, none seemed to link to his vanished memories—except for the final one, dated about six months prior, which raised suspicions.

It was a poem, apparently penned in his own handwriting:

My lady looks so gentle and so pure.
When yielding salutation by the way,
That the tongue trembles and has nought to say,
And the eyes, which fain would see, may not endure.
And still, amid the praise she hears secure,
She walks with humbleness for her array;
Seeming a creature sent from Heaven to stay.
On earth, and show a miracle made sure.
She is so pleasant in the eyes of men.
That through the sight the inmost heart doth gain
A sweetness which needs proof to know it by:
And from between her lips there seems to move
A soothing essence that is full of love,
Saying forever to the spirit, "sigh!"

These were Dante's Renaissance verses, intimately familiar to Lee.

Many years ago, on the day he encountered Sharmin Haelion for the first time since she had grown up, their eyes locked, and a powerful tremor surged through his heart. In that moment, he was reminded of Dante and the profound meeting between the poet and Beatrice. Therefore, he copied the poem into his diary on the very day.

Yet, Lee couldn't recall any motive to transcribe this particular poem once again, as it was solely linked to the specific moment in his life, not to mention the hand-drawn pattern at the bottom of the page—the same pattern from his dream. Following that, his diary entries consisted of just blank pages. The frequency of his diary wasn't regular, with instances of no entries for half a year or even one year. However, it struck him as peculiar that he ceased writing just after transcribing this suspicious poem. Even more bizarre was that, from this point forward, his memories seemed to vanish into thin air, leaving a vast blank space in his mind.

Several times, Lee almost convinced himself that this dream was related to his inexplicably lost memories—or perhaps the dream itself was the memories. However, each time, this notion was decisively dispelled. The place in the dream obviously didn't exist; Lee knew every nook and cranny of the Foundation, and no secret places should have been beyond his awareness. Moreover, there was no conceivable way for him to encounter Sharmin there in the Foundation.

Perhaps it stemmed from his profound longing for Sharmin. The investigation committee's preliminary conclusion seemed to align with these thoughts: "Due to the long-term isolation in the alien environment, the Foundation's chief and some Pioneers suffered from mild or severe deep space hysteria, confirmed as the main cause of the accident."

On the surface, the aforementioned conclusion had been officially endorsed by the authorities, and the leave notice had circulated widely within the Corporation, echoing the same narrative. Psychologists had even been enlisted to aid in what they term "rehabilitation." While it appeared that the matter had reached its conclusion, Lee couldn't shake the feeling that covert investigations were unfolding behind the scenes.

Despite his reluctance to believe it, peculiar events had occurred. The gravity of the reported "accident" is significant enough to pose a severe threat to the Foundation's existence. Furthermore, the unexplained disappearance of a spaceship couldn't possibly be attributed to so-called deep space hysteria. Initially, the investigation committee had intended to conceal the fact that a spaceship was missing. However, at that point, they were oblivious to his memory loss and leaked it inadvertently. He promptly checked the status of the Prometheus and received a jaw-dropping result: "Unknown."

"The current state of the Prometheus is inconclusive, please keep it secret!" Victor Zhukov, the head of the investigation committee, handed Lee an electronic form, urging him to sign the pre-drawn confidentiality agreement. As the director of Comprehensive Investigation Bureau in the Corporation, Zhukov had been holding the position for more than a decade. His rank wasn't higher than Lee's; however, as he had the privilege of reporting directly to President Hun, he always looked arrogant and domineering, earning him no favor within the Corporation. It was widely acknowledged that his presence typically heralded trouble rather than anything favorable. Everyone knew that when Zhukov appeared at the door, something very bad was about to happen.

Lee shot him an incensed glance and handed the signed document back, wordlessly. At that moment, Zhukov, sensing Lee's silent frustration, realized that if he had been aware of Lee's amnesia, the entire process wouldn't have been as exasperating. He appeared relieved anyway, noticing no doubt from Lee. Without delay, Zhukov proceeded to present the so-called preliminary conclusions. These were later confirmed by the headquarters. In the aftermath, Zhukov requested that Lee and the remaining Pioneers, believed to be affected by *deep space hysteria* be *escorted* back to Earth.

"Mr. Lee, it's almost time to let go of this matter. We're going home soon, be happy!"

During the spaceship journey back to Earth, Zhukov persisted in trying to engage with Lee. Already having an unfavorable impression of Zhukov from the beginning, Lee felt a heightened sense of anxiety now, rendering himself even less inclined to respond.

"Still worried? In my experience, these matters tend to pass quickly. Big issues become small, and small ones fade away," Zhukov continued, undeterred.

"Why don't I think it's that simple?" Finally, Lee couldn't hold back, his retort revealing the heightened unease and hostility he felt.

Zhukov, unfazed, responded with a smile, "the Old Man will make his decision. As soon as news reached Earth, multiple proposals flooded in. Everyone wants their person in your position, you know?"

Lee's face showed a little consternation. He didn't expect that the undesirable bench he had been occupying would suddenly become a coveted seat in the eyes of others. Zhukov noticed the subtle change and couldn't help but feel proud. "Surprised? The

Old Man scolded them all back. He said, 'No one is allowed to mention this topic until the investigation results are out!' He simply doesn't believe anything went wrong on your end." Zhukov paused for a moment, adding meaningfully, "he has faith in you."

Lee closed the diary, signaling the beginning of the next step in his ritual.

"Huh, where's the thing?"

An immediate sense of unease washed over him. He scanned the room, searching the floor without success. In a rush, he darted back to the bedroom, frantically rummaging under the bed. His search continued to the bathroom and then the entrance, but the object was just nowhere to be found.

"Oh, geez! Could it be that the kid picked it up?" Temur's image flashed in Lee's mind. Without hesitation, he called out, "Gia, pull up the surveillance for me, yesterday's footage. Show me what that child did?"

A 3D hologram materialized in the center of the living room, displaying Temur's movements—entering, wandering to the living room, inspecting the surroundings, taking the liquor, and then turning back towards the hallway, crouching down, picking up the card…

"Pause—Wait!" Lee shouted.

Stepping closer, he immediately spotted the ring on the floor in the hologram, capturing the moment Temur inadvertently carried it away.

"Damit ! " His brow tightened.

For Lee, the ring bore immense significance. It wasn't just because of the special pattern etched along its outer edge—the identical pattern that had occupied his thoughts for days after appearing in his dreams. More profound was the fact that the ring was the sole memento from his mother since she left.

Lee's knowledge about his mother was limited; she left abruptly soon after the family moved to San Francisco. Whenever his father broached the subject of her departure without a farewell, he would say, "Lee Nan is something we couldn't hold onto. She said, 'Come,' we followed. She said, 'I'll go,' and left without a word!"

Indeed, whenever referring to his mother, his father always used the name "Lee Nan," avoiding terms like mother or mama, which might have seemed more affectionate and natural. The memory of his mother had nearly faded from Lee's memory over the years. She left behind no words, photos, or video clips. There was also the unsettling possibility that his father had hidden or perhaps destroyed them all long ago.

Lee still vividly remembered that during the days when his trip to another planet was imminent, he had flown back to San Francisco and visited his father in the hospital ward, intending to see him one last time. Upon his arrival, his father, visibly shaken, propped up his frail body and handed Lee an object he had tightly held.

"This... this belongs to Lee Nan. She left it to you, and I kept it for you for so many years. It's time to have it back."

When Lee took it, his hand slightly trembled. It was a metallic ring, deceptively weighty, inconspicuous in his palm, dark gray like a discarded screw nut, with faint lines of pattern along the outer edge. After a few glances, he placed it gently on the small table at the head of the bed. Coincidentally, a ray of sunlight came through the window and landed on the ring, and an unexpected transformation unfolded—the dark gray surface dissipated like water mist, revealing a hidden golden sheen, and the pattern on the edge became distinct, unveiling a meticulously designed geometric pattern.

At that time, many things had not yet happened, and with years of knowledge, Lee recognized the pattern as a relatively simple mandala. Uninterested in religion, he dismissed it at the time. What intrigued him then was the material of the ring and the mesmerizing color changes under the influence of light. However, those concerns took a backseat to thoughts of Shallow Harbor, Sharmin, and the impending journey of self-exile that loomed ahead.

Now the situation was completely different, especially after Lee discovered that there were others interested in the ring. Lee's desperation to retrieve it grew, fueled by a burning curiosity about the secrets it might hold. When Gia mentioned that Temur was one of the Scavengers, a faint worry crept into Lee's heart. He knew these individuals were often unpredictable and willing to take risks for their livelihoods. It was entirely possible that someone had hired them to infiltrate his home. As Lee sifted through his thoughts, contemplating how to reclaim the ring, no clues surfaced.

From the first day in the Corporation, he wasn't exactly the one who was adept at navigating office politics, and without Chen's consistent support, reaching his current position wouldn't have been possible. When Chen fell, while Lee remained intact, the connections he once relied on were purged completely.

"Shiaojun Chyi."

The name, long pressed in Lee's subconscious, popped up eventually. He had to admit that this was the only person he could rely on to locate the ring from the thousands of Scavengers. The question lingered: Had he finally retrieved the courage to face him now?

Lee rose from his seat and poured a glass of Brandy, vividly recalling the pivotal moment from many years ago:

It was a summer afternoon after a heavy rain, the western sky bathed in a rare shade of red reminiscent of old movie lighting. Though the scenery was meant to be appreciated, Lee found himself distraught, hiding alone in a parked Mercedes sedan with windows tightly shut. Not far ahead lay a luxury villa, its iron gate locked, the gate vicinity was empty except for rain-scattered parasol leaves on the clean road, casting a slight bleakness. Suddenly, fallen leaves danced as a small flying car descended from the air. A sturdy figure emerged, helping a woman get out of the car. In that moment, a ray of sunlight illuminated the burgundy body the car, making it gleam like a burning flame. Lee, feeling a block in his chest, hastily secured the car door and activated the protective tint.

If time could smooth the creases left in the flying years, then a decade should be enough. As Lee contemplated, his heart settled into calm assurance.

3. RING

After a restless night, the clouds gracefully parted, allowing the southern city to be caressed by the gentle sea breeze as it welcomed a new morning bathed in sunlight. The robust rays dried the lingering moisture, leaving the residents with a dreamlike sensation, as if the fleeting storm had been nothing more than a distant reverie.

Temur sat motionless on the edge of the bed, appearing as though he hadn't fully awakened yet.

His attention was drawn to the glistening squares that stretched on the floor—fragments of sunlight that rarely slipped into the room through a narrow window above. He knew their presence was ephemeral, and as the sun rose, they would slowly move towards the bed, only to be swallowed by the darkness underneath. Intriguingly, as his gaze lingered on the bright patches, they seemed resistant to departure, as if determined to forge a perpetual presence in the room.

With a final rub of his eyes, Temur halted the futile observation. Leaning in, he seized the bun his sister had left him on the bedside and chewed it laboriously.

At this moment, the door was pushed open with a *creak*. Temur's sister hurried in, her body shivering, her face paler than usual.

Temur asked in surprise, "sister, why are you back so early?"

"Temur! Pack up! We must leave now. Let's go, get out of here!"

His sister, who had always been peaceful and calm, appeared to be extremely panicked at the time, which gave Temur a very bad feeling. He started searching around the room vigilantly, only to find that the pistol he was looking for was tightly held by his sister.

"Sister, what happened? What's going on? Tell me!" Temur pressed, growing more anxious.

"I shot the guy... multiple times. He was harassing me in the store, and wouldn't stop. I had to, I had no choice..." His sister's words were disjointed, her body trembling. Before she could finish, she slumped against the wall, squatting on the floor with a plop. Only then did Temur spot fresh bloodstains on her once-spotless dress.

"Boom... Knock, knock... Knock, knock..."

Outside the house, a jumble of footsteps echoed, accompanied by aggressive shouts. "Go in and see if that bitch is still there!"

No sooner had the words faded than two burly men burst in. One of them glanced at Temur's sister in the corner and excitedly bellowed, "she's still here, boss!" A figure swaggered in, surveyed the room, and spoke with a sinister grin, "ah, my lovely Teresa. I didn't expect you to be so violent! Taking out such a good man in such a gruesome way! How am I supposed to explain this mess to his family as the boss?"

Temur, enraged, jumped several steps in front of his sister, wrested the gun from her hand, and aimed it at the person who spoke.

"Coyote, what the hell are you doing here?" He shouted.

In response, the two men drew their guns simultaneously. Coyote waved his hand at them and addressed Temur, "put away your gun, kid! Your dumb sister already fired all the shots!"

Upon the boss's signal, a henchman advanced, attempting to restrain Temur. Temur kept pulling the trigger desperately. Despite his attempt, all he heard were a series of disappointing *clicks*.

The henchman laughed, seized Temur's arms, and hoisted him up. Temur struggled fiercely, kicking with all his might. The man, growing annoyed, threw him toward the head of the bed with force.

"Bang! Pong!"

Temur's head slammed into the low wooden cabinet next to the bed. A distinctive *snap* followed while the tin box on the cabinet crashed to the ground. Subsequently, a ring rolled out from the box, gracefully arcing across the floor, and finally settled in the lattice of light that Temur had been staring at just moments ago, emitting a faint *buzz*.

"Teresa, if you're not insane, just come with us, and as for how you pay, you have to let the brothers decide, and it's—"

Coyote abruptly halted; his gaze fixated on the row of light grids that had nearly been swallowed up by the shadows.

Simultaneously, the two henchmen sensed something amiss, discarding their lewd expressions. Their eyes shifted from their boss to the floor, exchanging puzzled glances.

The ring lay undisturbed in the remnants of sunshine, its bright golden light dancing rhythmically like a small flame in the dim basement. Coyote bent down, intending to pick it up. A strange expression flickered across his face, and finally, he grasped it firmly, holding it in front of his eyes with slightly parted fingers, examining it carefully.

"Ahh!"

A startling scream erupted from Coyote's throat. He tightened his grip on the ring and paced thoughtfully to the edge of the bed. He picked up the fallen tin box from the ground with his free hand and delicately placed the ring back inside.

"Where did it come from?" Coyote asked in a hushed voice.

Only Temur sensed the panic deliberately concealed by Coyote and hastily replied, "that belongs to my sister, and it's always been hers!"

Coyote promptly returned the box to its place, waved at his men, and declared, "let's leave!"

"Boss…" One of them, perhaps reluctant, elicited a kick between his legs from Coyote, causing him to scream.

"Do you want to end up like Sanier, fixed by a pussy? Can't you see this girl isn't to be messed with?"

Coyote exited the door, still cursing, while the injured man limped behind.

Meanwhile in Lee's home, he paced anxiously around the living room, preoccupied by thoughts of the ring, yet without a clear plan for contacting Chyi.

Over the decades, they hadn't exchanged any messages. Since the Lady Snow Incident in Shallow Harbor, Lee held a grudge against Chyi. However, their relationship hadn't reached the point of complete estrangement. Perhaps what held Lee back from reaching out was an unresolved feeling deep within him, something he couldn't shake off, maybe due to a lack of courage. For the time being, it didn't feel like the right moment.

"Forget it!" Lee shook his head and told himself, "maybe I should consider reaching out to Daewoo Chyi instead? Perhaps that's the way to go."

The Chyi family was hit hard by the Lady Snow Incident. Had it not been for their longstanding friendship with Chen, who mediated and intervened, their fate wouldn't have been much better than Consul William's, who was dragged to the square by the mob and publicly dismembered. During that turbulent time, Chen showed his kindness to the Chyi family, and Lee himself played his part too.

Finally, Lee convinced himself to open the terminal and write a text message that was overly polite:

My Dearest Uncle Chyi,

It has been far too long since our last correspondence, and I find myself reminiscing about you frequently. The passage of ten years feels like mere moments, and this recent return from the station has been unexpectedly swift. I deeply regret not notifying you sooner.

I express my sincerest apologies for any oversight on my part. In the coming days, I earnestly desire to visit your abode and pay my respects. It is my humble wish that you would graciously receive me.

Wishing you to endure good health and well-being.

Yours faithfully,

Yiming Lee

"Dear Lee, there is an incoming call from Daewoo Chyi," just after the message was sent, the crisp voice of Gia echoed.

The response arrived much faster than Lee had expected. He cleared his throat and said, "accept the call, Gia."

"Yiming, this is Uncle Chyi. I saw the news of your return, but unfortunately, there was some urgent matter requiring my attention. See, just as I was about to send for you, your message came in! How about having Shiaojun pick you up this evening? I've arranged a banquet for you...By the way, you should still live in the same place, right?"

Though Lee had been under Chen's mentorship for several years, he had yet to acquire the tactfulness and sophistication expected in the Corporation bureaucrat, and his response was rather blunt. "Uncle Chyi, in fact, I didn't want to bother, but I do have a small favor to ask. Maybe Shiaojun or you could help."

"Of course, Yiming. Whatever you need, big or small, consider it done. We're always here to help in every way possible."

"Thank you, Uncle, then I'll go over this evening...but don't bother too much. I'll just talk to Shiaojun, it would be inconvenient if there are too many people."

"Totally, that's perfectly fine."

Lee heard that Uncle Chyi's tone was slightly displeased, but he didn't care so much.

Back in Shallow Harbor, while it was Shiaojun Chyi who caused things to spiral out of control, the brunt of the suffering fell upon his father, who had slumped ever since. Shiaojun himself not only evaded responsibility but also assumed control of all significant and minor affairs from his father.

After the arrangement was settled down, Lee waited at home until dusk approached. The growing irritability compelled him to seek some fresh air outdoors. Quickly deciding, he headed to the rooftop of the apartment building. There, he walked across the empty parking lot designated for flying cars, leaning against the guardrails, lost in the view.

The sky bathed in a beautiful purple-red hue, yet the sunset remained invisible.

Innumerable giant towering structures, symbols of the era and emblems of the Corporation's power, dominated the entire landscape. These colossal monsters, high enough to reach the clouds, interwove and spread from the city center in all directions. Their imposing presence not only projected strength but also had a way of overshadowing harsh realities, making people turn a blind eye to them—like the area beyond the city where the sun quietly descended.

That was Abandoned Harbor, once known as Shallow Harbor before its fall.

Despite the towers obstructing his view, Lee strained to peer into the distance. Could these modern giants erase the existence of what lay beyond? An existence that may have long decayed, crumbled, and forgotten by the world?

While Lee was lost in thought, a bright spot flashed into his sight, pulling him back to reality.

Growing larger, it resembled a gliding eagle as it silently and swiftly passed over Lee's head. Suddenly, it decelerated, shifted into hovering mode, and readied for landing, emitting a faint light blue ion beam toward the ground. After touching the roof, its two hatches unfolded like the wings of an eagle, revealing a middle-aged man sporting sunglasses who jumped off from the cabin. From the distance, he lightly tapped his temple with his right hand before stretching it forward as a friendly wave.

"Shiaojun?"

"What's up, Bro? Didn't recognize me, huh?" The man took off his sunglasses.

"I recognize you, but that car is something else!" Noticing that Chyi still carried the air of a wealthy brat, Lee felt the initial distance between them dissipate somewhat.

"That's not just any car—it's the new *Mercedes Raptor*: light nuclear power, an ion engine, vertical landing, and foldable wings, limited edition with more than 100 in the world!" Chyi proudly rattled off the features, then gestured to Lee. "Come on, hop in and experience it!"

Lee showed no interest in his flying car, nor did he bother to correct Chyi's terminology from his perspective of being the space base commander.

Throughout the flight, Lee listened quietly to Chyi's exaggerated boasts, hoping to catch a trace of the information he had been eagerly seeking. As darkness fell, the flying car stealthily left the city and soared over the shadowy mountains. After a few circles in the darkness, it finally located an open space and gently touched down.

Lee found himself in the brightly illuminated courtyard of the Chyi Family's residence, where several servants bustled about. Upon landing, a clumsy robot servant rushed over, extending a greeting, "welcome!"

Without missing a beat, the robot scuttled toward a charming, old-fashioned building nearby, its voice echoing as it announced, "the young master has returned, and guests are alongside!"

"Ha!" Lee couldn't suppress a laugh.

"Don't. It was for my old man's entertainment." Chyi quickly explained.

As they reached the gate, a young woman emerged to welcome them, who was in a delicate Chinese cheongsam, had a plump figure, and wore a warm smile. With a slight bow, she greeted Lee, "welcome, Mr. Lee. My name is Atsuko Chiba. It's a pleasure to meet you."

Back at home, Lee had made various predictions about the night's meeting, but he hadn't anticipated the presence of such a woman. Consequently, he found himself a bit at a loss, stunned and speechless for a moment. Chyi noticed Lee's bewildered behavior, lightly patting him on the shoulder while introducing, "this is my wife, Atsuko."

Only then did Lee become aware of his embarrassment and quickly corrected himself, "Miss Atsuko—sorry, Mrs. Chyi, how are you?"

Then, he glanced at Chyi with an apologetic smile before following him inside.

Chyi's father also came out to greet him and kept saying, "Yiming! You're back anyway, and it's good to have you back. Really good!"

Lee, in his current state, felt like a different person. The heavy burden that had weighed on his heart for so long seemed to be lifted effortlessly, transforming his previous entanglements into a sense of hope.

During the meal, Lee refrained from mentioning the ring in front of everyone, and Chyi's father mostly led the conversation, delving into old stories about Chen. At the time Chen's accident occurred, Lee was far away, and the Corporation's internal announcement just stated that he killed himself unexpectedly with no details. Initially, Lee accepted this information without much scrutiny. It was only when efforts began to erase all traces of Chen from the world that Lee sensed something amiss. He speculated that someone might be seizing the opportunity to eliminate opponents, but since it didn't directly impact him, he dismissed it as a scandal. The suicide of such a high-ranking leader was generally deemed politically incorrect, and it had to be concealed.

However, today, as Chyi's father talked about Chen with a sorrowful expression, Lee couldn't escape a sense of guilt. He began to question whether, during his supposed "self-exile" process, he had truly been oblivious to the suffering of others.

Halfway through the dinner, Chyi mentioned fetching some wine, and Lee opted to accompany him. As they reached the wine cellar, Chyi began, "I know you've got something on your mind, but you seemed reluctant to speak. Is it something we can't chat about openly?"

Lee replied, "well, I'm here to ask for your help. If I brought it up in front of everyone and you're not on board, it would be rather embarrassing for me, you know?"

"Fine. Tell me what it is…By the way, I remember this is your favorite." Chyi tossed a bottle of XO Cognac to Lee.

Setting the bottle aside, Lee got straight to the point, "Shiaojun, the Scavengers, do you still have ties with them?"

"Of course, why not? My old man is afraid, but what do I have to fear? Besides, I've never believed I did anything wrong in the execution of Lady Snow. Though people all took it as the spark that ignited the Shallow Harbor bomb. But, deep down, you must know that what's bound to happen will happen sooner or later!"

Lee realized that Chyi had misinterpreted his intentions and viewed the question as a tease about his past decisions. He quickly clarified, "this isn't about Shallow Harbor. I just need your help to retrieve something. Some Scavenger took it from my home yesterday."

"Oh? Simple enough." Chyi, now holding a bottle of Zinfandel, showed it off. "North American goods, you know how rare they are these days! So, what is it?"

Lee activated the portable holographic projection, revealing an enlarged image of a ring in the dimly lit wine cellar. "Here it is, take a closer look."

Frowning and examining the object closely, Chyi finally broke the silence with a puzzled expression. "Is this… a nut?"

"Look again," Lee urged, showing the ring shining in the sunlight.

Chyi's eyes sparkled as he shouted, "heh! This is quite interesting!"

However, as he noticed the pattern on its edge, his expression suddenly changed. After a momentary shock, he questioned in a totally different tone. "*Have you ever met Mia?*"

This time it was Lee's turn to be confused. "What? Say it again?"

Chyi quickly brushed it off, returning to his casual demeanor. "Never mind. The thing is peculiar. Where did you get it?"

"My mom left it for me. Why?"

"Nothing," Chyi assured him, "no big deal. Give me a copy, and I'll have someone look into it. If they find anything, you'll know soon enough."

Lee handed the projection to him, "take it, I have the copy!"

Chyi caught it and gestured toward the door. "Let's head out. Time to have some drink."

Lee stood still, waiting for Chyi to disappear at the door before he finally blurted out, "where did Sharmin go then?"

Chyi responded, "she left, heading towards her own path, doing whatever she pleases!"

Left alone in the dark wine cellar, Lee felt a mix of relief and regret. Standing there, lost in thought, he felt a sudden surge of emotion, and a few warm tears rolled down his face.

In the dimness, a robot servant emerged all of a sudden, asking, "sir, do you need any help?"

4. REMEMBRANCE

Lee enjoys a bit of drinking but rarely goes all the way. He loves that sweet spot of being buzzed, a feeling like wandering in a dream without losing his wits.

However, that night at Chyi's house, he found himself thoroughly drunk. Even though there was a guest room ready for him, he insisted on leaving, even creating a ruckus fueled by the effects of alcohol. In the end, it was Chyi who guided him to the car, personally accompanied him home, and assisted him all the way to the living room, where he settled onto the sofa and succumbed to sleep.

As Chyi departed, Lee stirred awake. Opening his eyes, all he could discern was the blurry outline of Chyi's retreating figure—a dreamlike sensation enveloped him, transporting him back to the brilliantly illuminated night from many years past.

It was in Consul William's opulent mansion that Yiming Lee got to know Sharmin Haelion officially.

That evening, the Consul hosted an extravagant reception to mark the 10th anniversary of the Exclusive Market Treaty with the Corporation. The venue teemed with local celebrities, creating a vibrant and bustling atmosphere. Lee had to concede that it was his first exposure to such opulence, but this was clearly not a setting where he felt at ease. The dazzling lights, clamorous voices, and the shimmering dresses of the ladies overwhelmed him, leaving his mind in a whirl. Were it not for his duty, he might have slipped away quietly since he couldn't bear it. As it stood, all he could do was find solace in a quiet corner with a glass of champagne. Pensively positioned, he scanned the room for Chyi's familiar figure, hoping to follow him every step of the way to navigate through the night.

All the while, Lee sported a perpetual frown, appearing apprehensive.

Just a month prior, the shocking incident involving Lady Snow's murder of her father unfolded. The deceased held a pivotal role as the Corporation's representative in Shallow Harbor, and the adjudication process of the case dragged on due to its entanglement with the leader of Scavengers. Simultaneously, an unprecedented protest erupted among the Scavengers, vehemently demanding the release of Lady Snow and other implicated individuals. Acting as Chen's de facto representative, Lee was temporarily dispatched by the Corporation to coordinate between the Chyi family and William's government in the name of attending the anniversary celebration, so that they could properly handle this thorny matter finally.

Lee recalled that day when Chen broached the subject; he was taken aback. "Boss, let's face it, it's a bit out of my league—This is not any engineering problem."

"Yiming, this is no problem at all. All they want is your presence. You don't have to do anything; you can't do anything. But with you being there, the Chyi family can do something," Chen said, patting him meaningfully on the shoulder.

During that time, the Chyi family held an unrivaled status in Shallow Harbor, solidified through their longstanding friendship with Chen, which garnered special treatment from the Corporation for Shallow Harbor, including a more inclusive policy toward Scavengers. Consequently, they earned the support of influential Scavengers like General Chu, the leader implicated in Lady Snow's murderous act, who claimed brotherhood with Chyi. Because of this, the Chyi family saw the situation optimistically: If they could compel the Shallow Harbor government to release Chu and others with the Corporation's endorsement, they believed they could effectively downplay and even nullify the entire issue.

Ahead of the trip to the Shallow Harbor, Lee met Chyi in person for the first time.

The flamboyant man arrived in a popular rotary-wing flying car, its burgundy hue catching eyes. He proudly displayed the vehicle and brought up the topic, "Mr. Lee, don't worry about affairs of Shallow Harbor; everything is under control. Just come with me to the Consul's residence for a tour, and it will be all set!" Then, with a snap of his fingers, the flying car lifted into the air.

However, Lee couldn't overlook the gravity of the situation, which had already become a concern for Chen, indicating its complexity, especially with its involvement with the Scavengers, an issue everyone sought to avoid.

During that time, only those in authoritative positions discerned a growing dilemma: The Corporation's influence appeared robust, with the market steadily expanding to encompass nearly the entire Eurasian continent. Governments, both large and small, were scrambling to join the Exclusive Market, in exchange for the Corporation assuming regional economic responsibilities. However, these apparent successes were superficial, and it led to the issue of Scavengers. Among them were locals deprived of citizenship by the governments for various reasons, illegal immigrants who had smuggled in from outside the Exclusive Market to earn a living, and some disgruntled dissidents of the Corporation. The issue was slowly developing into a destabilizing factor that could bring the entire system to its knees. Those folks were ineligible for the credits distributed by the Corporation and had to find various means to live. With the majority of jobs replaced by artificial intelligence, their options were limited to the marginalized occupations excluded by the authorities, including roles like sex workers, pimps, fortune tellers, killers, and information traffickers—livelihoods that the Scavengers reluctantly embraced in their desperation.

Efforts to address this dilemma weren't entirely absent. The Titan resettlement plan which had been actively promoted by Chen was once regarded as a comprehensive solution. Yet, within the Corporation, the initiative faced widespread suspicion as a squandering of resources and manpower, and it garnered minimal support from the high-rank officials, with the notable exception of President Hun himself. With Hun's support, few dared to openly challenge the project, understanding that Hun had complete trust in Chen and even saw him as a potential successor.

After decades of unwavering dedication, some modest

achievements finally began to emerge. A significant milestone was the creation of an experimental zone on Titan's surface, rendered nearly hospitable for human settlement through a meticulously designed terraforming process. This Development sparked a surge in calls to station people on Titan within the Corporation. Propaganda videos, which had been strictly controlled ever since, even began publicly advocating for immigration.

However, Chen himself believed that the timing was not opportune. He was aware that someone sought to exploit this chance as a checkmate, compelling him to navigate through challenging circumstances. Such calls reached President Hun's desk anyway, and Hun summoned Chen multiple times, urging the expedited inclusion of advance personnel selection on the agenda.

A common saying goes, "distant water won't quench present thirst." When practically addressing the Scavenger issue in reality, both local governments and the Corporation's actions appeared more as superficial gestures than genuine work. Neither entity displayed a willingness to tackle the Scavenger cases, operating under the collective assumption that such pursuits would prove fruitless. Rather than confront the matter head-on, the prevailing sentiment leaned towards maintaining a façade of normalcy, avoiding the necessity of providing a comprehensive public explanation. This passive approach, seemingly clumsy and often likened to an ostrich burying its head in the sand, was effectively complemented by adept public opinion manipulation, and it generally worked for many years. To the average citizen, Scavengers were perceived as a sporadic and manageable presence, notwithstanding the inherent dangers they posed. The adopted strategy bore resemblances to governmental approaches during the last pandemic: Without testing, there would be no reported increase in cases.

If the situation were to escalate significantly, the Corporation could still swiftly strip the affected area from the Market as a last resort, thereby leaving the inhabitant of the region to fend for themselves by cutting off their supply of material and energy entirely. Such cases were rare, as a lose-lose situation was undesirable. Activists with leadership qualities, often from the upper echelons and possessing considerable influence, would always emerge. These individuals tirelessly maneuvered between the public, the governments, and the Corporation, skillfully

maintaining a delicate balance to avoid the catastrophe.
In the case of Shallow Harbor, Chyi Family played such a role.

Absorbed in reflection, Lee released a quiet, introspective sigh. With the last drop of champagne drained, he lifted the empty glass, signaling the waitstaff weaving through the crowd.

While Lee was surrounded by singing and dancing, a nagging thought lingered in his mind. "Are these festive displays just a clever cover-up for the unease and panic concealed in every heart? Or do people genuinely remain oblivious, enjoying a tranquil moment before the inevitable storm? Perhaps they choose to immerse themselves in the transient beauty of good days, fully aware that they are on the verge of complete end?"

Just then, his attention was abruptly drawn to a figure in the distance—a young woman who, for a moment, seemed to exist in a world of her own. Their eyes locked without warning, but inevitably, and in that electric instant, Lee felt an involuntary surge in his heartbeat. It was her—the same girl who had brushed shoulders with him in the courtyard of William's office just days ago. Tonight, however, she radiated stunning elegance, adorned in a gorgeous ensemble and a delicately crafted hairstyle. Yet, the tumultuous emotions that gripped Lee were identical to those he had experienced during their initial encounter. Even at that moment, he started realizing that these were more than some fleeting attraction or the typical flutter one feels in the presence of a beautiful woman; instead, it was akin to the sudden arrival of a long-lost soul in the cycle of samsara—a cascade of familiarity and memory, rather than shyness and unfamiliarity.

In an instant, she walked straight towards him, closing the distance between them. Now he could effortlessly notice the slight flush on her fair cheeks and the eagerness in her dark green eyes. The sequence of events unfolded so suddenly that Lee was completely unguarded.

"Follow me," she greeted him in the tone of an old friend, her eyes quietly watching him, not allowing him to run away or refuse. So he followed, tracing her steps up the spiral staircase of the hall and through a short corridor, eventually entering a room adorned with paintings and sculptures.

The girl knelt down and opened a cabinet, as if searching for something. "You must remember me?"

"Yes, we seemed to have a run-in in the courtyard that day," Lee replied.

The girl slightly stirred, halted her search, stood up, tidied her dress, and addressed Lee, "my name is Sharmin Haelion. It's nice to meet you!"

"I... I am Yiming Lee, nice to meet you too!" Lee responded somewhat embarrassedly, then looked around the room and asked, "are you... an artist?"

"I don't know if it's counted, I went to San Francisco Art Institute and studied prehistoric art there."

"Oh, you're from San Francisco too?" Lee inquired in surprise.

"I have been there for only a few years," she responded softly, a hint of shyness passing across her face.

Lee knew nothing about the prehistoric art, but he did know about the San Francisco Art Institute. "I studied in Berkeley, applied physics and aerospace engineering."

"Wow, that sounds awesome!" Sharmin deliberately opened her mouth slightly, smiled, and immediately added, "that fits this era!"

Lee gradually relaxed, paced to the small table in front of the window, and his eyes fell on a crystal-clear vase, inquiring, "is this vase prehistoric?"

Sharmin giggled, "underestimated your engineering students' sense of humor!"

She slightly patted her chest and stopped laughing.

"Look at the reflections! It's really beautiful," Lee admired solemnly, but his attention was unconsciously attracted by a small painting next to him—by the woman in the painting, to be precise. She was dressed in white, sitting elegantly on a sun-drenched terrace, with a bright orange starfish in a bun behind her ears, and a pair of clear eyes looking into the distance. Needless to say, the figure must be Sharmin herself, but Lee always had a strange feeling, as if he had known the woman in the painting for a long time.

"It's so beautiful..."

"If you like it, have it as my gift. Crystals are all like this, there is an inexplicable beauty."

Sharmin walked quickly to the table, took out a few sunflowers that were about to wither in the bottle, threw them into the trash, turned around and picked the bottle up, poured out the water inside, wiped it with tissue, and stuffed it into Lee's hand.

Lee was caught off guard by her swift actions, so all he could do was stand there bewilderedly and explain, "uh... actually I was talking about that little painting. Is it you?"

This embarrassed Sharmin, and her cheeks flushed. "That... that's scratchy work..."

"Yiming, how could you be here? Sharmin, why did you bring him here? You guys know each other?"

Shiaojun Chyi appeared at the door unexpectedly, his face was full of impatience and surprise. "Took me a while for you!"

"Er...We Just met; you know her?" Lee was momentarily at a loss for words.

"Sharmin was my middle school classmate, and she is Consul William's niece." Chyi grabbed Lee's arm, urgency evident in his actions. "Come with me, let's talk to William. It is almost done!"

Lee hurriedly followed Chyi out of the door, still clutching the vase, and glanced back at Sharmin, uncertain of what to do.

"Sharmin, let me borrow him for a minute, and you guys can catch up later, sorry!" Chyi symbolically apologized to Sharmin, snatched the vase from Lee, and handed it back to her.

"You guys really had so much time... Get it back later, let's hurry up!" He muttered to Lee.

In the following years, Lee always had a vague impression of what happened next, as if it were a fleeting morning dream. He could only recall being distracted all night after leaving Sharmin's room. What remained certain was that three of them—actually two—determined Lady Snow's fate in less than ten minutes. Simultaneously, the destinies of Shallow Harbor, and even their own fates were sealed, encompassing him, Chyi, and Sharmin.

Three days later, after waking up in the early morning, Lee saw the official news release, revealing that the court had swiftly sentenced Lady Snow to death and the execution would be immediate. As for the accomplices, considered coerced, they received lenient sentences and were all released on the same day. The public narrative was carefully steered, emphasizing the rare cruelty of Lady Snow's crime and suggesting that only a harsh punishment would satisfy its people.

The news didn't affect Lee much. His foremost concern at that moment was Sharmin, and with everything concluded, he contemplated leaving the place in the coming days. However, he couldn't yet decide whether to find an excuse to visit the Consul's residence once again.

"Knock, knock!"

Lee has been staying in the Chyi family's mansion these days, and the knock on the door should be reminding him to go to breakfast, he thought.

When he opened the door, he saw Chyi, and then noticed Sharmin close behind. She was once again wearing the Prussian blue English trench coat from the day they had passed by. With her coffee-colored hair pulled back, she held a rectangular package in her hand.

"Someone's got something for you!" Chyi said.

Lee hurriedly took the package and thanked Sharmin repeatedly.

"You don't look like you've had breakfast, so we'll wait for you in the dining room and let's talk while eating." Chyi proposed.

Lee nodded, watched the two leave, closed the door and returned to the bedroom with the package.

After he carefully tore open the thick package, he was surprised to find that hidden inside was an oil painting on the wooden board—the very one that had made his heart flutter. A sudden joy immediately filled his heart.

Lee rushed into the bathroom, quickly took a hot shower, shaved, blow-dried his hair, and changed into a clean shirt from his suitcase before heading to the dining room with impatience.

However, upon entering, he sensed an unsettling atmosphere. Sharmin's face was turned stubbornly away, her eyelashes fluttering in what seemed like anger. Meanwhile, Chyi displayed his typical self-righteous demeanor, sporting a somewhat contemptuous smile and sneakily glancing at an unnoticed corner.

"What's wrong with you two?"

"Right on time. Sharmin thinks the court rushed the verdict, but, Lee, don't you think it's as close to fair as we'll get? Considering the public's opinion."

"Public's opinion—but what about Lady Snow? Did anyone bother inquiring her and investigating the details of her case?" Sharmin questioned.

"Sure they did. She just didn't say anything."

"Maybe she chose not to say. Silence doesn't mean she agreed to the fabricated facts. She knew no one cared about the truth. You all just wanted to close the case quickly. But don't you think she was ready to sacrifice herself?"

As Sharmin spoke, a visible tremor ran through her, surprising both Chyi and Lee. They couldn't help but ask in unison, "you know Lady Snow? You've met her?"

"No," Sharmin rubbed her nose, seemingly to collect herself. After a moment, she continued slowly, "I've only seen her once, outside the court this morning. It was a brief scene, but I have read volumes from her eyes..." Sharmin's gaze drifted into the distance, and a faint melancholy settled on her face.

"The pain she endured—unbearable humiliation, despair, and hope—the sudden hope a man brought her," Sharmin continued, her tone calm but filled with intense emotion, like a rising tide.

Concerned she might cry, Lee interrupted, "maybe let's pause for a moment. It's all in the past."

"No, it's just beginning. I can already sense a surge of rage—his rage and their rage."

"Sharmin, are you okay? How about I accompany you back home for some rest?" Chyi sensed that something was amiss—an obvious observation, yet he attributed it to the emotional nature of women and refrained from making a fuss.

Sharmin nodded, prepared to leave. Then, she turned to Lee, "now that everything is over, are you leaving too?"

"I might leave in a day or two. Not sure if I'll get a chance to see you again."

"Goodbye, then—"

Sharmin waved to Lee, fell silent, and left with Chyi.

Lee found himself holed up in that room for an entire day, his soul adrift and his thoughts consumed by Sharmin's image. Particularly vivid were her turquoise eyes, which seemed to peer into the depths of everything, triggering an intense déjà vu but failing to unearth any relevant fragments from the deep soil of memory.

Over the years, Lee had sensed a lingering shadow in his heart, a residue from his mother's sudden leave during his childhood. Instead of dissipating, this shadow had expanded, causing him to involuntarily associate women with ruthlessness. As time passed, he became increasingly hesitant to easily approach any woman in his adulthood. He never doubted his sexual orientation; rather, he firmly believed that one day, he would encounter a woman with whom he felt familiar and intimate. Even if they were meeting for the first time, it would feel like a reunion. Now, the person he had long anticipated had appeared, but her abrupt entrance left him completely adrift, lost, confused, and in a state of panic.

"Knock, knock, knock!" As darkness settled in, a rapid series of knocks on the door snapped Lee from his daydream. Before he could open the door, Chyi burst in.

"Things have gone to hell!"

Panic rarely seen on Chyi's face, he slammed the door behind him and continued urgently, "the mob has taken over the Consul's home; we need to find a way out quickly!"

"What? What mob?" Lee, still half-asleep and half-awake, seemed indifferent, which angered Chyi. In a terrible mood, Chyi grabbed Lee's body and shook him. "Wake up! Dude! Shallow Harbor is about to fall! Why don't you hurry up and report to your boss?"

"Report what? Haven't you always claimed mission completed?"

"How could I know the asshole, Chu, would be so obsessed with that whore? He had so many girls before, but I've never heard of him fighting for anyone!" Chyi's words were filled with complaints. "After Chu was released, not only did he not dismiss the protesters, but he also added fuel to the fire, instigating the mob to occupy the Consul's home and threatening to avenge Lady Snow!"

Lee grew anxious. "What's the current situation of it? Is Sharmin still there?"

Chyi pleaded, "Mr. Lee, please, report to the Corporation immediately and ask for help!"

Lee finally sobered up. "Okay, I'm calling."

"Boss, the situation is developing badly. There's a local riot here in Shallow Harbor!"

"It's a mass revolt!" Chyi interjected. "Lady Snow incident wasn't handled well, and I messed it up... I don't know if there could be any way to fix it?"

"Forget it. Come back, the plane will arrive in thirty minutes!"

Chyi, anxious, pressed further, "Mr. Chen, what about Shallow

Harbor? Can't the situation trigger the mutual defense treaty?"

"Shallow Harbor—I have long anticipated it—would have sooner or later reached such an uncontrollable situation. You all know the cause and effect. It is your business not to handle it well! Soon, the Corporation will activate the suspension clause of the treaty."

"Mr. Chen, are you abandoning Shallow Harbor?"

Without answering, Chen switched the subject, "Yiming, get ready to come back! By the way, the Chyi family can go with you."

"But boss—" Lee tried to say more, but Chen had already hung up.

Lee turned to Chyi and said, "take me to the Consul's office; I must see Sharmin again!"

"Are you crazy? I don't understand. Shallow Harbor has been abandoned!"

"Okay, where's your car? Set the route for me!" Lee dragged Chyi out without looking back.

"Fine… Hold on. How about this? You find my dad and get him ready to leave. I'll go pick up Sharmin and join you in half an hour! If I don't arrive, you leave first! Shallow Harbor will be blockaded soon; you must hurry!"

It wasn't until many years later that Lee had to admit that when he made this decision, it wasn't out of trust in Chyi but stemmed from the cowardice hidden deep in his heart.

From childhood, Lee was never one to embrace responsibility. Accustomed to a life of apparent tranquility, he consistently leaned towards the status quo, opting for the predictable rather than venturing into the unknown. As a result, life rarely saw him make decisive choices.

"Was leaving North America to join the Corporation an exception?" Lee asked himself.

Back then, when Chen visited Lee from thousands of miles away, he was impressed by Lee's breakthrough in the technology of extracting helium-3 from Saturn's atmosphere. Knowing little about Lee's character, Chen believed that an inspirational talk could persuade him to dedicate his enthusiasm to the Titan project, which seemed unattainable at the time.

In that era most young people might be easily convinced; however, Lee showed no interest.

"By the way, if you join the Corporation, at least you can have a visible future in the next few years. Look at the current Northern California, look at it! Totally mess, aren't you annoyed here?"

Lee replied hesitantly, "well, um… I need some time to think about it."

Among Chen's persistent efforts, it was the last casual remark that truly moved Lee.

If Lee had his own answer now, he would say that the only real choice he made was that decade-long "self-exile."

After withdrawing from Shallow Harbor, he felt a profound sense of depression.

On one hand, he blamed himself for the incident, believing it was his negligence that played the role. The riots, having lasted over ten days, resulted in the deaths of nearly a hundred government officials and tens of thousands of civilians in the city. Most tragically, many were killed by the defense system while attempting to flee across the river in a panic. Lee wondered if a small intervention during the three-person meeting could have altered the course of events. He found no answer. Surprisingly, Chen showed exceptional tolerance, displaying no intention of holding Lee accountable. Instead, he praised Lee for his efforts and spared the Chyi family too, as if the unfolding tragedy had been inevitable.

"Rain drops fall, and girls get married." He threw out an old saying that not many people knew anymore.

On the flip side, Sharmin's fate continued to tug at Lee Yiming's heart, causing persistent distress and sleepless nights. He grappled with regret on a daily basis, reproaching himself for relying too much on Chyi and not going to find Sharmin himself. He believed that, had he taken action, whether it was to rescue her or face dire consequences together, it would have been a preferable outcome to the ongoing anguish.

The first time Lee heard from Sharmin again was during a discussion about the Titan mission with Chen. Chen was anxious, highlighting a disagreement with Hun on sending landing personnel. Chen favored large-scale recruitment of Scavengers for *voluntary immigration*, citing the colonization of North America as an example, which was characterized by its low cost, large scale, and inclusion of such early immigrants like social hooligans, fugitives, dissidents... Chen wanted the immigrants to fend for themselves there, alleviating the economic pressure and social burden at the same time, "shooting two birds with one stone," in his words. Hun, however, preferred loyal and capable *Pioneers*, citing the break of North America from the control of its colonizer through a revolution.

The voice of Hun naturally prevailed, but the task of selecting the Pioneers fell on Chen's shoulders.

"It's a real puzzle, you know!" Chen complained to Lee with a self-mocking laugh. He then switched the topic, "Shiaojun is back. The guy is really bold and capable. He swam back from the other side, and he brought a woman with him."

Lee's heart trembled.

Chen glanced at him, and continued, "go see him. Tell him it's not entirely his fault. Deliver my message."

Lee never informed Chen that he hadn't even entered Chyi's house when he saw Chyi with Sharmin at the time. Chen never brought it up again, as if he had forgotten about it.

After returning home that night, Lee downed a bottle of Brandy in one go and then, fortified by the alcohol, called Chen on his secure line, "boss, regarding the candidate for Titan, I think I am the most suitable." Clearly, this lifted a weight off Chen's shoulders. He reassured Lee, emphasizing he had not misjudged him. Before Lee departed, Chen deliberately sent over more than a dozen boxes of fine French Cognac, allocated to the necessary materials of the advance team.

5. VISITORS

"Dear Lee, I'm sorry to disturb you, but I have to wake you up. I hope you rested well last night…"

Gia tirelessly repeated her gentle wake-up call to Lee, apologizing for the disturbance while urging him to rise. The soothing tone resembled the nostalgic voices from radio broadcasts of old times.

Finally succumbing to the persistent summons, Lee, still hungover, sat up slowly, realizing he had spent the whole night on the sofa.

It appeared well into the day, with the gentle sunshine filtering through the blinds and casting gleaming patterns on the floor in front of the window. The comforting warmth and humid essence distinctive of winter noontime permeated the room gradually.

"What time is it?" Lee inquired.

"It's 11:18 a.m.," Gia replied apologetically, "I'm sorry to wake you, but two visitors have been waiting at the apartment door for a while."

"Visitors? Who are they? Show me," Lee asked, intrigued by the unexpected guests.

A hologram materialized in the living room, revealing a woman and a teenager anxiously pacing outside. At first glance, Lee recognized the teenager. "Wasn't this the kid who stole the ring from his house just the day before yesterday?" He thought.

"Heh! Shiaojun's efficiency is impressive; the guy does have some capability. Gia, let them in!"

Deciding to meet them, Lee headed to the door after a hasty trip to the bathroom, where he quickly washed and changed his clothes.

Wearing a scowl, he awaited their arrival.

As the elevator doors opened, the woman, followed by the hesitant teenager, stepped out. She approached Lee promptly but remained silent. Perplexed, Lee studied her thin frame, pale face, and neatly tied hair, sensing a familiarity that suggested they should know each other. As he quickly sifted through past memories, he found nothing, but that wasn't unusual given that he had lost more than one piece of memory.

"Are you..." Lee began, only to be interrupted by the woman, "Yi—Mr. Lee?"

She stammered, prompting Lee's eyes to widen in recognition.

"You... you're Lyur, aren't you?"

"Yes, it's me, Mr. Lee," she replied, her voice barely above a whisper.

"Ah!, Lyur, is that really you? Come in, come in!" Lee exclaimed, ushering Lyu into the house. Temur, the teenager, followed, moving slowly and muttering under his breath. "So you two know each other!"

"Temur, this is Lee, once a friend of my father's—or you might as well call him Yiming."

Lee's emotions swirled in a complex mix of surprise, joy, and uneasiness, making it challenging for him to articulate his feelings. He never anticipated seeing Chen's only daughter, Lyu Chen, again, especially under such unusual circumstances.

Lee had once been genuinely impressed by the earlier little girl, now a young woman. During those earlier days, he was a frequent visitor to Chen's family, and each time he arrived, Lyu, then a mere fourteen or fifteen years old, would eagerly greet him at the door, playfully shouting "Uncle Lee!" with infectious enthusiasm. This always left Lee somewhat embarrassed, especially considering he was not yet thirty at the time. Unable to ignore the teasing, especially when Chen was present, Lee would jokingly emphasize his faculty position at Berkeley, expressing a preference for being addressed as "Mr. Lee."

Lyu, a witty young girl, clearly understood the game. She froze her smile, muttering, "I don't like the title; it's not intimate at all!" After a pause, she added, "anyway, it was either uncle or brother –

you decide."

In response, Lee found himself flushed and momentarily speechless.

Lyu's father interjected, "wouldn't it be nice to let the girl just call you Yiming?" This suggestion left Lee without any viable excuses, and from that day forward, he became accustomed to being addressed by Lyu as "Yiming" instead of "Mr. Lee."

However, in this moment, as Lee observed the thin and seemingly distant girl in front of him, it was difficult to associate her with the Lyur from his memories. Still, he harbored no doubt about her identity. His immediate thought was that she must have endured significant hardships, and her family likely underwent profound changes following Chen's accident. This realization filled him with a mix of sadness and a bit of guilt.

"Temur, why haven't you returned the ring yet?" Lyu turned around, addressing his younger brother sternly.

"This troublemaker is my younger brother. He's not easy to discipline, always making trouble. But I never expected him to take something of yours this time," Lyu explained.

"Brother?" Lee asked with a puzzled expression.

"It was my sister who took me in when I was dying of illness on the street!" Noticing the confusion on Lee's face, Tumer offered a brief explanation before retrieving the ring from his pocket and handing it back to Lee. "Regret taking your stuff, now the whole city is after it. If it weren't for my buddy this morning, we wouldn't have got away. Here, take it back!"

"Lyur, what has happened over the years? Is Auntie okay?" Lee finally asked, unintentionally touching the scars Lyu had hidden in her heart.

Overwhelmed, Lyu finally broke down crying. Temur had always viewed his sister as strong and resilient, so her sudden vulnerability deeply unsettled him, prompting an anxious exclamation. "Sister, what's wrong? Are you okay?"

Lyu paused her tears and wiped her reddened eyes, reassuring Temur, "I'm fine, just recalling some past events I never told you. Maybe it's time to let you know."

"Gia, can you prepare something to drink? Tea or coffee," Lee asked as he rushed into the kitchen, hoping to find some beverages to help soothe her emotions.

"I'm sorry, dear Lee, I haven't ordered any drinks yet, but I can place an order now." Gia responded.

In desperation, Lee poured half a glass of Brandy and handed it to Lyu, feeling somewhat embarrassed. "Sorry, uh, I've just returned. There's nothing prepared at home, only this—give it a try. It might help you feel more comfortable."

Lyu took a sip from the glass and immediately began coughing violently.

Seeing her reaction, Lee blamed himself, saying, "geez, I forgot. It's actually quite strong!"

"No worries, it's just a little too bitter. I'm fine, really!" Lyu was amused by his awkward reaction. Trying to ease his embarrassment, she took another sip, enduring the stimulation of the alcohol. "Well, I do feel much better now."

Feeling more at ease, Lee settled in to listen as Lyu began recounting everything that had happened with her family over the years.

"The unsettling chain of events commenced with my father. Absent from our family's radar for over half a month, we groped in the dark until official confirmation finally reached us. My mother, tirelessly trying every conceivable means and reaching out to virtually everyone within her network—considerable at the time—persistently sought information about my father's whereabouts. Day after day, her inquiries echoed into the void, met only with silence. She recounted how people, once seemingly approachable, had turned cold and indifferent. Their responses either flickered ambiguously or they outright concealed themselves, displaying a collective lack of surprise, empathy, or solace. This peculiar atmosphere, void of sympathy and consoling words, cast a sinister shadow over our days. In the face of this ominous silence, my mother and I harbored a growing sense of foreboding. We steeled ourselves mentally, preparing for any unexpected turn of events. Yet, when the grim tidings finally arrived, they struck us like a thunderbolt from a clear sky. The heartbreak was profound, and the facts they presented were almost impossible to accept."

"I'm sorry," Lee whispered.

What Lyu heard might have seemed like an ordinary expression of sympathy, but didn't it also carry the guilt that Lee had been harboring in his heart all along?

In fact, the day after Chen's accident, Lee received a top-confidential notice from the Corporation. The content was brief and solemn: "It is with profound regret that we inform you of the untimely demise of Shannon Chen, Head of the Space Exploration Division and Senior Vice President of the Corporation. Following a comprehensive investigation, it has been determined that the cause of death was suicide. Any discussion regarding this matter is strictly prohibited until the official announcement is released to the public."

This news didn't surprise him too much.

As early as when the Titan Terraforming project was abruptly halted, Lee had a bad feeling. Lee knew better than anyone that Chen had dedicated his whole life to this project. If not for some drastic changes in the political landscape, possibly wrestling within the Corporation, Lee couldn't fathom why the authorities would make a decision almost abandoning the huge achievement that had already been made.

Of course, from the executive level, there could always be a reasonable explanation. They argued that the process of extraterrestrial migration needed to be both reasonable and gradual. As a result, they decided to construct a *Foundation* above Titan, which would become a miniature Earth ecological simulator, a super starship capable of sailing the universe indefinitely, and a space city with ample capacity for thousands of people.

They emphasized that nothing achieved in the early phase of the project would be abandoned. Any plan would remain mere fantasies without the numerous super-automatic factories already erected on the ice field of Titan's land, not to mention the material transformation engine operating around the clock inside.

While it sounded reasonable, Lee couldn't ignore the fact that the entire project's purpose had undergone a complete transformation. The large-scale immigration advocated by Chen would never be realized in the so-called *Foundation*.

"Foundation, what is this? A lavish tourist resort?" He murmured.

Because of this, Chen didn't hesitate to use his private channel to send a secret message to Lee, which constituted an extremely grave violation according to Corporation discipline. He told Lee that "the Old Man must have been controlled." Lee might have thought it was nonsense at the time, so he didn't care much. Although somewhat confused, he wasn't too averse to the Foundation. He believed the bitter life of hiding under the ice for the past few years was enough, and moving to the sky might offer him more comfort.

Lee didn't mention this message in several rounds of internal investigations afterward. Despite understanding that the private channel wasn't secure, he chose not to disclose it, perhaps to demonstrate his loyalty to Chen to the greatest extent possible.

"The formal notice was chillingly simple, stating that my father committed suicide. They verbally claimed that his act had reverberated with catastrophic consequences within the Corporation and the society at large. We were instructed not to speak out, purportedly for the greater good, while still preserving the remnants of my family's reputation. On that fateful day, Zhukov, a functionary from the investigation department whom we knew well, delivered the message at our doorstep. I discerned a nuance of emotion in his demeanor that set him apart from others. Beyond the dreary notification, he offered condolences, expressing the ephemeral nature of existence and wishing my tearful mother to subdue her sorrow and allow it to wane with the passage of time."

As Lyu spoke, a torrent of tears cascaded down her face, unchecked. She delicately dabbed at them with her hand, wiping them away, and raised a glass to her lips, fortifying herself with a sip before resuming her narrative.

"My father's disappearance was ethereal. Soon, his name vanished from public media, and even archival remnants underwent deletion, rendering him a phantom in the collective consciousness. Yet, as the world diligently forgot, my mother and I clung tightly to our memory. Devoting all her energy to investigating my father's death, my mother adamantly believed that something shady lurked beneath the surface. 'Your father couldn't have committed suicide; he feared not death but the idea of being dead. A man with such fears wouldn't choose suicide!' Obsessed with this notion, she quit her respectable job, lost her Devotee status, and, as a consequence, I was forced to drop out of college."

"And what did she uncover?"

"Nothing." Lyu shook his head and sighed. "Or perhaps something, I don't know."

"May I meet her?" Lee tried asking.

Lyu remained silent, continuing her narration.

"I recall one day when my mother returned home with

exceptional passion. She claimed to have found a key clue by analyzing my father's location data over the years. In his records, she discovered an unusual trajectory leading to an underground arena the night before he disappeared. The arena was situated in lawless zones frequented by Scavengers, hardly a place where a high-ranking official as my father would go without any specific reason, risking his life. Moreover, he had a phobia of blood and couldn't bear the sight of bleeding. Undeterred, my mother ventured into this unknown territory herself. As a brahmin, she never would have expected herself to be in such a place. Upon returning, she was very excited, telling me she had figured out what happened that night—my father met a fighter named Danny there, and they talked extensively. She stated she confronted Danny the night and even showed him a picture of my father. His reaction was one of horror; he pushed her away and fled."

"What happened next? Was this Danny found?"

"No," Lyu replied. "After my mother returned to the arena, the owner denied the existence of such a person and presented her with surveillance footage, asserting that she had met no one that night. Depressed, my mother insisted she couldn't be mistaken, citing Danny's distinctive feature—the absence of a nose, leaving a hollow cavity above his mouth—a haunting reminder of some past trauma."

Lyu's face revealed a trace of fear as she spoke, as if recounting a nightmare. She took a small sip of Brandy, awaiting the restoration of composure before continuing.

"The subsequent day, the Corporation dispatched several individuals who claimed to be from the psychological intervention team to our house. They stated they were there for PTSD diagnosis of my mother. We refused and an argument ensued, resulting in my mother's being forcibly taken away. Days later, they informed me of her alleged severe insanity, deemed genetic, and revoked my legal status. I was evicted and had no choice but to stay with an old maid my mother had brought earlier."

With her narrative seemingly concluded, Lyu appeared to have regained some composure. The influence of alcohol lent her cheeks a rare, crimson hue, reminiscent of the beautiful young girl Lee had met years ago.

"Where are you staying now?"

"In Snake Field, like all the undocumented ones."

"Things have changed. We don't even have a place to call home anymore!" Temur, breaking his silence, interjected. "All because of your mess. The entire Snake Field is after us, and it's likely they've taken over our place by now!"

"Is that so? Then come stay with me. There's plenty of space, though it's a bit bare. But we can arrange for whatever you need—food, clothing. That won't be an issue."

"It sounds logical. Everything spiraled from that ring, which belongs to him anyway. Living in his home makes sense," Temur preemptively voiced his agreement, not waiting for his sister's response.

"Temur, mind your words!" Lyu gently scolded. Without explicitly accepting or declining Lee's offer, she silently trailed behind as Lee led Temur to explore the accommodations.

That night, Lee found it extremely hard to fall asleep. He tossed and turned, restless, until he finally gave up trying altogether. Rising from his bed, he grabbed a glass and made his way to the living room. Settling onto the sofa, he poured himself a drink.

"Dear Lee, you seem sleepless, would you like some soft music to soothe you?" Gia asked and turned on the light.

Lee was a little annoyed. "Turn off the lights and hibernate yourself!"

With the room darkened once more, the faint light of dawn seeped in through the window, casting a gentle glow. Lee leaned back on the sofa; his eyes inevitably drawn to the expansive painting adorning the wall. Memories from his youth surged back—the melancholic blue sky, the vast African savannah, and the bustling village markets. What was it about this painting that captured his attention once? Dominating its center was an indigenous girl, seated on the ground with bound hands, her face reflecting profound sorrow, surrounded by men in intricate dances and poses.

Suddenly, an overwhelming sense of melancholy washed over Lee. Startled, he accidentally knocked over his glass. And he rose abruptly, approaching the painting with intent to remove it. But his hands trembled, causing the entire frame to crash to the ground unexpectedly.

Upon waking the next morning, Lee immediately sensed a

change from his usual routine. Breakfast, meticulously prepared, awaited him on the dining table. Sounds emanated from the kitchen, signaling activity. Moments later, Lyu emerged, holding a pot filled with steaming soup.

"Apologies for waking you," she began, her voice tinged with caring. "I've compiled a list for Gia based on your preferences. Most items have already arrived, while a few are still in transit. I hope breakfast suits your taste."

Still groggy, Lee hesitated before responding, "anything works for me. I'm not particular... well, I mean, I appreciate it."

Lyu smiled gently. "This soup might help you rest easier."

Lee's face flushed slightly. "Did my restless night disturb you? I've been plagued by nightmares lately. Sometimes they're so intense, and in my solitude, I may not realize how loud I become."

Lyu shook her head while serving the soup. "Your restlessness didn't bother me. My father, before his accident, had nightmares that were truly horrifying. He would awaken in a frenzied state, causing chaos until he could calm down."

Intrigued, Lee asked, "did he ever share what haunted his dreams?"

"He believed everyone around him was an imposter. Everyone except himself," Lyu replied.

"Imposter?"

"Yes, that's the word he used, and we couldn't even have a single idea when we heard it." Lyu put the soup bowl in front of Lee and continued, "my mother used to say the most horrifying dreams are those where you relive past traumas endlessly."

Lee sighed deeply. "I resonate with that sentiment. The challenge lies in discerning if my dreams are mere fantasies or fragments of reality."

Lyu tilted her head, asking, "how come? When you wake, can't you differentiate?"

Her words carried an air of indifference and casualness, yet beneath them lay an unmistakable warmth and concern. This unexpected blend caught Lee off guard, stirring within him an urge to open up.

"it's complicated and hard to articulate briefly. when I was over there, something inexplicable occurred, and I don't know what it was because part of my memory is gone. Ever since then, I was haunted by the dream."

"What? Was this considered an illness? I had heard about your situation and initially thought it was severe. Now that my mind is at ease, perhaps I could introduce you to the Lady of Oblivion; she might be able to help."

"Lady of Oblivion?" Lee echoed with curiosity.

"She is the maid my mother brought into our household. Skilled in interpreting dreams, her family has lineage of mind readers. After relocating here, she's opted not to secure a legal identity. Perhaps those with official identities don't seek out dream interpretations. My mother once tried convincing my father to consult her, but he declined. Now, she resides among the Scavengers. Yet, her reputation has grown; many now refer to her as the Lady of Oblivion. I can inquire about her on your behalf."

Lee quickly shook his head, declining, "appreciate it, but I would rather not."

6. LADY OF OBLIVION

Ethelinda didn't mind when the locals referred to her as "Lady Meng," or perhaps "Lady of Oblivion." Their dialects twisted the words, rendering them nearly interchangeable, and she didn't bother to clarify. However, she had a slight preference for the latter one. Whispers of legends painted her as the custodian of memories, a notion that resonated deeply with her own livelihood.

Much like the poor folks who turned to her for help every now and then, Ethelinda was one of the outsiders without legal status. In principle, they were not entitled to any of the resources of the place—not the sunlight, the air, or the water. Yet who could stop a few sunbeams from sneaking into the darkest corners? Or prevent the stale air from circulating in this filthy space? They couldn't even get the city's maze-like water supply network properly maintained. Leaks were everywhere due to man-made damage or age-induced erosion, yet these unintended openings became vital water sources for these poor people. And then there lingered another possibility: Perhaps the authorities let it slide intentionally, keeping the underprivileged in check, always condemned to live like rats in the dark, without the courage to have even the slightest defiant thought.

Unlike those displaced souls, Ethelinda possessed an innate spirit for freedom, a legacy from her ancestors that coursed through her veins from the moment she took her first breath. Different from the displaced, humility found no refuge in her heart. She ventured alongside Subhashree to this place as a maid to the Chaturvedi family, yet their connection was never substantial; she merely offered occasional help at their estate in the past. Her true reason for leaving with them stemmed from the characteristic in her blood, which explained why she gave up her legal status as their maid. Subhashree was surprised by the decision, indicating that she simply didn't understand the Romani people well enough.

In Ethelinda's eyes, reading and interpreting dreams was merely a livelihood, a fragment of her overall life. The true gift passed down through her lineage was a profound sensitivity to all things imbued with spirit. This unique ability transcended barriers of language, imagery, and distance, allowing her to perceive the emotional nuances of any spiritual entity—whether distant or near, gentle or tempestuous, joyful or melancholic.

In moments of rest, Ethelinda would brew a robust bowl of black tea with a handful of tea dust, settling onto a bench by her window. Here, she would silently tune into the emotional currents within her surroundings, akin to one reclining on a beach chair, attuning to the ocean's whispers.

Rather than dwelling in underground confines like moles, as others did, Ethelinda fashioned her home within an abandoned train car at the obsolete Chiwan Station. This once-vibrant hub from the era of the Grand Construction now stood as a relic of the past, its high-speed rails and platforms left to the ravages of time. The rusted tracks, fractured platforms, and forgotten carriages were overtaken by encroaching weeds, signaling a stark contrast to their former glory. The metal carriage, while offering basic shelter from the weather, was frigid in winter and searing in summer. Having endured the ravages of time, it was widely infected with rust and barely sufficient to shield from the wind and rain. Few chose to live in such a place. Yet, amid such desolation, Ethelinda's sanctuary stood out distinctly. She diligently cleared encroaching weeds, filled her surroundings with vibrant blooms, drew wires from afar to illuminate her carriage at night, and strung a clothesline to hang her laundry. Those dresses with vibrant floral patterns swayed gracefully in the air, serving as beacons for those seeking her presence. Ethelinda's intentional isolation mirrored a scientist's meticulousness in antenna placement: maintaining a precise distance from societal noise while connecting with profound emotional frequencies.

That morning, Ethelinda brewed her customary black tea but unusually prepared three cups, sensing the arrival of an old friend. Along with her would come two companions with intricate connections. One had recently returned from a distant, elusive place, bearing tales of unique experiences.

Sure enough, even before she could finish straining the tea dregs, Ethelinda discerned the faint footsteps outside. With a knowing smile, she rose and opened the iron door of her carriage. There, not far off, she spotted three figures approaching: a man, a woman, and a child.

The woman's eyes locked onto Ethelinda, and with swift strides that seemed to cover double the distance, she stood before Ethelinda in moments. Ethelinda gazed at the woman, a wave of melancholy washing over her. "Could this be my dear Lyur?"

"Ethie!" Without hesitation, the woman embraced Ethelinda tightly, and both were overcome with emotion, tears streaming down their faces.

After a while, wiping away her tears, the woman introduced the two accompanying her, "Ethie, meet my brother, Temur, and my friend, Lee Yiming. Lee has been tormented by a recurring dream, and I've brought him here in hopes that you might help him out."

Lee offered a symbolic nod to Ethelinda, clearly indicating his lingering reluctance about this trip.

Had Zhukov not abruptly summoned him for a mandatory session with all the returning Pioneers, Lee would have never considered seeking aid from what he perceived as a medieval sorceress. The briefing revealed an unsettling truth: Those afflicted by what was termed *deep space hysteria*—himself included—were trapped in an endless cycle of the same haunting dream, leaving Lee profoundly shaken.

As for the notion of *medieval sorceress*, it had never truly taken form in Lee's mind until this moment. Previously, his imagination had conjured images of charlatans lurking in dim marketplaces— cunning figures adept at eloquence, skilled in deception, and capable of offering elusive psychological comfort. Yet, as his eyes settled on Ethelinda, he immediately felt the situation was far beyond absurdity, surpassing the limits of what he could endure— the woman appeared to be in her late fifties or early sixties, yet her attire defied any semblance of age, with dark green eye shadow and thick scarlet lips. A vibrant dress, adorned with oversized florals, clung to her form. Her cheeks, while showing signs of age, were marred by an excessive layer of rouge. Two lengthy braids, a blend of brown and yellow hues, cascaded down her front, crowned by a gleaming golden rose, still in its nascent stage of bloom.

"Lyur, perhaps we should leave," Lee suggested while considering a retreat, noticing that Lyu and Temur had already boarded the carriage one after the other.

"Mr. Lee, why not join us for a cup of tea? Your tale intrigues me. While recurring dreams might be common for me, it becomes unusual when multiple people share the same nightmare!" Ethelinda leaned out from the carriage, extending her hand in a welcoming gesture. Caught off guard, Lee found himself compelled to grasp her hand, allowing the enigmatic sorceress to guide him aboard.

"And how could you possibly know? I wasn't even aware until recently," Lee queried, settling onto a bench beside the window, his unease palpable.

"Observe this table. How many cups are there?" Ethelinda prompted.

While being baffled, Lee scrutinized it and finally responded, "three."

"And yet, how did you know there were three cups?" she probed further.

"Because they were already there," Lee replied, masking the rising irritation within him.

"Exactly. You might have been irritated when I questioned you about these cups. Yet, just as you recognize those cups, being aware of your dreams is as natural to me."

With a graceful motion, Ethelinda sprinkled dried mint leaves into three steaming cups, cautioning, "be careful, they're still hot." She paused to sip her tea.

"You might as well share the dream troubling you," she advised, her voice measured. "As of now, all I perceive is a nebulous vagueness. If you withhold details, I fear my insights may fall short of your expectations, merely labeling it as peculiar, without providing genuine help."

"So, you acknowledge something odd within my dreams?" Lee queried.

"It's not the content that's peculiar," Ethelinda clarified, "but the essence of the dream itself. After years of interpreting dreams, this sensation is unparalleled. Yet, I would be happy to hear it firsthand."

At this point, Lee had no choice but to let down all his psychological defenses and recount the dream that he had been familiar with for a long time.

Ethelinda listened intently, her countenance grave. When Lee finished, she posed her first question, "do you recognize the woman from your dreams?"

Lee responded, his uncertainty evident, "it's hard to explain. Seems I know her, but not exactly the same person I've known."

"And the others who share this dream? Do they know her?"

"Those people?" Lee suddenly recalled, "I remember now, they seemed to call her *Mia*."

"Mia?"

"Indeed, Mia—the name sounds vaguely familiar, but I can't exactly remember where I've heard it before. There's a lot slipping through my memory."

"How long has it been since you've touched a woman?" Ethelinda asked inadvertently, seemingly shifting to some unrelated topic. Lee, feeling embarrassed, hesitated for a long time and stammered, "seven or eight years. But you see, how could there be any woman in the place I was stationed? I mean women in the real sense, not those *women*."

"Poor lad." Ethelinda sighed, slightly shaking her head as she grabbed Lee's hand gently, giving it a comforting pat. Simultaneously, as her gaze shifted to Lyu, she noticed the sudden blush that colored her cheeks.

"Mr. Lee, what you described doesn't sound like a dream. Rather, it's more like a piece of memory."

Lee vehemently countered, "impossible! I'm pretty sure that I have never been to the place I've dreamed of. I am familiar with the blueprint of the entire station, and I've scrutinized every detail; such a place cannot exist!"

"I merely suggested it resembled a memory, not definitively stating it is one. While you can create dreams, you cannot fabricate memories. Everything you described wasn't of your making; it doesn't belong to you."

"Not belong to me?"

"Right, it doesn't belong to you, but I can't explain how or why it found its way into your mind!"

Ethelinda continued to shake her head, and said in disbelief, "your dream is so unique that I'm at a loss for words to explain it. It's as if something was planted deep within your consciousness. I sense its presence, yet I can't grab onto it, much like a child trying to catch a fish in a river, only for it to slip away at the last moment. Rarely have I felt so uncertain in my life."

"Why, Ethie, haven't you always said that every dream had its origin?" Lyu's voice tinged with anxiety. "True," Ethelinda replied, "but his experience isn't just any dream. It feels more like a memory someone implanted—or perhaps messages, narratives, or something else. Can't find the right word."

"But how can that be? Often, you read people's thoughts so easily, even without them being around!"

Ethelinda offered a comforting smile, sensing Lyu's dissatisfaction with her explanation. She reached out, taking Lyu's hand reassuringly. "Lyu, I may have insights, but I'm not all-knowing. Besides, the world is growing increasingly perplexing, with more and more stuff that's hard to figure out…"

She paused to take a sip of her tea, then brightened, seemingly recalling something. "How about I share a story?"

"A story?" Lyu and Lee asked simultaneously.

"Yes, a story from years past. I've long sought the right person to share it with, and it happened that you came by. The world has transformed so much, I often wonder how many peaceful moments I have left…"

Ethelinda let out a long sigh before continuing, "it must have been some winter, and a late night. There arrived a guest unexpectedly. You see, my place is hard to find, and very few visit me at night. Besides, I always have a hunch when people are about to come. The guest was a large man with a daunting face. You know, I've never been one to be easily frightened by appearances alone. Yet, behind his unusual face, there was a sort of hollowness that I had never felt before, dark and bottomless, it was this eerie feeling that truly terrified me. I've spent most of my life reading the emotions of living beings, and it's never once unsettled me. Yet, that particular night, with him seated opposite me, I was gripped by an inexplicable fear and couldn't even speak. It felt as if I was standing on the edge of a deep well, just one step away from plunging in. He himself was frank, telling me why he came, that he stopped dreaming at some point. You should understand, people can go mad when they stop having dreams, so I tried my best to comfort him, to read his mind as much as I could, and to calm myself too. But no matter how hard I tried, there came nothing, I felt nothing, and this never happened before, unless—"

When Ethelinda said this, her body trembled slightly, and she was no longer the calm person she had been minutes ago.

Lyu grabbed her hands and asked softly, "unless what?".

"Unless it wasn't a living thing sitting across from me. Anyway, I was so frightened the night that I didn't know what to do. Eventually, I had no choice but to force him away. Surprisingly, he remained calm throughout, neither arguing nor lingering, simply leaving in silence."

"Gosh, you've never told me about it?"

Ethelinda sighed. "It was shortly after you left, Lyur. Those times were filled with unrest. By the time it ended, you'd moved on, and I thought it best to forget."

Lee interjected, "you mentioned his horrible face, can you describe it?"

"His face was quite unusual, let's say, where his nose should've been, there was nothing but a vast void."

A collective gasp filled the room as all three exclaimed in unison, "Danny!"

"Danny…" Ethelinda murmured the name, as if a foggy memory had been lifted. "No wonder I was suddenly reminded of this today when you were here. There's really some connection. You've met this man too, haven't you?"

"Ethie," Lyu whispered, her voice trembling with emotion, "this man is tied to my father's accident. I never shared this before, but my mother met him once right before she was confined." Holding back tears, Lyu implored Ethelinda, "can you help us find him? Figuring out this mystery might reveal the truth behind my father's death."

Lyu's plea was laden with yearning and sorrow, and while Ethelinda knew the challenge of the task, she offered a comforting smile. "If you're set on finding him, we'll do it, as I can still recall his face precisely, despite the years."

"I've got an idea!" Lee interjected, "let Ethelinda describe him for Gia. With Ethelinda's memory and Gia's technology, we can recreate his image."

Harnessing Ethelinda's remarkable memory, Gia swiftly

reconstructed a detailed three-dimensional image of Danny's face. Together, they fine-tuned it until Ethelinda finally nodded in approval.

"What's our next move?" Temur inquired, his eyes scanning the group.

Lee hesitated, directing his gaze towards Ethelinda, silently seeking guidance.

She exhaled slowly, her voice measured. "I'll need time. I can sense his presence faintly, but it's strongest when he's near."

"Head to the pawnshop and seek out the proprietors, but only if he pays," Temur suggested, pointing at Lee.

Pawnshop was the term Lee had only recently become acquainted with. In this context, it referred to the place of so-called information dealers—Scavengers who specialized in procuring illicit information for a living. While the Corporation's control over information was very strict, it had faced criticism even from some of its top-tier executives. In certain cases, they executed *hard destruction*, which erased data so comprehensively that even if they regretted it later, recovery was impossible. Thus, the rise of information traffickers in the black market became inevitable. There had never been a thorough crackdown. Most of the time the authorities provided guidance instead, since many officials themselves occasionally sought help from the dealers.

Lee was not against the idea. He asked, "do you know someone with better a reputation? Those people are complicated, and if we pick the wrong one, not only will our goal not be achieved, but it could also bring a lot of trouble!"

Grinning, Temur responded, "certainly, as long as you offer them quality goods. By the way, they don't accept Corporation credits and you'll need something substantial. Do you have Bitcoins?"

Lee also smiled, "no, but you can take anything from my home, except for the ring and the small painting on the wall!"

"Who'd want your paintings?" Temur retorted.

With their plan set, the trio prepared to depart. As they did, Ethelinda stood by the carriage door, waving. "Mr. Lee, take good care of our Lyur!"

The unexpected remark left Lee momentarily speechless. He managed to reply, "ah? Oh, yes, of course."

Lyu's face flushed with embarrassment, with a stomp she

protested, "Ethie, why are you talking about the nonsense!"

7. MYSTERIES

Red Phoenix's pawnshop was tucked away in an old shipping container, just a brief five-minute walk from Snake Field Station. Such containers, rust-stained remnants from the days when Snake Field thrived as a port, dotted the landscape for miles around. Legend had it that in 2048, when the port was closed off due to the blockade on adjacent Shallow Harbor, several bold lads from the neighborhood sneaked in for a thrill ride. Little did they know that bullets show no mercy, and within moments, they tragically became mere cannon fodder. This unforeseen bloodshed threw the community into chaos. Fearing widespread instability, authorities swiftly sealed off the entire Snake Field and relocated all its residents—men, women, and children—to distant locales. Yet, an unexpected lapse occurred during the evacuation due to someone's oversight. The port's facilities remained intact, and even more astonishingly, the vast underground subway station remained operational, which inadvertently transformed the area into a magnet for refugees. Risking perilous journeys across the channel, thousands of fugitives established themselves here. By the time officials recognized the gravity of the situation, it was already too late, and no one was willing to step up to clean up the mess, so they had no choice but to let it go. Over time, Snake Field Port's former glory faded into obscurity, replaced by its infamous reputation as a sanctuary for the Scavengers.

While the black market was rampant in this area, traders weighed their options carefully. The advantages were clear: a steady influx of people and convenient accessibility. However, the drawbacks were significant too—the area's notoriety made businesses easily targeted by both sides of the law and a single misstep could lead to disasters. Thus, only the most audacious and capable ventured here, individuals like the aforementioned Coyote and the soon-to-be-introduced Red Phoenix.

Red Phoenix's true name was rarely known. She was widely believed to have come from Persia, arriving with her father decades ago. Back then, the Corporation's reach was far more limited, primarily extending to a few less prominent regions abroad, including remote areas in the Far East and the Middle East, such as Persia.

Individuals as smart as Red Phoenix's father, who possessed a keen sense for assessing situations, smelled the opportunity. They seized upon the Corporation's strategy for large-scale expansion, flocking in to capitalize on it. If fortunate enough, they could quickly secure a profitable position. In this way, her father transitioned into a minor bureaucrat overseeing information control. Leveraging this access, both he and Red Phoenix began their illicit business endeavors. Simply put, they covertly backed up data destined for destruction, later selling it to interested parties at premium prices.

Eventually, they must have displeased someone, leading to their activities being exposed. Yet, due to their foresight, and with plenty of dirty materials in hand, the fallout was minimal. In the end, her father was investigated and got dismissed, with his legal status revoked. However, in terms of their livelihood, not only was it unaffected, but it also became increasingly prosperous.

After her father's passing, Red Phoenix assumed control of the business. With her shrewd character and adept handling of various situations, she quickly gained renown in Snake Field, eventually becoming the proprietor of the largest pawnshop in the area. Red Phoenix was widely recognized for her capabilities, and she charged steeply. When clients approached her, they had to provide valuables upfront, even before stating their request. Ultimately, Red Phoenix would decide whether or not to proceed and choose when to act, all based on the value of prepayment.

Red Phoenix deeply disliked being pushed. If she achieved results, one would know; if not, it was likely because the offer wasn't sufficient or the information one sought was too costly—

both are essentially the same. Given that those who sought her services endorsed her abilities, even if things didn't work out, they would hesitate to reclaim their prepayment.

Temur stressed Red Phoenix's rules to Lee several times before they set out, yet Lee merely nodded, absentmindedly toying with the two bottles of Brandy.

Growing increasingly frustrated, Temur remarked, "my sister is deadly serious about your matter, shouldn't you be taking hers just as seriously too?"

Lee responded, "to be frank, we're giving it our best shot. You see, if that shopkeeper you boasted could track down the man, the authorities would have done it long ago. I don't see anyone else succeeding where they haven't."

At this time, Lee wasn't neglecting Lyu's affairs intentionally; rather, he felt suffocated by the mounting pressures surrounding him—there had been so many things unfolded in days and the situation escalated too much since his last meeting with Zhukov. The intensity of investigations had surged. Within a span of days, Lee found himself meeting Zhukov thrice, conversing with his direct superior, Dave, head of the Space Exploration Division, and facing questioning from Elizabeth, a vice president overseeing Mind Exploration. All these were unusual, and the latter was particularly surprising, given Lee's limited prior interactions with Elizabeth. When Lee was initially stationed on Titan, this lady was relatively unknown. However, her meteoric rise within the Corporation was undeniable. In just a few years, she ascended to her current position, overseeing a rapidly expanding Mind Exploration Division that rivaled the Space Exploration Division in prominence. Within the Corporation, rumors swirled about her close ties with Hun, fueling speculations. Lee had once envisioned her as a captivating figure, only to discover she was an austere old woman with a rigid posture and an icy demeanor that unsettled him.

Each encounter shared a common thread: an insatiable curiosity about Mia. While some inquiries were direct, others were more veiled. Elizabeth stood out by merely throwing a probing gaze without uttering a word, which disarmed Lee in a few minutes, compelling him to echo responses he had previously shared.

"Very well, is that all?" Elizabeth asked, her subtle smile concealing deeper implications. Lee wiped the sweat from the tip of his nose, feeling a surge of surprise. He couldn't fathom why he would divulge such confidential information to someone he had just met. Although she held a high rank, she hadn't even begun to inquire deeply.

"That's all. But is that the information you're seeking this time?" Lee responded cautiously.

"Exactly. Mia is an intriguing subject, she holds more significance for our division than any other!" Elizabeth elaborated, hinting at layers of unspoken intent behind her words.

Over the years, rumors circulated about the Mind Exploration Division's discreet research endeavors in the spiritual realm. Several of these studies might have some scientific basis, while others ventured into the domains of mysticism and the supernatural completely. Given this background, their vested interest in the current unusual circumstances seemed only logical.

"Do you really think there's a woman named Mia... and we've met?"

Elizabeth again shot him a cryptic smile. "Deep down, you probably know the answer."

After exiting Elizabeth's office, an unsettling sensation lingered with Lee. He tried to reassure himself that such feelings were commonplace among those interacting with the Mind Exploration Division. The division's rapid rise within the Corporation had raised eyebrows, but what truly fueled concerns was its research direction, which diverged significantly from the Corporation's science-centric ethos. Still, it would be simplistic to label them as mere practitioners of the occult. Their track record boasted notable accomplishments; for instance, the Pioneers dispatched to the Foundation all underwent the so-called "mind purification" process, which seemingly transformed them, stripping away inherent selfishness and fostering unwavering loyalty.

"Ridiculous," Lee muttered to himself while thinking about it, offering a wry smile.

"What?" Temur asked.

"Oh, nothing. But you might not be aware that these two bottles of Brandy in my hands are quite precious. Back in the '50s, wildfires raged in Cognac for five months, reducing those vineyards to ashes. People died or fled, and since then, genuine Cognac has become a rarity." Lee gestured with the bottles, attempting to emphasize their value to Temur.

However, in the old shipping container, the rarity Lee offered didn't impress Red Phoenix at all. Having encountered countless rare treasures over time, she hardly flinched at such offerings.

Setting the bottles down with a hint of frustration, Lee asked and activated Gia, "Can you help find this man? Gia, project Danny's image for her."

"You're connected with the inside, aren't you?" Red Phoenix delicately brushed a fiery red strand of hair from her face, meeting Lee's gaze.

"Does that matter?"

"Truthfully, I have reservations about those on the inside," Red Phoenix remarked dismissively, gesturing as if ushering them out.

Sensing the negotiation faltering, Temur intervened, "what if we increase our offer?"

"That depends on what you're offering," she replied coolly.

"Good stuff," Temur replied, withdrawing his right hand from his jacket pocket.

He clenched it into a fist before slowly extending it toward Red Phoenix. Just as he neared her, he opened his hand to unveil a ring. Upon seeing the ring, Lee erupted, "why did you take my stuff again?"

Intrigued, Red Phoenix reached out, attempting to snatch the ring from Temur. However, her grip slipped, causing the ring to clatter loudly onto the floor.

"Careful! It's super heavy!"

"Interesting." She leaned over, retrieving the ring from the floor. As she examined it, a faint pattern on the ring's edge captured her attention, causing her expression to shift drastically.

"This... Who the hell are you?"

A triumphant smile spread across Temur's face. "Don't sweat it. This should be enough to get you on board, yeah?"

Shaking her head, Red Phoenix decisively put the ring back onto the table. "This item isn't yours!"

How could Red Phoenix not recognize the ring? Wasn't it the very one rumored to be associated with a hefty bounty from the Chyi Family? Its distinct features might not be discernible to the average person, but Red Phoenix was well aware of the significance behind the symbol engraved on its surface. Given the complexities of the situation, she believed it wise not to get entangled in unnecessary complications.

"That ring belongs to me," Lee interjected, seizing control of the conversation.

Red Phoenix cast a disinterested gaze upon this middle-aged man with a weary demeanor, his face marked by fatigue and there was nothing about him that piqued her curiosity. Yet, a fleeting thought crossed her mind. "What if he was telling the truth?"

She was fairly certain the ring had no ties to Chyi. Given his track record, he must be searching for the ring on someone else's behalf, as he often does. And if the ring truly belonged to the man standing before her, wouldn't his identity alone warrant her assistance?

"Well, give me a copy of the man's image. As for the ring—I can't afford it. But remember, I've done you a favor and you must pay me back, perhaps someday in future!"

Upon hearing this, Temur grinned, snatched the ring, and handed it back to Lee, jesting, "see? They're not interested in your ring at all!"

As soon as Temur returned home, he eagerly shared the latest developments with his sister. He found her in the living room, balancing on a chair while attempting to hang a painting on the wall.

Observing this, Lee rushed over to assist. To his surprise, he recognized the painting as the one he had taken down that night. Hastily, he explained, "you don't need to hang that up. I intentionally removed it."

Lyu looked puzzled, commenting, "but it's a nice painting!"

Lee paused for a moment and explained, "you know, this painting reminds me of this weird dream I keep having. Still trying to figure out what their connections are."

"Ah? But this depicts the Dogon people performing a ritual sacrifice." Lyu took off the painting and handed it to Lee.

Lee's eyes widened in curiosity. He asked, "what? Dogon people, sacrifices?"

Lyu nodded. "Yes, it's a depiction of a ritual from the Dogon tribes. Although it may seem gruesome, this theme gained popularity in Africa. They believed in sacrificing young women to gods from the Sirius star."

"Hey, how do you know that?"

"Interestingly, my college thesis focused on the Sirius culture of ancient African tribes. The Dogon people, despite their seemingly primitive practices, accurately predicted the trajectory of the Sirius binary star system."

"Really?" Lee put down the painting in his hand and helped Lyu jump down from the chair gently. "I was not aware of you knowing astronomy?"

Lyu chuckled, wiping sweat from her brow and explaining, "it was related to my thesis and became a side interest, especially since my father introduced me to an astronomical expert specializing in Sirius. If you need any information on the Dogon people to interpret your dream, I can assist."

Lee shook his head and replied, "no, let's concentrate on investigating your father's affair."

Red Phoenix was impressively efficient, responding within just three days—a timeframe that caught Lee off guard.

"Mr. Lee, we've gathered the information you sought," came the voice on the other end. Lee immediately recognized it as that of Red Phoenix.

"Regarding Dan, the last confirmed sighting was in January 2053. Based on our findings, it's highly probable he was smuggled to the other side."

Lee's voice trembled with anxiety. "By *the other side*, do you mean Abandoned Harbor? Is he… Is he still alive?"

Silence greeted him. After what felt like an eternity, Gia's reminder signaled that the call had already ended.

Given that it is connected to Abandoned Harbor, who else could Lee turn to for help besides Chyi? With a wry smile, Lee instructed Gia, "connect me to Shiaojun Chyi; we need to discuss something."

But before Lee could react, Gia interjected, "actually, Mr. Lee, there's an incoming call from Chyi right now!"

"Put him through!" Lee said, sounding surprised yet eager.

"Yiming, we need to talk," Chyi's voice came through, sounding weary. "Would you mind if someone picks you up and brings you to my place so we can discuss things privately?"

"Why not?" Lee agreed eagerly. "Sure, certainly!"

At that moment, Chyi lounged in solitude within his seaside villa, a drink in hand. The ring had consumed his thoughts for days. Despite the bounty message being out for a week, the only piece of substantial information he had received was about a child taking the ring. However, this child, accompanied by his sister, had suddenly vanished without a trace. For Chyi, this had evolved beyond a mere favor for an old acquaintance.

Ever since that pivotal night when he noticed the distinct pattern on the ring, his fascination had only grown. Lee's mention that the ring was left by his mother as a memento didn't sit well with Chyi. While Lee's seemingly indifferent response to Chyi's probing might have suggested otherwise, Chyi wasn't easily swayed. He believed there was more to it than mere coincidence.

Currently, the news of Mia's return resonated deeply within the Organization. Whispers circulated that the High Priestess had summoned trusted chiefs, directing them to gear up for an impending search and rescue operation. Although such a significant responsibility had yet to be bestowed upon Chyi, he couldn't help but contemplate the possibilities. If destiny presented him with the chance to locate Mia ahead of others, could he finally shake off the lingering frustrations that had plagued him for years? Would he reclaim the fearless and spirited demeanor of the Shiaojun Chyi before the Lady Snow incident? For over a decade, the Lady Snow incident weighed heavily on Chyi like a covertly growing tumor, continuously causing discomfort and ensuring he never forgot its haunting presence. He believed that unless he addressed it head-on with significant action, it would continue to burden him indefinitely, leaving him perpetually unsettled.

That's why in the past few days, Chyi pieced together a compelling theory: This ring with the intricate mandala pattern wasn't necessarily unique worldwide, but its distinctiveness made it improbable for anyone outside the Organization to possess a matching piece. Given Lee's prominent stature within the Corporation, the likelihood of him obtaining the ring from Mia, rather than inheriting it from his mother, seemed more plausible. This led Chyi to speculate: If Mia wasn't directly in Lee's grasp, their paths must have intertwined more than once for him to get such a coveted item.

Chyi firmly believed in this deduction, a process he was deeply obsessed with. He was always one to delve into what he deemed "logical," regardless of any apparent gaps. Once he settled on a conclusion, it became unassailable. This very reasoning had once driven the execution of Lady Snow. Now, it bolstered his confidence to locate Mia. But the ring's whereabouts remained unknown, and time was not on his side. He had no choice but to abandon his attempt to find the ring and discern its identity, deciding instead to confront Lee directly and question him about the matter.

So, the call to Lee was initiated eventually.

After speaking to Lee, Chyi set down his wine glass, stretched, and approached a vast glass wall. This wasn't just any wall; it transformed the space into an expansive aquarium. Through the dim lighting, the muted hues of the gray reef, swaying aquatic flora, and clusters of dull corals were discernible. A solitary lemon shark, previously concealed, stirred and darted away into the shadowy depths upon sensing Chyi's presence.

Chuckling at the shark's abrupt departure, Chyi strolled alongside this expansive aquatic scene, reaching what appeared more like a luminous glass wall than a mere window. This vast expanse illuminated the entire hall, reminiscent of a vintage theater screen. Beyond this luminous barrier, nature presented a breathtaking tableau of lush mountains, crystalline waters, and azure skies. Intriguingly, within this expansive window, a concealed door was nestled, leading to a corridor that guided visitors to a pavilion perched above the tempestuous sea, a completely different realm echoing with the thunderous cadence of waves.

This architectural marvel bore the signature touch of Chyi. After escaping from Shallow Harbor, Chyi's gaze immediately settled on the majestic rock formation protruding from the cape. Consulting several Feng Shui experts confirmed its potential, as it offered a strategic position facing the sea with mountains at its back, symbolizing both defense and power. Sensing his energy wane at that time, Chyi meticulously surveyed the surroundings and actualized his vision, erecting a traditional pavilion against this formidable backdrop, dubbing it the "Retreat Pavilion," reminiscent of a famous garden in Jiangsu. This retreat became Chyi's sanctuary. Here, he evaded incessant familial chatter, sidestepped the unpredictable tensions of the outside world, and crucially, concealed his affiliation with the Organization from his unsuspecting family. It served as his clandestine hub, allowing him to manage secretive endeavors occasionally. Initially, joining the Organization seemed like a desperate measure, a means to preserve his own life and even save Sharmin's in the chaos. However, over time, Chyi began to perceive that to the Corporation, individuals were mere expendable pawns, easily discarded as seen in the incidents at Shallow Harbor. This realization led him to reconsider his loyalties. And he gradually began feeling committed to the Organization, though whether or not the Organization truly trusted him remained an entirely different matter.

After Chyi departed, the expansive window gradually dimmed, transforming back into an ordinary wall that lacked its earlier luminosity. The entire hall plunged into darkness, save for the faint glimmers emanating from the aquarium.

Darkness persisted until Chyi returned, accompanied by Lee.

Looking around curiously, Lee began with a clumsy apology, "really sorry about my ring, Shiaojun. I should have informed you as soon as I retrieved it. But, you know, things have been crazy busy lately. So much going on."

Chyi sneered, "you still refer to it as *your* ring?"

"What do you mean?" Lee looked genuinely puzzled.

"Cut the act, where is Mia?"

Lee's eyes widened in surprise, questioning, "how could you know about Mia?"

"Just tell me her whereabouts. You've got her ring," Chyi continued, his tone calm but insistent, revealing his determination to uncover the truth.

Lee was confused again. "How does the ring have anything to do with Mia? I've had it for years, as I told you, ever since my mother gave it to me!""

Chyi paused, a brief silence settling as he sensed the futility of his inquiries.

At the same time, Lee activated the projector and resumed their conversation, saying, "let's set aside the ring for now; I approached you with another purpose."

As the 3D holograph materialized, a stunning face suddenly took center stage in the expansive hall, prompting Chyi to exclaim, "who is this?"

"That's Danny. He's supposed to be in Shallow Harbor. He's an underground boxer, tied to Shannon Chen's suicide. Chen visited him right before taking his own life."

Chyi's expression darkened at the mention of Chen. "You're not seriously reopening Chen's case, are you? It's been concluded for years. Stirring that up could cost you your life."

"I can't shake the feeling that something is weird. If I can find some answers, it might bring closure for his family and make up for the mess they've been through. We're all friends, aren't we? After all, it was related to human life."

Chyi scoffed, "friends? After what happened in Shallow Harbor? You talk about friendship and lives, but wasn't it all suspicious? Weren't the thousands who died there human lives? Where was the friendship then?"

Lee's face flushed with emotion. "Why do you keep bringing that up? Do you know you're the one who can't move on?"

Chyi pressed on, "sure I can't move on as I am not like you! Can't you see, Yiming? You were just a pawn in this game. You were manipulated, yet you still harp on about loyalty and friendships. Did you ever stop to think about how suspicious the events at Shallow Harbor were? Why would Chen assign you a role that was clearly out of your depth? Shallow Harbor was abandoned too effortlessly, and yet, you never questioned it. I bet you felt guilty, didn't you? Chen probably anticipated you would botch things up, leading you to willingly accept that isolated assignment, to a barren place in the middle of nowhere. This was all part of his scheme! While it's understandable to navigate through the Corporation's intricate plots, only someone as naive as you would still cling to notions of friendship amidst all this."

Lee's eyes fell, his voice barely a whisper, "can you help me or not?"

Chyi calmed down a bit. "I could, but I won't. This case is a minefield. You'd be wise to steer clear."

After a tense silence, Lee ventured, "what if I told you about Mia?"

Chyi's eyes narrowed, disbelief washing over him. "What did you just say?"

"Mia. You want to find her, right?" Lee's words came out more forcefully than he intended, surprising even himself, and he pressed, "do you want help or not?"

"I do, of course!" Chyi leaned in, patting Lee's shoulder, his tone serious. "We've got a deal."

8. TRUTH

The roar of the crowd surged like relentless waves crashing upon the shore. Yet, amidst this tempest of noise, Uritu remained an island of tranquility, his face devoid of panic. Hidden in a discreet corner, far removed from the piercing lights overhead that illuminated the ring, he shielded himself from the brutal and savage fighting on the field—not out of indifference, but to escape the unsettling aroma of blood and sweat that pervaded the air, a smell he found truly disgusting. In fact, the outcome of the fight held immense significance for him.

For this reason, Uritu's gaze remained fixed on the expansive screen suspended from the steel framework of the ceiling. Displayed on it were alternating sets of red and green numbers, pulsating with intensity—these were not scores but rather the fluctuating odds of the fighters. When the particular red number Uritu monitored surged past a hundred, the crowd's tumultuous cheers crescendoed to a deafening peak before abruptly dwindling into an unsettling silence.

Motionless as a statue, Uritu betrayed only the faintest twitch at the corner of his eye; otherwise, one might have believed time itself had come to a standstill. The once clamorous arena now lay blanketed in silence, and its very atmosphere growing palpably dense. The pervasive smell of sweat and blood appeared to freeze, as if poised to shatter upon the ground with a mere flick of one's finger.

The silence persisted for several tense minutes, with Uritu

holding his breath. Abruptly, the numbers on the giant screen began to fluctuate again: 100, 87, 50, 17...

At first, boos emanated from the opposite side of the ring. Then, like a bursting dam, the crowd unleashed a torrent of curses, shouts, and even howls. Eventually, as a bright red number remained steadily displayed on the right side of the screen without wavering, the tightly circled spectators around the boxing ring began to disperse amid shouts and rebukes.

At that pivotal moment, Uritu seized the chance to assess the scene in the ring. As anticipated, Beast remained steadfast, never failing to meet his expectations. Though weariness seemed to shadow Beast from a distance, a subtle nod followed Uritu's snap of his fingers, reaffirming their unspoken understanding. Despite this reassurance, a pang of sorrow washed over Uritu as he observed Beast through the blood-red mask veiling his face. He could never decipher whether the hidden expression behind it was one of joy or sorrow. In his estimation, the sentiment likely skewed 90% toward joy and 10% toward sadness, leaving him hopeful that Beast hadn't fared worse emotionally.

Beast stood as Uritu's last remaining card—indeed, his sole card. Over the years, Uritu had watched as his other fighters met their demise one by one, leaving Beast with an unblemished record. While staying alive in the fighting arena equated to never losing, the longevity of a fighter's life remained as unpredictable as a lottery number, eluding any attempt at prediction.

From the moment Uritu first laid eyes on Beast, a peculiar certainty settled within him: This fighter was destined to reign supreme in the Abandoned Harbor's fighting scene, a fact he declared by refusing to recruit any more fighters. His peers scoffed, attributing his insane decision to the sting of losses. They argued that diversifying one's assets was the golden rule—a sentiment echoed even by Tana, who viewed Uritu's stance as mere superstition. Yet hadn't her unwavering loyalty to Uritu stemmed from her own superstitions?

Consequently, Uritu's unwavering faith in Beast bore fruit, reaping substantial profits that left his once-skeptical rivals simmering with envy and resentment.

After tallying his earnings for the night, Uritu signaled for the Beast to approach, displaying the numbers as was their routine. Without hesitation, he transferred half of the sum to Beast on the spot—a generous gesture uncommon in their clandestine circuit. While cunning brokers found various means to thrive without relying solely on gladiators, the fierce and trained minds of fighters like Beast proved insufficient for survival in Abandoned Harbor.

Beast showed minimal interest in the figures, offering only a nod as acknowledgment before uttering, "water," in a low, raspy voice. Reacting swiftly, Uritu retrieved a cylindrical military canteen from his bag and handed it over.

Beast slowly lifted the mask up, revealing a disproportionately large mouth, and "purred" the water into it. "Buzz…" Suddenly, a chime emanated from the watch on Uritu's wrist, prompting him to rise urgently. "Quick! Tana's here to collect us!"

Returning the emptied kettle to Uritu, Beast wiped away the lingering water, releasing a sound that hovered between contentment and a deep sigh.

As soon as they settled into the car, Tana's voice cut through the tension. "Our house was broken into today, but strangely, nothing seems to be missing."

"Damn it!" Uritu cursed under his breath.

The vehicle they rode in was a worn gasoline car, cobbled together from various parts. With a press of the accelerator by Tana, the engine roared to life, propelling them forward with a loud *boom*.

"No gasoline or water was taken, and the food remains untouched, but the place is a mess," Tana continued, her voice tinged with unease.

Sensing her apprehension, Uritu sought to reassure her, "it's all right. We're nearing our goal, and once we have enough funds, we'll leave this cursed place behind. And I've already asked Kevin to arrange for the ship bound for Northern California. It's set to depart from Hanoi and will arrive in two or three months, carrying a shipment of steel bars. It should be a secure passage. I've reserved three spots, assuming—"

Interrupting himself, Uritu turned his gaze to Beast and said, "you mentioned hailing from NorCal, didn't you? In that case, you're free from fighting. Return to your kin. Your share remains untouched."

Beast nodded without a word.

"Dear, something feels off… I've never felt this way before. Open the window and look back. Do you see anything?" Tana's voice quivered with unease.

Alerted by Tana's words, Uritu rolled down the window and leaned out, scanning the sky. He noticed an unusual flicker, distinct from the stars.

"Find a wooded area near the river and take that path, you know it!" he instructed tersely.

Tana maneuvered the car with a sense of urgency, the mysterious flicker trailing closely behind. As they neared a dense forest, she abruptly veered off the road, plunging the vehicle into the shadows.

"Quick! Kill the headlights!" Uritu commanded, barely getting the words out before darkness enveloped them.

Navigating cautiously through the dense forest for a long time, Tana heard the soft babble of a stream. "We're nearly there," she whispered, relief evident in her voice.

The car clumsily turned onto a road in disrepair, and Uritu leaned out again, glanced around, and comforted everyone, "shook it off!"

The car lumbered onto a crumbling road, eventually halting in front of a grand yet decaying iron gate. This once-majestic mountain mansion hinted at a bygone era of opulence.

At first glance, anyone could discern that this was once the mountain mansion of a wealthy tycoon. It appeared that the original owner had either relocated or fled overseas when Uritu seized it, making it their home. In Abandoned Harbor, only individuals like them retained some hope for life. They sought refuge in such secluded, abandoned residences to escape the senseless violence that plagued the streets. These remote locations offered a degree of protection, deterring casual intruders. However, Uritu's apprehension stemmed not from petty thieves but from potential conflicts with influential figures, the *big men* who wielded significant power and posed greater threats.

Beast was the first to step out of the car, carefully swinging open the rusted iron door to reveal an unobstructed path. Meanwhile, Uritu retrieved an H&K caseless submachine pistol from a compartment. With practiced ease, Tana released the brake and steered the car inside.

The piercing glare of the headlights revealed a rotorcraft stationed in the courtyard's center, slowly emerging into their view. Startled, Uritu sprang out of the vehicle, weapon at the ready, only to discover the rotorcraft unoccupied.

"Uritu, we're here to negotiate!" The unexpected voice from behind caught Uritu off guard. He pivoted to find three armed men positioned near his car: one holding Beast captive, another aiming a gun at the vehicle's cab.

"Easy there... Let's keep things civil." Uritu promptly discarded his firearm.

The apparent leader of the trio asserted, "General Chu wishes to converse with this guy," gesturing toward Beast.

"And who are you guys working for? General Chu?"

Ignoring Uritu's query, the leader continued, "we know the guy helped you make a lot of money. Rest assured. General Chyu's compensation will be more than generous."

"Beast? Why would General Chu be interested in him?" In his panic, Uritu momentarily forgot his maneuvering skills, making the trio frustrated. One of them thrust the barrel of his gun into the car window.

Tana cried, "dear... Help me!"

Uritu caught Tana's muffled pleas from inside the car and his voice softened. "If you want to take him away, go ahead! What's stopping you? Just let my wife go!"

Without hesitation, the leader yanked open the car door, releasing Tana before seizing the other man's firearm, pressing it menacingly against her temple.

"Excellent," he affirmed, signaling his cohorts.

The other two seized Beast, propelling him forward several steps before boarding the flying car together.

As the vehicle ascended, the leader retracted his weapon, allowing Tana to rejoin Uritu. With a backward glance, he briskly retreated, vanishing into the shadows of the night.

Finally releasing a pent-up breath, Uritu enveloped Tana in a comforting embrace as her tears threatened to spill, saying, "it's all right. We'll find Kevin and leave this place immediately."

Gazing skyward, Uritu watched the rotorcraft wobble in the distance, gradually diminishing into a mere speck. Moments later, a fleeting red streak darted across the night sky, flickering briefly like a spent firework before vanishing altogether.

Yiming Lee's eerie dream persisted, but over time he grew accustomed to it. No longer paralyzed by fear, he found himself increasingly adept at recognizing its illusory nature while still within its confines. Seizing these moments, he meticulously scrutinized every detail, searching for any possible clues. As he pondered Ethelinda's words, he started to consider the notion that perhaps this wasn't merely a dream. The dome, the platform, the flashes, and the peculiar expressions on the faces—all remained consistent with each recurrence. Each visitation intensified his suspicion that someone might have embedded this experience into his consciousness deliberately. Perhaps it was a carefully orchestrated plot, its essential clues cunningly hidden within. And each time Sharmin—or Mia—disintegrated into ashes amid the glaring light, he awoke consumed by grief.

During breakfast, Lee still appeared fatigued.

"That dream again?" Lyu, seated across from him, inquired with evident concern. She had been diligently researching the Sirius and Dogon people, driven by a quest to unravel the mystery surrounding the painting. Although Lee had long ceased to be interested in the painting itself, realizing he had been overly suspicious before, he couldn't bring himself to dampen Lyu's enthusiasm, especially when she approached the task so carefully and earnestly.

"I'm fine, I've grown used to it."

"Speaking of which, haven't I been assisting you with research on the Dogon people? There's something off..."

Lee responded with a distracted "Oh?"

"I mentioned before that my father connected me with an astronomical expert from the Corporation. He's extensively published on Sirius. I asked Gia to look into his work, but she couldn't find anything—despite me citing some of his papers in the past!"

"It's not surprising. Much of the information available for public access has undergone substantial redaction, you—"

At first, Lee contemplated discouraging her from pursuing what he deemed futile efforts, but as the words surged to his lips, he clamped down, stifling the urge to voice his reservations. Yet, Lyu effortlessly sensed the unspoken sentiments and addressed them in a hushed tone, "I know what you're getting at. You think I'm chasing shadows, wasting my time. In fact, I just want to help, though I can't help on anything."

Lee could hear the hint of hurt in her voice. He quickly

reassured her, "that's not what I meant. What was the expert's name again? Let me check our internal database."

"Saeed Hosseini."

"Gia, search for information on Saeed Hosseini and grant me the maximum access."

After a brief pause, Gia responded, "I'm sorry, Lee. There's no information available on Saeed Hosseini."

"That can't be right. Dad had invited him to our family several times—I've met him!"

Lee tried to explain. "Unless…"

"Unless he was implicated by my dad's incident?" Lyu hesitated, her voice dropping, and her words hung heavily in the air. Lee felt a jolt of unease, Danny's ominous visage flashing across his mind, compelling him to find a way to keep Danny at bay.

"Lee, there's a message from Shiaojun Chyi!" Gia alerted him.

Lee sensed the timing must signify an important update. "What did he say?"

"He simply said, 'Come quickly!'"

Though brief, the urgency of those words wasn't lost on Lee. Pushing aside thoughts of breakfast, he directed Gia, "arrange a car to the location where we last met."

Upon hearing this, Lyu's excitement mirrored Lee's own. "Does this mean there's news about Danny?"

"It seems likely. I'm heading there immediately!"

This time it was a servant who guided Lee into the dimly lit hall. The expansive window remained shuttered, casting the hall into near darkness. Only the faint glow from the aquarium provided enough illumination for Lee to discern a figure seated on the sofa.

"The man is dead, and I have no intention of involving myself further," Chyi declared wearily.

"Dead? How? Where?" Lee pressed.

"In Shallow Harbor, at the hands of the EOS." Chyi replied.

Lee's disbelief was palpable. "The Eyes of Sky? You can't mean Danny was targeted by the Corporation's orbital laser system."

The *Eyes of Sky* was a formidable high-energy laser weapon system stationed by the Corporation in outer space. It served as a critical bastion of global peace in the post-collapse era, following the dissolution of the old world order. However, its influence as a deterrent far surpassed its actual combat capabilities. Due to this formidable reputation, the system has seen limited activation. Notably, during the Shallow Harbor blockade, it mercilessly obliterated hundreds of thousands of ships and flying vehicles attempting escape, underscoring its devastating potential.

"The activation of the EOS requires Hun's authorization!" Lee reiterated, seeking clarity.

Chyi sighed, his demeanor heavy with fatigue. "I have no intention of involving myself further in your affairs. Look, the man was located, and their aircraft was downed shortly after its takeoff. Everything was eradicated."

Despite Chyi's reserved demeanor, Lee ventured, "is that all? You don't want to know about Mia?"

Chyi responded with a hint of detachment, "I possess a recording if you're inclined to hear. As for Mia, she's returned. My involvement ends there."

As Chyi finished his words, a hushed conversation between two men crackled from the darkness:

A: "Tell me about that man!"
B: "Beast?"
A: "…"
B: "He slipped away from the other side, unbelievable, wasn't it? He's a puzzle, keeps his secrets tight, and I can't know much."
A: "Just give me the facts. What do you know?"
B: "He's from NorCal and has family there. He left because someone offered him a lifeline."
A: "Who? How?"
B: "He didn't tell the name, but whoever it was had clout. Said they could fix his head. Given he had taken too many hits from boxing, doctors in NorCal had grim predictions for him They anticipated he would lapse into a coma within a year or even shorter. Yet the man coaxed him into a clinical trial, saying it would restore his brain to its previous state."
A: "Did it work?"
B: "Yeah, he survived, obviously, but it's hard to say that he's in good condition as promised."
A: "Elaborate!"
B: "He told me he had changed, that he had lost something fundamental."
A: "People change; get to the point."

B: "But he said he couldn't dream anymore!"
A: "Trivial matters! Anything else?"
B: "He can no longer feel pain."
A: "To the point!"
B: "He can't be harmed either."
A: "I meant, what's the bottom line?"
B: "He believes he might be immortal."

Upon hearing the cryptic exchange, Lee felt an inexplicable chill creep over him. He waited in silence, expecting Chyi to break the quietude, but the guy remained silent on the sofa.

"Can we at least have some light?" Lee finally broke the uneasy silence. The prolonged darkness weighed heavily on him. At Chyi's gesture, the room flooded with light. The expansive aquarium wall captured Lee's attention first. A lemon shark, previously hidden and resting, darted away, startled by the abrupt brightness.

Lee was startled too. He instinctively stepped back, then approached the aquarium once more, as if drawn to something specific. Bending down, his gaze settled on a dark red entity nestled among the rocks—its contorted shape reminiscent of an inverted banana peel, twitching slightly.

"Starfish? Alive?" A strange thought flashed across Lee's mind but vanished just as quickly.

Without responding to Lee's question, Chyi reclined, his voice tinged with exhaustion, "that's all I can offer. Additionally, there's an electronic document detailing the clinical trial they spoke of. It's been sent your way. Now, if you'll excuse me, I'd like some time alone."

With an implicit dismissal hanging in the air, Lee departed, a whirlwind of unanswered questions swirling within him.

Meantime, Lyu had anxiously awaited Lee's return. Spotting him, she hurriedly inquired, "any updates?"

Lee nodded, masking the growing unease within him. "Danny's gone, but he's left behind some clues."

"Clues?" Lyu's eyes widened, "do they connect to my father?"

"Hard to say for now," Lee replied cautiously. "There were unusual aspects about Danny that your father must've sensed, prompting his investigation."

"Unusual how? Just because he lacked a nose?"

Lee hesitated, grappling with how much to disclose. "The clues are elusive, Lyur. I'm still piecing them together."

"So, my dad was killed because he was tracking down Danny?"

Lee paused, struggling with the weight of the information and the dangers it hinted at. This wasn't merely an old, forgotten case; it felt like a deep-rooted conspiracy ensnaring everyone involved. Shannon Chen's demise hinted at its gravity, yet it lacked definitive proof of foul play. Sensing Lyu's desperation for answers yet reluctant to entangle her further, Lee replied cautiously, "possibly. I need to delve deeper to understand."

Retreating to his room, Lee accessed the message from Chyi. It unveiled an agreement dated 2045, signed by *Daniel Nikolayevich Ivanov* and *Great Evolutionary Biotechnology Co., Ltd*. The latter's signature was simply a scripted initial of "D. W." While most of the document droned on with legal jargon, one detail stood out: the signing location, San Jose, Northern California.

Lee swiftly accessed the intranet to search for *Great Evolution Biotechnology Co., Ltd*. As anticipated, the system yielded no results—a clear indication of intentional redaction. This only deepened Lee's suspicions: Powerful entities were meticulously concealing whatever secrets Danny held. The fact that they activated the EOS (Eyes of Sky) suggested the gravity of these secrets. The same enigmatic information seemed to be at play in Shannon Chen's death, a realization that heightened Lee's growing apprehension.

As Lee mulled over these revelations, he felt trapped, ensnared in a web of intrigue and danger. It was as if an unseen net, intricate and impenetrable, was closing in on him. Uncertainty gnawed at him. Was he unwittingly stepping into a carefully orchestrated snare, or was he merely the long-waited prey of others? This pervasive sense of lurking peril was even more disconcerting than Zhukov's scrutiny. Perhaps the nebulous, unseen threat was more unsettling.

Overwhelmed, Lee reached for a bottle of Cognac, seeking solace before succumbing to an uneasy sleep.

9. SOUVENIR

The dream remained steadfast in its repetition. Once the blinding glare faded, Lee found himself enveloped in utter darkness, with only the residual mandala pattern on the dome lingering in his vision. Unlike previous instances when he would snap awake, this time he opted to remain, squatting on the altar-like platform with a deliberate intent to see what would unfold next.

A surprising chill, accompanied by an unsettling silence, surrounded him, prompting him to instinctively curl into a tight ball and clutch his arms around himself for warmth.

Lost within the nebulous confines of the dream, Lee had lost sense of time. Yet, a subtle warmth began to seep through, emanating from beneath the platform. As his attention was drawn to this gentle heat, a faint orange glow materialized—reminiscent of the final vestiges of a setting sun left to the dark night.

Soon, he realized that the light was not as far away as he had first thought, and as he moved his body and held out his hand to the light, he saw it, forgetting the concept of light that had just flashed through his mind.

That was an orange star-shaped object, resting silently on the plane where Lee found himself (the notion of an *altar* had faded from his awareness). No larger than his palm, it radiated a soft orange glow in every direction. The concept of optics seemed to elude him too; in fact, the shimmer illuminated its orange body, yet the source of the light remained an enigma.

In an instant, a surge of warmth welled up from the depths of

Lee's heart, coursing through him until he felt immersed in a comforting ocean. It was a sensation suffused with joy, cordiality, familiarity, a hint of shyness, and a profound sense of déjà vu. As this warmth intensified, a tunnel of memories unfurled before him. Drawn to the luminous glow at its end, he glimpsed scenes of a vivid blue mist, pristine white sails dancing atop azure waters, a bustling marketplace, and animated crowds...

"Is that star on your head real?" the little boy asked, his eyes wide with curiosity.

"Of course, silly! Want a closer look?" The little girl delicately unpinned the dried starfish from her hair, offering it to him. Gently cradling it in his small hands, the boy wrinkled his nose and said, "smells... fishy."

She giggled, rolling her eyes. "That's just the scent of the sea, Mr. Nose!" She thought to herself, only grown-ups would say something like that.

"Give me back!" she lunged for her starfish, but the boy lifted it high above his head, just out of her reach.

"Come and get it!" he teased.

"Give me! Give me!" Frustrated, she hopped and leaped, trying to retrieve her treasure. Her efforts only made him chuckle more. Her cheeks flushed with anger, and she wrapped her arms around his neck like a little monkey, throwing him off balance. The two wrestled and eventually tumbled together onto the soft grass.

Concluding their playful tussle, the little boy sprawled on his back, the starfish momentarily forgotten. He gazed upward, captivated by the cerulean expanse above, where seabirds darted and danced amidst the billowing clouds. Abruptly, a droplet touched his cheek, drawing his attention upward to a pair of shimmering eyes reminiscent of brilliant emeralds, glistening with tears.

"Boohoo... you broke it!" the little girl cried, tears streaming down her face as she rose from the ground to retrieve the starfish now shattered into two pieces.

Realizing he had gone too far in their play, the little boy scrambled to his feet, his gaze lowered in remorse.

"I'm sorry, I didn't mean to. Please don't cry," he pleaded.

The little girl wiped away her tears, attempting to fit the fractured starfish pieces back together.

"Come on, I'll show you something special!" The little boy said, seizing the moment. Then he tugged at the girl's arm, leading her toward the bustling farmer's market, whether she resisted or not.

"Sample! Sample! Free Sample!" echoed the vibrant calls from various stalls.

Amidst this market scene filled with an array of colors—deep red cherries, radiant golden navel oranges, a spectrum of bell peppers, verdant mint leaves, rich purple grapes, and translucent gooseberries—he found it unusual such vivid hues could manifest in a dream. Yet, it wasn't merely the visual spectacle; the air itself carried an ethereal blend of the rich aroma of caramel, the delicate fragrance of apricots, cinnamon's sweetness, and the robust scent of rosemary, all set against the backdrop of the sea's salty tang.

"Ding-dong-cling-clang-ding-dong-cling-clang..."

The bells of the Ferry Building chimed, their melodic toll echoing through the bustling atmosphere.

Lee finally opened his eyes, trembling with an unexpected rush of emotion. Still nestled in his bed, he saw the afternoon sun filtering through the blinds. To his astonishment, tears had welled up without his noticing.

A thought flashed in Lee's mind. *I must make a trip back to NorCal.*

Without second thoughts, he swiftly filled out an application and submitted it into the system.

"Yiming, up already?" Lyu paused her tidying of the living room, noticing Lee's emergence. She retreated to the kitchen, offering, "you seemed so exhausted. I didn't want to disturb your rest earlier. Let me warm up some food for you."

"Thanks," Lee replied.

Almost immediately, regret gnawed at him. Proposing a trip to Northern California at this moment seemed ill-timed. Wouldn't it raise suspicions of an escape plan? In truth, he wasn't even sure if he had considered the idea himself.

"I've come to terms with it," Lyu continued, mistaking his unease for concern over Danny's matters. "Whatever I discover about my father's tragedy, it won't change the outcome. But at least I've known the truth about my mother; she wasn't delusional, and the stories they told are all lies."

Lee felt a pang of guilt at her comforting words. Trying to reassure her, he stuttered, "I'll dig deeper into your father's affairs.

If I get the chance to confront Hun, ahem—"

Eventually, even he felt embarrassed about his boastful tone and feigned a cough.

Lyu passed a glass of water to him. After taking a few sips and clearing his throat, he continued, "Lyur, I think I might need to take a trip—"

His words were abruptly cut off by Gia's urgent interruption.

"Lee, Dave needs to see you right away!"

Upon hearing this, Lee inwardly lamented, "screwed now!"

Dave's office boasted a prime location on the 88th floor of Block A in the Corporation's headquarters, chosen meticulously by Shannon Chen earlier for its serene bay views. Upon entering, Lee found Dave alone, and a subtle sense of relief washed over him.

"Lee, I can't recall you having any other relatives in Northern California," Dave cut straight to the chase.

"No," Lee hesitated, considering retracting his earlier decision, "actually I contemplated going back to pack, but soon realized there's nothing of value to bring. So I reconsidered it for now."

"It's okay. I've already approved your return, and I've discussed it with Zhukov and others, and they all agreed it might be good for you to have a trip back to your hometown."

"Huh?"

Lee was taken aback by Dave's unexpected response, growing increasingly suspicious about the real reason for this meeting.

"You've really put in the work over the years. How about taking a breather? I'll find someone to step in temporarily for the Foundation. Your dedication hasn't gone unnoticed. You know, back in the day, you were the only one in the company with the guts to step up and shoulder that responsibility. I've always admired that, even the boss has praised your commitment multiple times."

Lee finally caught on to the implication and asked, "who's stepping in for me?"

"Liam, Liam Mohammadi. I'll set up a meeting so you two can get acquainted beforehand."

Recalling Zhukov's earlier words about Hun not being urgent to replace him, Lee queried further, "is everything set in stone?"

"It's pretty much settled," Dave affirmed. "Head back and prepare. Oh, and there's some intel… A transport ship crashed in Brittany from outer space. We suspect it might be the lost Prometheus. Rumor has it there's a survivor, possibly this *Mia* person you've heard about."

Just as Lee was about to exit, Dave's revelation stunned him. His body stiffened, and after a brief pause, he whispered, "have they... found her?"

Observing Lee's reaction, Dave appeared satisfied, and he replied softly, "rest assured, we're on it."

When Lee was on his way back home, it was nightfall. Encased within a nimble rotorcraft, he skimmed through the city's lower reaches. As twilight enveloped the horizon, vast holographic displays materialized, seemingly out of nowhere. These projections, appearing as numerous and relentless as mushrooms after a downpour, filled every available space between the towering structures. They showcased the Corporation's illustrious history and monumental achievements, casting the entire scene in an eerie, dreamlike glow.

For the first time since his return, a disgusting sense of boredom consumed him. He found himself reminiscing about those seemingly endless days and nights of solitude, which he once believed would never conclude. Now, in hindsight, He recognized that during his time concealed beneath the ice and later within the so-called "City in the Sky," he had experienced a unique sense of serenity and calm.

While Lee held the title of commander-in-chief appointed by the Corporation, He rarely needed to delve deeply into the day-to-day operations. Over a decade prior, the Corporation had developed an unparalleled artificial intelligence named Eve, dispatching her to Titan. Eve's relentless and meticulous oversight managed both the unmanned factories on Titan and the artificial ecosystem at the new station. To Lee, those coordinated drone swarms, organized robot tribes, and the intricate nuclear power facilities felt as fundamental and integral as Earth's natural landscapes; they neither owed their existence to him, nor would they fade with his absence.

A peculiar notion began to take shape in Lee's mind. Perhaps that distant place, millions of miles away, held his true sense of belonging. This realization clarified why, upon Dave's suggestion of finding a replacement, a profound and indescribable sense of loss immediately engulfed him.

Then he thought of Mia, a woman who had only appeared in

his dreams, yet at that moment, he felt a profound depth of concern for her well-being.

And then there was Brittany.

Located as a promontory of the European continent extending into the North Atlantic, Brittany had once been a part of the French Republic during the era before the collapse of the European Union. As nations disintegrated and republics fell, most disconnected governments gravitated towards the Corporation's Unified and Exclusive Market to secure essential energy and resources. However, Brittany stood apart. The locals, inherently resilient and distrustful of the Corporation, clung to their independence. As a result, Brittany emerged as one of the rare regions in the Old World untouched by the Corporation's influence.

"Brittany," Lee whispered, perplexed by the unexpected warmth and familiarity he felt towards this seemingly ordinary geographical reference.

He also reminisced about his father's words: "Stay optimistic! Forge your path! Those old days are gone; you'll usher in a new era, akin to a modern Middle Ages!" These relentless teachings reflected a distinct pessimism.

His father constantly perceived the world as teetering on the edge of ruin due to factors like dwindling oil reserves, environmental decay, erratic climate patterns, societal stratification, widening wealth disparities, and escalating social unrest. His father's natural admiration for visionaries like Elon Musk shaped his beliefs. From a young age, his father imbued him with the idea of interstellar migration, pushing him towards aerospace studies and space science. Essentially, his father propelled him onto this irreversible journey.

Lee, inherently lacking grand ambitions, was acutely aware of his shortcomings. Throughout college, he struggled with feelings of isolation. Beyond his academic pursuits, he found solace either deciphering enigmatic symbols from ancient Babylonian civilization on his computer or gazing at the cosmos late into the night from the Lawrence Science Museum's platform. Had it not been for Chen's persuasive visit to Berkeley, enticing him to join the Corporation, Lee might have settled into a tranquil life in Northern California, complete with a loving spouse and a family of his own.

Finally, memories of his mother flooded back. The same

mother who had forsaken him, fracturing his childhood in the process. And the starfish, a precious recollection he had ruthlessly discarded to break ties with a past he wished to forget. Yet, its allure remained irresistible to him. The radiant orange starfish, shimmering with a faint light, felt like a key unlocking a door. In his analogy, he likened himself to an individual confined in a darkened room for an extended period. Despite the lurking dangers or uncertainties outside, the innate human desire to break free from confinement remained overpowering.

The starfish had served as a beacon, guiding him through the obscure corridors of his dreams. Yet, beyond that tunnel lay a memory, dormant for countless years, awaiting its natural resurgence. Initially, only fragments of recollections surfaced, leaving him puzzled about their coherence. However, as these fragmented memories collided and intertwined, a vivid tableau began to unfold:

He was leading her through a bustling marketplace, her tiny hand nestled securely in his. At each stall, he would eagerly present a variety of fruits—vibrant red oranges, deep blackcurrants, sunny yellow cherries, succulent blueberries, and exotic passion fruit. Handpicked, one by one, he fed them to her, perhaps in an attempt to atone for an earlier misstep. Yet, the genuine happiness radiating from her smile resonated deeply within him.

Only when she bid farewell, gripping his hand tightly as if reluctant to release it, did he realize the clarity in her eyes.

She pressed half a starfish into his palm, declaring, "I'll give you this half!"

Soon after, she was whisked away by her stoic mother, one of the purportedly esteemed guests of the new Republic invited to participate in the fleet parade celebrating independence. As armed soldiers forcibly distanced him, a fleeting glimpse of her retreating figure lingered, her parting shout echoing, "hey! My name is Sharmin Haelion, remember it?"

It was only now that Lee understood why Sharmin Haelion was full of kindness and familiarity when she walked towards him lightly at the banquet in Consul William's mansion that night, and why he had a strange feeling of déjà vu when she took his hand and walked in a fly.

Now was the time for him to retrieve that piece of starfish, a cherished souvenir from memories both lost and rekindled.

10. HOMETOWN

For Yiming Lee, memories of his hometown felt like ancient glaciers—frozen and obscured from view for ages—until the right emotion acted as the thaw, unleashing them like a sudden burst of spring water. When long-forgotten scenes reemerged with startling clarity, he grappled with a sensation that old experiences were both fresh and elusive, like wisps of smoke he couldn't dispel.

Take, for instance, his encounter with young Sharmin near the ferry building. Before ever finding the starfish in his dream, or more precisely, before glimpsing a real starfish in Chyi's aquarium, he had no recollection of that moment. Yet now, he struggled to accept its reality. The vividness of the memory transported him so completely that amid the dampness of an Asian metropolis, he could still feel California's sun warming his skin. The mingled smell of marijuana and excrement wafted back to him, along with the distinct aroma of various berries tantalizing his palate.

Such uncanny recollections, appearing with such tangible realism, fueled Lee's growing skepticism about their authenticity. This skepticism compelled him to delve into his past with an uncommon intensity, inevitably leading him back to the decaying remnants of his once-forgotten hometown.

Lee never witnessed San Francisco's golden age, nor did he harbor a fascination for its bygone splendors. The nostalgic tales adults spun about the city's illustrious past failed to resonate deeply with his youthful sensibilities. While he recognized the city's historical significance and its association with prominent figures, his sentiments toward it mirrored his indifference to the once-glorious cities of Rome or Chang'an.

Born in the 2020s, Lee was plunged into an unprecedented era of upheaval, a time unlike any other in human history. His youth was marked by a relentless succession of transformative events: a global pandemic, waves of New Affirmative Action, the challenges of Great Stagnation, the De-federalization Movement, the ascendance of Neo-orthodoxy, the disintegration of the European Union, the emergence of the Central Christian State, a Brief Civil War, the formation of the Northern California Republic, and the inexorable rise of the Corporation amid the prevailing chaos. This series of events, unfolding like a never-ending storm, gradually eroded the foundations of the once serene and delicate Old World, leaving its frightened and desperate people in ruins. While adults could still seek solace in nostalgia, young individuals like Lee naturally drifted towards forgetfulness.

Indeed, amidst the relentless turmoil, moments of magic occasionally pierced through, such as his encounter with Sharmin. On a rare, sweltering morning that brought an unusual calm, his father announced they would visit the ferry building to witness a spectacle—the entire fleet of Northern California anchoring in the bay to commemorate the birth of the new republic. While his father's excitement bubbled over, Lee remained indifferent to the looming warships. Instead, he found himself captivated by the sky's unusual hue, a delicate, ethereal blue reminiscent of aged oil paintings. Its unexpected appearance lent the surroundings a dreamlike quality that left him momentarily adrift. Lost in thought, he wandered the bustling docks until a glimmer caught his eye—a vivid orange star shimmering in the sunlight. Drawn to its allure, he met the gaze of a curious little girl adorned with the captivating ornament.

Yet, ultimately, Lee chose to suppress those fleeting memories, including that specific one, knowing that clinging to them would usher in darker visions. These haunting scenes would infiltrate his dreams, rousing him from sleep in the dead of night, leaving him restless and tormented.

He couldn't shake off memories of the era of citizen autonomy, when his typically frail father wielded an AR-15 from the stairwell, defending their home against intruders, felling more than four in a single, harrowing confrontation. The aftermath lingered as a grim reminder, with father and son spending a day grappling with the remnants—bloodstains stubbornly defying their efforts to erase them.

He had vividly remembered the height of the Secularization Movement. Enraged protesters ignited the nearby Grace Cathedral, just blocks away. The ensuing night was in chaos—thick smoke, agitated crowds outside their windows, and the unsettling repetition of gunfire.

Perhaps most chillingly, Lee had been haunted by memories of Andrew, his childhood friend—a cheerful boy whose father was one of the active conservatives. On the day of the Republic's founding, a brutal act led to Andrew's family being lynched, with their recognizable heads displayed ominously on the porch.

Even now, the mere thought of the traumatic scenes would send involuntary shivers down Lee's spine.

This time, however, Lee chose not to abandon the idea of heading to Northern California. Instead, as forgotten memories persistently resurfaced, he found himself increasingly inclined to embrace them. Driven by a newfound determination, he resolved to actively explore the events of his past, understand the realities of the present, and anticipate what the future might hold.

More than three decades had passed since the termination of the transpacific civil route. Yet, now, Lee found himself aboard a dedicated weekly flight bound for a singular destination: the Northern California Republic. This republic stood as the sole independent entity on the North American continent with a favorable disposition toward the Corporation. The relationship between them remained delicate, being marked by mutual interdependence and caution. Specifically, Northern California's reliance on the Corporation was palpable. Only the Corporation's power could help shield the republic from looming threats, primarily emanating from the Central Christian State to the east and the southern anarchists, both vying to reclaim this *rebellious land*. However, this dependency came with conditions. What set Northern California apart was its unique landscape amidst the chaos that had set back societies across the North American continent by over a century. Northern California, in contrast, thrived. Its authorities' lenient policies toward technology and innovation rendered it a sanctuary for liberals globally. Consequently, the region attracted a myriad of scientists, artists, ideologists, and others who found themselves at odds with the Corporation's ideology. This influx positioned Northern California's scientific and technological advancements leagues ahead, perpetually astonishing the Corporation. Recognizing this value, the Corporation fostered close business ties across a broad spectrum of entities, all in pursuit of harnessing Northern California's cutting-edge scientific achievements.

Consequently, the flight carried only a handful of passengers: officials with business within the Corporation, Northern Californian traders engaged in various transactions with the Corporation, and individuals labeled as terrorists—disguised as the aforementioned groups. Media outlets often sensationalized these potential security risks, constantly highlighting isolated incidents of terrorist activity to perpetuate a pervasive yet somewhat distant sense of threat. However, for those passengers compelled to undertake this journey for diverse reasons, the immediate concern wasn't the threat of terrorism. Rather, it was the deafening roar and tumultuous vibrations accompanying the rapid ascent of the aircraft that instilled a palpable sense of impending doom.

Ironically, the genesis of this revolutionary flight concept could be traced back to Elon Musk, a renowned entrepreneur from Northern California's early years. While the foundational idea bore resemblance to Musk's initial vision of intercontinental travel via rocket, the aircraft's propulsion system evolved from chemical combustion to nuclear fusion ion power. This innovation allowed for swift point-to-point transit, enabling passengers to traverse vast distances and arrive at their destination in less than an hour.

While ordinary passengers struggled to acclimate to the abrupt hyper gravity, contorting their faces in discomfort, Lee remained unfazed. To him, such sensations had become routine. His eyelids grew heavy, and before he knew it, he had drifted into a peaceful slumber.

As the landing platform floated on the waters of San Francisco Bay, the early morning sky was alive with the buzzing of drones. From a distance, their collective hum resembled a swarm of bees awaiting their next directive. Once the plane touched down, passengers began to disembark, descending the gangway with anticipation. In synchronized motion, drones swooped down, each carefully selecting its designated guest, ready to take them to their next destination.

Lee stepped into the awaiting rotorcraft and was surprised to find a dark-skinned girl already seated inside.

"How did—?" He was stunned and almost jumped out, while being pulled back into his seat by the girl.

She began with a cheerful introduction, "hey there! First time in NorCal, huh? Lucky you! I'm Talma, and trust me, when it comes to guiding, I'm your go-to gal!"

"I didn't ask for a guide," Lee retorted, attempting to activate his personal assistant to replace the drone, but it remained unresponsive.

Talma chuckled. "Look, your signals won't work around here. That's why you need us, the guides!"

"What happened? Wasn't it reported?" Lee questioned.

A hint of annoyance crossed Talma's face. "If you're not interested, you can step out. Plenty of others would love my guidance!"

"Fine, take me to 1219 Lombard Street," Lee relented.

"Got it, 1219 Lombard Street!" Talma confirmed, signaling the rotorcraft to ascend.

As they soared over San Francisco, Lee's gaze wandered to the city below. Despite all the devastation, the city retained its unique charm. Spotting Fort Mason, he even caught a glimpse of his home's distinctive orange roof.

Upon landing, Lee was eager to get off, but Talma held him back with a surprised expression.

"I don't carry Northern California dollars," he said. "I can only offer Corporation credits instead You'll need to manage the exchange."

"Costs you a hundred!" Talma claimed, a boldness that momentarily caught Lee off guard. Yet, he yielded, inputting the necessary amount on the electronic card she proffered.

Grinning, Talma remarked, "you're getting the best guide in the Bay—yours truly, the all-knowing Talma!"

As Lee began to depart, she called out, "you'll find my details in your records. Trust me, you'll soon realize it's money well spent! Call me when you are in need!"

Without a backward glance, Lee briskly moved on, an air of disdain trailing behind him.

The landing spot stood a mere hundred steps from Lee's residence. Climbing a slope, he caught sight of the two-story structure, its familiarity almost uncanny. While the façade seemed largely unchanged, years of exposure to wind and sun had transformed the once-dark brown walls to a faded hue. The white fences flanking the stairs had also weathered, showing hints of mottling.

Ascending the steps, Lee reached the porch and pressed the doorbell. "Tim, it's Yiming. I'm back!"

The door swung open to reveal a young woman with fair skin and ear-length silver hair, accentuated by a shimmering chip nestled above her eyebrow. "Lee! You're here!" She exclaimed, ushering him inside. Casting a quick glance outside before shutting the door, she continued, "I've been counting the days; it was utterly boring. So, tea or coffee?"

Lee, still processing the unexpected turn of events, managed to stammer, "wait—where's Tim? Have we met before?"

"Oops! My bad! I should've filled you in earlier." The girl chuckled, catching her oversight. "Tim headed to Napa before Christmas to spend some time with his brother. He rented out the place to us. Oh, by the way, I'm Sophia. Been holding down the fort here, waiting for you, and voila, you've finally made it!"

Lee raised an eyebrow, skepticism evident in his gaze. While he wasn't particularly intrigued by this surprising twist, as long as it didn't interfere with his primary mission, he remained indifferent. However, a sense of unease crept over him, particularly as Sophia's words hinted at an anticipation of his arrival.

So, he questioned, "you were expecting me? You knew I was coming?"

Shrugging nonchalantly, Sophia responded, "didn't have that intel. Just passing along what I was informed." She then busied herself with an espresso machine, preparing a cup which she handed to Lee.

He took a sip, but a strong, unpleasant bitterness made him involuntarily spit it all out, complaining, "what is this?"

Sophia's expression soured; annoyance evident. Swiftly retrieving the cup, she downed its contents in a single, satisfying gulp. "Beans are a rarity these days, can't afford wastage. Sure, it's a tad past its prime, but it's still recognizable as coffee!"

Up to this point, Lee hadn't formed a favorable impression of the girl before him. Her abrupt demeanor and seemingly off-kilter responses made him wonder if something was amiss with her. Choosing not to engage further, he stated firmly, "I'd like to return to my room. Tim should have informed you that it's not meant for renting." Casting a discerning glance at Sophia, who appeared nonchalant, he added, "there are personal items there. You shouldn't have touched..."

Sophia responded with an air of casual indifference. "Only ghosts care about your items. Had it not been for my mission, I wouldn't linger. But our task nears its end and may fortune favor us!" She offered a cryptic wink, leaving Lee puzzled.

Eager to leave the living room, Lee rose to head back to his room. Just as he ascended the stairs, Sophia's voice cut through the silence.

"Lee, be ready. Someone will fetch you tonight."

Caught off guard by the unexpected remark, Lee contemplated seeking clarification. However, after a moment's pause, he decided to hold his questions back, suspecting that Sophia wouldn't give him a straight answer anyway.

Upon pushing the door open, Lee felt a wave of poignant nostalgia sweet over, reminiscent of the emotion he yearned for when he first entered his apartment in the city not long ago—a feeling that had eluded him then. He stood rooted in place, his gaze drifting across the familiar yet altered surroundings. Eventually, his eyes settled on the astronomical telescope positioned by the window. Overwhelmed by a cloud of dust, he blinked back moisture and slowly lifted the blinds, allowing sunlight to flood the room and illuminate the accumulated cobwebs and dirt. As he tenderly wiped the telescope's tube, the metal gleamed anew.

As Lee surveyed the room under the sun light, memories flooded back to him—the timeworn wooden bed, the clutter beneath the makeshift table, the closet—all laden with boxes he'd intended to take through maritime shipping. In the end, he decided to leave them behind, a bid to break ties with his past, which now seemed ironic as he found himself back in this very room years later.

With a resigned sigh, Lee began methodically examining all the boxes one by one, carefully resealing them before returning them to their original spots. Yet, the wardrobe posed a challenge. Alone, with Tim absent and his reluctance to seek help from Sophia, Lee grappled with the stacked boxes. In a momentary lapse, the uppermost boxes tumbled, scattering their contents across the floor. Among the debris, an old tin cookie box resonated with a distinct *clang*.

Eyes widening in recognition, Lee exclaimed, "here it is!"

Hastening to the box, he lifted its lid, revealing the dark orange dried starfish—a relic from his childhood and souvenir of Sharmin.

He cradled it delicately, its faint fishy aroma serving as a subtle reminder, challenging the deliberate amnesia he once imposed upon himself.

11. LA RETROUVAILLE

As night enveloped the surroundings, an unsettling silence pressed upon Lee, casting doubt on the very reality he had accepted throughout the day. Was he truly lying on his childhood bed, within the familiar confines of his old home, or had he been ensnared in yet another fragment of his fragmented dreams? Restlessness overtook him, denying him the solace of sleep. With a sigh of resignation, he opened his eyes to an initial void of darkness. Gradually, familiar sights emerged from the shadows— the ceiling fan's gentle rotation, the wardrobe doors that had seen countless makeovers, the weathered shutters, and the cherished astronomical telescope by the window. All stood as silent witnesses to his past. The experience echoed a childhood experiment with film development. He remembered sifting through his father's storage boxes one day in some year, unearthing what appeared to be a roll of black plastic sheets. When they were exposed to daylight, shadowy images became vaguely visible, captivating his youthful curiosity. Recognizing it as old photographic film, Lee purchased the necessary chemical reagents and embarked on a DIY film development adventure with some tutorials. Images from years gone by began to emerge, a development that would have surprised the original photographer. Amidst various scenes of unfamiliar landscapes and fleeting moments, one photo stood out—*she* and his father captured in a moment frozen in time. They stood side by side on what appeared to be a college campus, their smiles genuine but distant. No embraces, no handholding. Yet, as he gazed at the image, an overwhelming surge of emotion washed over him. Tears formed in his eyes, and an unexplained conviction settled in his heart: She must be the mother figure who had left such a faint imprint on his memory.

In the quiet solitude, Lee lay on the wooden bed, his body tightly wrapped in clothes.

Everything became clearer now. Surrounding him were several storage boxes of varied sizes, their contours highlighted by the pale moonlight seeping in through the window. The room felt chilled, the moonbeams casting an ethereal glow that lent a frosty ambiance to the surroundings. A sense of unease gnawed at him. The absence of familiar urban sounds heightened his disquiet. He yearned for the distant echoes of engine roars or the sporadic pops of gunfire, the unmistakable auditory tapestry of San Francisco nights. Memories flooded back of nights spent with friends, their youthful laughter mixing with the challenge of identifying the types of weapons from distant shots. Among them, Andrew had a particular expertise in this. He boasted of his father's extensive ammunition collection, enough to equip an entire battalion, stored securely in their garage.

"Damn it!" Lee exclaimed, sitting up abruptly and shaking his head vigorously, attempting to banish the haunting image of the young boy's bloodied face from his thoughts.

A subtle wave of regret passed through him. Perhaps he shouldn't have declined Sophia's offer to let him stay in her room. She had knocked on the door when it was dusk, her expression shifting to disbelief after he turned down her hospitality.

"Are you seriously planning to sleep in the storage?"

Rather than appreciating her concern, Lee found himself frustrated, exclaiming, "it's not a storage room!"

"Whatever," Sophia dismissed, clearly exasperated. "If you don't heed my advice, you're putting me at risk. Remember, it's my responsibility to ensure you're safe!"

Once more, Lee let out a soft sigh as he rose and made his way to the bathroom.

Without flicking on the light, he simply turned the faucet, and splashed cold water onto his face. However, catching a glimpse of his weary reflection in the mirror startled him, causing him to stagger back. Unwilling to continue this way, he swiftly exited and descended the stairs to the living room. Feeling the familiar texture of the sofa from earlier, he reclined. Just as he began to relax, a brilliant light pierced through from the upper floor, flashing across his face and body. Startled, he shielded his eyes with his hand, attempting to discern the light's origin through his peripheral vision. As the living room lights illuminated, extinguishing the intrusive beam, he spotted Sophia descending the staircase, an automatic rifle in her grip.

"Are you out of your mind?" Lee's voice thundered with disbelief. "This is still my home!"

Without a word, Sophia shouldered the rifle and took a seat across from Lee.

After a brief silence, Lee asked, "any booze? Brandy?" His slow tone hinted at the opportunity for Sophia to offer some form of apology.

Sophia's lips curled into a knowing smile.

"Only Vodka or Tequila."

"Then, Tequila it is."

"Neat?"

"Exactly."

Sophia effortlessly retrieved two glasses, filling one with Tequila and the other with Vodka. With a playful wink, she extended one toward Lee. "Tequila, to us."

Lee raised an eyebrow, finding his glass suddenly empty. Having consumed nothing all day, he was hit by the alcohol hard. He observed Sophia's blinking, wondering if it held some hidden meaning or was just a mere habit. Pushing the thought aside, he asked directly, "you mentioned someone picking me up?"

"Yes," Sophia replied in a subdued tone, finishing off her vodka in a swift gulp. She set down the empty glass and glanced at her watch, reminding herself, "it's nearly time. Mia will be here soon."

"Mia?" Lee's voice cracked with palpable shock, causing him to rise abruptly. The glass slipped from his grasp, hitting the floor with a resounding *clang* before rolling to a stop near Sophia's feet.

Sophia retrieved the fallen glass, placing it back on the coffee table before responding nonchalantly, "that's right, Mia."

The room grew heavy with silence as Lee and Sophia sat across from each other. Sophia seemed aware of Lee's lingering hostility, choosing silence as her shield. With her head bowed, she absentmindedly caressed the cold metal of her rifle. Lee's suspicions churned within him, yet he hesitated to voice them. Memories of his prior brusqueness toward her made him reluctant to press further, leaving an uncomfortable silence hanging in the air.

Is she genuinely this bothersome?

Lee pondered, trying to pinpoint the cause of his discomfort with Sophia. Was it her silver-dyed hair, or perhaps the chip embedded above her eyebrow? These features evoked memories of the defiant anarchists from bygone eras, stirring a sense of unease within him.

Summoning courage, Lee finally broke the silence, his voice laced with caution. "Can I ask you something?"

Sophia met his gaze, her eyes narrowing slightly, "what's on your mind?"

Lee hesitated, momentarily pointing to his own eyebrow.

Sophia sighed, her demeanor softening for a fleeting moment, "it's a scar, a wound from the past. The bones were shattered, and I've covered it up ever since."

"Oh… it actually looks good now," Lee said, feeling a subtle heat rise to his cheeks. He could guess from her explanation about the shattered bones that it likely stemmed from a gunshot wound, probably in a brutal battle.

"Buzz….Buzz…"

Sophia's watch hummed softly, prompting her to rise with a sense of alertness. She hastened to the door, swung it open for confirmation, and then turned to Lee with a quick declaration, "she's here."

Lee's heart raced as he steadied himself, preparing to meet this awaited arrival. At the threshold stood a woman draped in a nondescript blue hooded sweatshirt. After exchanging hushed words with Sophia, she hastened toward Lee, removing the hood in a swift motion.

Though time had etched its lines upon her face—deepening her features with the weight of years—Lee recognized her instantly. The subtle indentations on her cheeks, the soft creases at the corners of her eyes, and the weary gaze that met his own; all confirmed that this was no illusion. It was Sharmin, standing before him after years apart.

Overwhelmed by the realization, Lee nearly blurted out her

name, "Shar…"

But she swiftly silenced him, pressing a finger to her lips with a hushed "Shh." Moving behind him, she meticulously examined his head, ears, and neck, searching with a purpose. After a thorough inspection, she gave Sophia a confirming nod. "All clear…" Then turned to Lee, adding, "and I'm Mia."

"Mia…" Lee murmured. The name had bothered him for so long, now it stirred a mix of confusion and astonishment.

Breaking the momentary silence, Mia's voice carried a familiarity that transcended the years. "Yiming, we're leaving now. Got everything you need?"

Lee locked eyes with her, recognizing the same spark of eagerness in her eyes—those deep emerald pupils—just as he remembered from years ago. It stirred a warmth within him, evoking a sense of familiarity and kindness.

"I do!" He replied. With a burst of energy, he dashed up the stairs, entered the bedroom, located the half starfish, carefully wrapped it in cloth, and swiftly tucked it into his backpack.

Mia waited anxiously at the foot of the stairs, engaging sporadically in quiet conversation with Sophia. As Lee descended, his bag slung over his shoulder, Mia swiftly opened a small door adjacent to the staircase. With urgency in her movements, she ushered Lee inside before following suit.

"I entrust this to you," she said to Sophia with gravity, pausing before shutting the door behind them.

"Have no fear, Comrade!" Sophia responded calmly. With a subtle wink, she added another layer of assurance before the door closed between them.

The space beneath the stairs was familiar to Lee; it led to the basement, often used for storage and, in his childhood memories, the place where his father had once confined him as a form of punishment. With practiced ease, he flicked on the wall switch, illuminating the room with a sharp *snap*. Catching sight of Mia, he was filled with a rush of surprise and joy.

"I never imagined we'd meet again like this!"

Mia's lips curved into a smile. "That's precisely what you said the last time."

Confusion clouded Lee's expression, he murmured, "last time?"

Mia's smile broadened as she gazed at Lee, her silence speaking volumes. In Lee's memory, Sharmin had never regarded him with such an expression. Yet, he couldn't deny the sense of warmth and comfort it brought him.

"You'll recall soon enough. But for now, it's time to move. They'll be here any moment." Mia's tone shifted to urgency.

Retrieving a portable torch from her backpack, she shined its light onto the dim stairwell ahead. "Come on!"

Feeling disoriented, Lee's thoughts became a whirlwind of questions, and he asked with confusion, "that leads to the basement of my home!"

Yet, as he descended, Mia revealed a hidden compartment beneath the floor, exposing a vast, dark passage below. Securing the torch to her side, Mia beckoned Lee, who remained rooted in astonishment.

"Follow my lead," she said. Noticing Lee's concern, she quipped, "don't worry, we're the ones who dug this hole, and we'll cover the damages, I promise!"

Lee hesitated. "Where does it lead?"

"The abandoned Hyperloop Tube," Mia's voice echoed faintly. "It's our ticket out tonight."

The urgency in her voice spurred Lee into action, and as he descended, he found the narrow tunnel walls equipped with handles to grab.

"Who's after us?" He asked.

"Your own people," Mia replied, her voice fading, "if they catch wind of us, Sophia's safety is uncertain."

The confines of the tunnel stifled conversation. Lee focused on the task, navigating the twists and turns, ups and downs, amazed at the enormity of the project and wondering how two seemingly frail women could have constructed it, especially if Sophia's claim about their recent arrival was accurate.

After emerging from the tunnel, Lee found himself on a spacious underground platform that he quickly recognized as the Maritime Museum Station of the Hyperloop MRT. The station had been abandoned soon after Northern California declared independence, leaving it surprisingly new. The floor gleamed, the solar-powered ceiling lights cast a gentle glow, and the state-of-the-art loop pipe stretched into the distance, its length indiscernible.

Mia was stationed at the far end of the platform, engrossed in a handheld device, attempting to establish a connection to the control system.

Rushing over, Lee queried, "is this even operational?"

"It's a gamble," Mia replied tersely.

"And our destination?"

"L.A."

A cloud of confusion settled on Lee's face. "But L.A. has been a ghost town for ages."

"Some may see it as a desolate land, but others don't. Like Shallow Harbor, it remains undiminished, doesn't it?" Mia remarked. As she spoke, a fleeting expression crossed her face, one that Lee managed to discern despite its brevity. So, he immediately retrieved the starfish from his backpack. "It's clear to me now. I now understand why you took me to that studio at the Consul's party that night. I see what you were trying to show me, and I remember... It's all coming back to me!"

Mia looked up, spotting the starfish in Lee's hand, and a relieved smile crossed her face. "You found it? Sooner than I anticipated. Let's move!"

As if on cue, a safety door within the loop pipe slid open with a subtle hum. Inside the secure enclosure, a capsule roughly the size of a lifeboat emerged. Mia lightly touched its outer wall, triggering an entrance to appear. She swiftly jumped in, then extended her hand to beckon Lee. He grasped her hand, and together they maneuvered into the compact space, pressed closely side by side.

"The capsule was designed for a single passenger, but for safety, we should stick together," Mia explained.

Lee felt the closeness, Mia's warm breath touching his face. He couldn't recall ever being this physically close to her before. Yet, despite the uncertainty and strangeness of the situation, he felt an inexplicable calmness, as if he were lying in his own bed.

It felt surreal.

Turning to Mia, he searched her face for some semblance of an explanation. She, however, remained fixated on the monitor above, her demeanor calm and collected. Their proximity didn't seem odd, transforming the tense situation into something resembling a routine family outing.

The capsule shot forward with sudden force, its acceleration pressing them back. While Lee was accustomed to such jolts, he hadn't anticipated how composed Mia would remain amidst it.

"With Hyperloop, experience the thrill of traveling from San Francisco to Los Angeles in just 40 minutes. Faster than you ever imagined!"

The propaganda slogan for promoting Hyperloop MRT in its early phase proved astonishingly true. Exiting the capsule in Los Angeles, Lee was surprised to find the station above ground, greeted by the sight of a brilliant moon in the night sky.

"Mia!" A burly man, armed with a rifle and dressed in combat gear, approached. Magazines adorned his shoulders.

"Comrade Ivanov," Mia inquired, "what's the status?"

"It's dire. We need to move quickly. Sophia is no more, and they might discover this location soon."

Upon learning of Sophia's death, Lee felt a sudden, searing pain in his heart, as if a sharp blade had pierced through. Overwhelmed, he couldn't stand and found himself squatting on the spot, consumed by grief. Mia stepped forward, offering a comforting pat on the shoulder, saying, "every day, countless lives vanish in such cruel and cold ways... in Abandoned Harbor, in L.A., and many other places... You just don't see it."

As Lee looked up at Mia in the moonlight, he discerned faint tear stains on her cheeks.

The man named Ivanov urged them to move, prompting Lee to stand and follow, with Mia trailing close behind.

The Los Angeles end of the Hyperloop wasn't far from the beach. The rhythmic sound of waves reached Lee's ears, and soon, he witnessed the sparkling sea under the night sky. A flying car awaited them on the deserted beach, and as they drew near, it emitted a sudden roar with its headlights piercing the darkness.

"Where are we heading?" Lee turned to Mia.

"Avalon, the floating city," Mia responded, her voice carrying a low and damp tone, revealing the lingering sorrow in her heart.

12. AVALON

"Avalon, an island adrift in the mist of the Summer Sea, the last sacred place of the Druids."

As the flying car swiftly traversed the dense fog enveloping the sea, a small island, emanating a crystal-like glow, gradually came into view. Lee could hear Mia's low and solemn chanting, a ritualistic undertone to her words.

"So, is this small island our destination?" Lee interrupted, curiosity evident in his voice.

"It's not an island; it's a floating city, the floating city of Avalon," Mia replied.

From the flying car hovering over Avalon, Lee, even without Mia's guidance, discerned its unique characteristics. Firstly, its shape was far from natural, resembling a circular or elliptical form. Secondly, unlike conventional cities visible from the air, aglow with scattered lights in the darkness, Avalon was bathed in a uniform, soft cluster of light, resembling a hemispherical lantern afloat on the sea.

Drawing closer, various buildings of diverse shapes emerged on the ground—towering structures, intertwining corridors, and tiled pavilions. What set them apart was the common feature of transparent outer walls. This design allowed for glimpses of the interior layout, furnishings, vegetation, and even the subtle movements of people within. A myriad of diffused lights cast a captivating array of colors, transforming Avalon into a mesmerizing spectacle.

The flying car began its descent, and in an imperceptible moment, a subtle transition occurred, casting the surroundings into a brightness indistinguishable from daytime. Lee, taken aback by the sudden change, peered outside curiously. The night that had tightly shrouded them vanished without a trace, as if they had unwittingly fallen into a wholly different time and space.

Gradually, the flying car touched down on a transparent platform. Below, a garden unfolded, its paths obscured by lush shrubs, and a pond adorned with five or six blooming lotus flowers came into view. Children played and chased each other in the vibrant scenery, visible from above. Stepping out of the car, Mia led Lee towards an area marked with an *entrance* sign. Initially, it seemed no different from other places, but as they bid farewell to Ivanov, the ground beneath them swiftly descended. In the blink of an eye, they found themselves in the garden. Surprised, Lee raised his head, and through the transparent ceiling, he beheld a bright white sky suffused with soft light, reminding him of nothing less than the fabled heavens.

Mia's footsteps echoed through the surroundings, fading as she approached the path through the bushes. Lee, standing still, could no longer contain his emotion and blurted loudly as Mia retreated. "One thing that has always weighed heavily on me is that when I was in Shallow Harbor, I shouldn't have left without saying goodbye!"

Mia paused, turned around, and responded calmly, "I know."

Lee felt a wave of disappointment. The surprise of the unexpected reunion was overwhelming, but Mia's unusually calm reaction, or rather Sharmin's, exceeded his expectations. Sensing his doubts, Mia retraced her steps, walked up to him, and offered comfort.

"Yiming, I understand that tonight, everything, including bringing you here, feels rushed for you. There's really no other way. I wasn't entirely sure whether you would come back or not, even though we've been waiting for you. Originally, we planned to wait until you fully recovered, but your return happened sooner than expected. That orange starfish—it's something I deliberately planted in your dream. Otherwise, you'd be like everyone else, unable to retrieve your memory. Maybe using it as a key to wake you up wasn't the best choice, but I miss it more than you can imagine."

At this point, Mia's eyes flickered, prompting her to pause. She raised her head, gazing at the sky for a moment before continuing, "I didn't anticipate your determined return. It's not what you used to tell me; you always said you weren't good at making decisions. Nonetheless, I'm genuinely glad, even if it deviated significantly from the original plan. Others seized the opportunity to follow us, and Sophia paid the price."

Mia's voice wavered as she mentioned Sophia, and she turned her head, discreetly wiping her moist eyes.

Lee still seemed to struggle to comprehend Mia's words, but the mention of Sophia's death left him with an unprecedented sadness. Despite knowing Sophia for less than half a day and exchanging only a few words, he was struck by a sharp pang, realizing the fair-skinned girl with silver hair, who once offered him tequila, would never stand before him again.

"I'm sorry. Since the day I woke up from that dream and contemplated returning home for the first time, I've questioned if it was the right decision. You're right—I'm not good at making decisions, and though I don't recall discussing it with anyone, I genuinely apologize," Lee attempted to justify his overwhelming sadness by attributing it to the guilt weighing on his heart, which sounded more reasonable to him.

"No, the apology should come from me. If it weren't for me, none of this would have happened. But dwelling on it won't change the past. We can only move forward now," Mia responded, beckoning for Lee to follow her. Noting the sadness etched on Lee's face, she comforted him, "don't blame yourself. Even if Sophia's death isn't directly linked to you, feeling sadness is normal. It's empathy—human beings experience it to varying degrees."

Finally, Lee began to move, following Mia slowly. As they walked, the two of them gradually vanished at the end of the path.

On the same night, across the ocean in San Francisco, a brief yet intense shootout erupted on Lombard Street. The exchange of gunfire lasted for about ten minutes, but in a city accustomed to turmoil, it went largely unnoticed. As the echoes of the gunfire subsided, a group of heavily armed militants emerged from a small house, swiftly taking strategic positions and adopting a defensive stance.

Two combatants walked out from a small house on the corner, carrying a lifeless body, and a man who appeared to be the lead casually closed the door. He nonchalantly rubbed the bloodstains on the ground with his boot and spoke into the intercom, "Operation Wolf Warrior is over. The target is lost; a stubborn bandit was killed."

With the immediate threat eliminated, the militants relaxed their guard, regrouped, and followed the lead and the two men carrying the corpse up Lombard Street to the nearby Russian Hill. At the hill's summit, an abandoned tennis court flickered with lights, and a massive light nuclear spaceplane stood like a nocturnal behemoth. A man at the gate anxiously smoked a cigar, the ember glowing in the darkness.

As the militants reached the court, the man hustled down the staircase and yelled at the lead, "what the hell happened? The target's out, and how the hell did so many screw it up?"

"Sir, didn't see it coming. They dug a damn tunnel underneath," the lead replied.

"And then?"

"That tunnel led to some abandoned Hyperloop MRT station. When we got there, poof! Nobody in sight."

"Dam it. They probably slipped into the loop pipe. Should've thought of this crap earlier. So, they're likely in L.A. now. Any idea where the Los Angeles Loop spits them out?"

"Hang on, checking... It's somewhere near the original Santa Monica Marine Park. Still want us on their tail?"

"Chase after what? By the time we rolled in, those folks vanished into the Pacific. Pack it up, retreat the team. Boss doesn't want us roaming too far. Gotta show some respect on NorCal."

"What about this, Mr. Zhukov?" The lead pointed at the corpse on the ground.

Zhukov strolled over, glanced down, and urged impatiently, "don't you hear me? Move out! Quick!"

In a matter of minutes, the soldiers ascended ladders from various directions and boarded the spaceplane. With a roar, the monster emitted a faint beam of ions, ascended into the air, and vanished into the night sky in the blink of an eye.

Lee slept for an extended period, waking up with a sense of

relaxation and comfort. Still enveloped in the spacious and soft bed, he contemplated the idea of just sleeping some more. Hugging the large elastic pillow beside him, he inhaled a faint fragrance that abruptly brought him back to wakefulness.

Mia wasn't around, nor was she in the room.

But it was the same room Mia had brought him to last night—or whenever that was. He had completely lost track of time. The room was still bathed in soft white light, just like when he first arrived.

He still couldn't believe everything that had just happened. The memory of them hugging felt so real, the softness and warmth of her skin seemed to linger in his fingers. But strangely, he didn't feel surprised at all.

All he could recall was that they were like a couple who hadn't seen each other in ages. No matter how close they got, it was just like revisiting the past. Mia had hinted that a significant portion of his forgotten memories belonged to the two of them. Yet, when he looked into her eyes, asking her to reveal the details, she insisted he would remember everything in due time, just like with the broken starfish. If she told him now, it might disrupt his memory recovery, blurring the lines between dream and reality.

But how could he be sure the scenes popping up in his mind now weren't just dreams? Lee started feeling a bit frustrated as he sat up, but the pleasant scent on the pillow didn't fade away. He also remembered the mandala pattern he dreamt about—the same pattern engraved on his mother's ring. Surprisingly, it was also on a similar ring Mia wore.

"That's the halidom of the High Priestess," Mia had explained when he inquired about it.

"Yiming, you up yet? Time to meet the High Priestess!"

Stirred by crisp voices, Lee glimpsed Mia in a white dress. Hastily, he threw on a sheet, wrapped it around himself, and headed to the bathroom. There, he spotted his clothes.

"Yiming, I brought you some new threads so the High Priestess won't be amazed when she sees you."

Upon the offer, Lee opened the door with one hand, taking the clothes through the gap.

It was a set of white cloth robes. Lee dried off, hesitated for a moment, and decided to put them on. Glancing at the mirror, he was taken aback by finding himself resembling a martial arts master. He remembered Mia mentioning that he had been associated with them before. If he chose to believe Mia and accept her into his lost memories, he was already a crucial member of the Organization.

Lee stepped out, and Mia eyed him from head to toe, akin to the inspection of a bridegroom poised to enter the wedding hall.

"It fits well, nice…" Mia complimented, "I didn't realize you were quite handsome before!"

Lee had grown accustomed to the indescribable intimacy that Mia displayed towards him. This mysterious closeness initially shocked him, but the joy it brought made him embrace a reality he hadn't known existed. In this newfound reality, he had become one of the Druids, ready to dedicate his life to fulfill the mission bestowed by the High Priestess. It was because of this commitment that, when he spontaneously appeared in Northern California, the High Priestess decided to take the risk and arrange this meeting in Avalon, even when the time wasn't fully ripe.

Mia checked the time on a vintage bell hanging on the wall, adjusted the belt on Lee's robe, and expressed satisfaction.

"All right, let's go!"

With that, he followed her as they left the room.

Navigating through the garden, they entered a winding corridor with oriental characteristics. Rose vines adorned the sides, climbing to the top, and vibrant flowers competed for attention, casting a colorful tapestry that veiled the boring white light of Avalon. It was the first time Lee felt a connection to the real world.

Unable to resist his curiosity, he asked, "is there no night here?"

"No, the sky above the floating city is filled with invisible skylight collectors, storing the sun's energy to provide continuous illumination. This blurs the distinction between day and night, and the seasons aren't as clearly defined as they are outside, so the boundary between the ephemeral and the eternal is not as clear."

"Did the High Priestess build Avalon?"

"No, the ruler of Avalon is a woman named Lake Kim—we all call her Lady Kim."

"Is she a Priestess too?"

"No, she's a devout Druid, but not part of the Organization."

So far, Lee comprehended that the term *Organization* referred to themselves—a faction known as *saviors* in Druid society.

Embracing this new reality meant accepting a new identity bestowed upon him.

Towards the end of the curved corridor stood a magnificent pavilion adorned with high cornices and scattered bucket arches. A small bridge connected the corridor's end to the pavilion, and the gentle gurgling of water accompanied its flow. Mia gestured for Lee to ascend the bridge, but she made no move to follow.

"Just me?" Lee expressed deep surprise.

"Yes, the High Priestess has not met any other followers other than you."

"What? How is that possible? Haven't you even met her?"

"Nope," Mia replied calmly.

This sudden revelation shattered Lee's calm and comfort in this alternate world, triggering an instant collapse. The panic, patiently awaiting an opportunity, swiftly reoccupied his mind.

13. PRIESTESS

"You're here, and I'm truly happy!"

Lee followed the voice and spotted the High Priestess in a black robe.

She sat on a chair against the wall, wearing a hood and a veil over her face. All he could vaguely see were a pair of eyes hidden in the shadows—or so Lee thought, considering the room's size, dim lighting, and the distance of more than ten steps between them.

Despite the hoarse quality, the High Priestess's voice carried kindness. A fleeting thought crossed Lee's mind, making him wonder if he had heard this voice somewhere before. The notion gripped him, and he found himself asking in a trance, "have we met?"

The High Priestess remained silent, gesturing for him to sit first.

Until now, Lee didn't notice the other chair on her right, which was identical to the one she occupied, and placed on the side of a mahogany high table. Both chairs were close to a white wall adorned with a mottled old painting—easy to identify as "Fishing Alone in the Cold River" by Yuan Ma. Glancing around, Lee couldn't spot any other furniture. The room had windows on one side, adorned with bamboo-colored curtains, casting the entire space in a dusky tone. This unique dusk, like all the light in Avalon, appeared intentionally crafted. It remained constant, creating an illusion of eternal time.

Lee hesitated but eventually walked over to the empty chair

apprehensively, facing the entrance, now void in his vision. The High Priestess sat beside him, positioned so that Lee would need to turn his head to see her. However, he refrained from doing so initially.

"Turn your head!"

When the High Priestess commanded, Lee initially dismissed it as a hallucination, considering his internal struggle to resist doing so in the moment. Yet, his apparent indifference compelled the High Priestess to change her tone and ask again, "Yiming, can you let me take a look at you?"

Unexpectedly startled, Lee felt a strange connection between the voice and his memories.

"Are you all right?" the concerned tone of the High Priestess brought him back.

Finally, he turned sideways and saw the High Priestess's eyes for the first time. Contrary to his expectations, the black pupils held a faint sadness, lacking the depth and mystery he anticipated. He noticed wrinkles and bags under her eyes, revealing the experiences of wind and frost, but not disclosing her exact age. A fleeting thought crossed his mind once again, suggesting that he had seen these eyes somewhere before.

As the High Priestess continued to gaze at him, Lee felt a sense of shyness and turned his face away. In that moment of turning, he thought he caught a glimmer of light in the High Priestess's eyes.

"Why summon me, and what important commands do you have?" Lee, having calmed down, voiced the pressing question on his mind.

The High Priestess sighed lightly, responding calmly, "if you still harbor resentment—"

"Resentment? What resentment?" Lee interrupted eagerly, as if he had been holding back these words for a long time.

"Don't you resent the man who entangled you in all of this? Perhaps you don't remember fully what happened before. We've put upon you a layer of invisible protection, but haven't you been grappling with pain and doubt every day lately?"

"No." Lee shook his head, reflected for a moment, and continued, "regardless of how I got involved, the decisions were made years ago—when I made that choice, attended that reception, or even earlier, when my father took me to the ferry dock to witness the fleets as a child. If there's any resentment, it might as well be directed at the mother who left us behind, whom I haven't even seen. You don't need to worry about my grievances; I've gathered some insights from Mia. Since she mentioned that I made a choice before and was willingly aligned with you, there's no need for concerns about my remorse or anything."

These words surprised Lee as much as they did the High Priestess, and he pondered how he could reveal so much to someone he had just met.

The High Priestess's body began trembling slightly, as if offended by Lee's words, and she remained silent for a long time. When she spoke again, her voice carried a majestic tone. "You have to be resentful; you have to hate Hun!"

"Hun?" Lee's body jolted, jumping up as if electrified. The name cut through the air like a cold sword, snapping him out of his reverie and prompting a re-examination of the *new reality* he had just embraced in the past two days.

The High Priestess, realizing her losing her composure, took a moment to calm herself before continuing. "Don't you want the world to go back to its old days?"

"I don't understand what you mean. If you're referring to my father's time as the old days, then I have to say that I—not only me—have no real impression of it. Yes, they always speak nostalgically about the past, but human memories are inherently unreliable. Painful memories tend to be filtered out unconsciously, and I'm well aware of that."

"Your father's time, yes! I mean exactly your father's time. Don't you feel sorry that the past, so close at hand, has left no trace in your memory? You doubt the memories of an entire generation, and you must know that their memories are fading, but would that imply the past we experienced hasn't existed at all?"

"The past is inherently insignificant, and many times, it's just annoying."

"No! You think that because you know nothing! I wanted to sit in front of you myself a long time ago and tell you everything about Hun. Those are things you should know. I hope you won't be too shocked by what I'm going to say next!"

Lee's heart raced in his chest, the rhythmic pounding resembling distant war drums.

The High Priestess spoke with a fluid eloquence, "you have to admit that he is a genius, a genius unparalleled in the entire history of mankind—extending even to the future, if mankind manages to endure. He was keenly aware of this uniqueness from an early age. Naturally, he cultivated a mindset of looking down on ordinary people, setting himself apart at any occasion and time. His innate ability to project an infinite sense of mission and responsibility, without pretension, made him a figurehead capable of influencing an entire generation. This invisible yet irresistible impact helped him dominate the value systems and social beliefs of his time, serving as both a spiritual mentor and a great leader. Together, they overturned the old but stagnant order. Some argued that the world's decline led to the rise of Hun, but in reality, it was the rise of Hun that hastened the world's decline. When his revolutionary theories in modern physics materialized, the world absorbed the colossal impact and subsequently crumbled. Yet, what did he offer to the people after dismantling the old order? Just a faint glimmer of hope amid infinite despair. Even that fragile hope, if not for the painstaking efforts to sustain it, would have dissipated at any moment. Does this make him truly superior to others? He must control the entire world by meticulously operating the behemoth that is the Corporation. You are more familiar than I with the extensive efforts they've invested, particularly in the ever-growing Mind Exploration Division. They concoct various materials to sustain people's dwindling hope, resorting even to special means to perpetually inject hope into their consciousness. Obviously, this cannot endure. The Corporation will fall apart one day, just like the old world. Everyone understands this truth, but few dare to voice it."

"Isn't that too categorical? Not all regions are under the Corporation's control, like Britain, Brittany, and Northern California... And, of course, Avalon."

"When there is only one model left that the world deems successful, is there a need to emphasize its superiority? The existence of Northern California and Shallow Harbor, these chaotic deformities of the world, serves as the Corporation's chosen therapy to delay its own demise. Pure fiction alone is insufficient to justify the Corporation's existence. They require narratives passed down through words, stories told by those who have escaped certain places and can speak of the true suffering they endured."

Lee fell silent for a moment. He comprehended that the High

Priestess's words were not baseless, especially after the recent encounter with Chyi's mockery. The words might not be beautiful, but they were enough to compel him to acknowledge the undeniable facts he had long resisted.

"But what's the point of you talking about that?" Lee hesitated, expressing a sentiment he felt wasn't entirely decent.

"He always liked to portray himself as omnipotent. In his heart, he believed he was *the one*. He even refrained from reproducing, fearing to leave his genes in this world."

The High Priestess, visibly agitated, paused to take a few deep breaths before continuing, "—but who doesn't know that a man cannot escape death? No matter how extraordinary he is, he is still a mortal."

Lee, unable to refute these words and choosing not to, felt a sudden surprise.

Over the years, he had never paid attention to Hun's age. In the Corporation-controlled areas, public information was meticulously curated, and there was no mention of Hun's age at all. It was only now that Lee realized this notable absence.

"In 2015, Dr. Hun revolutionized the global landscape with the invention of nuclear fusion particle synthesis technology. This groundbreaking achievement, akin to contemporary alchemy, enables the seamless reorganization of atoms, facilitating the transformation of matter from the molecular level to the atomic level, and from the chemical level to the physical level. It marks the complete liberation of the closed loop between matter and energy.

In 2025, recognizing the escalating threats from the global shortage of resources and energy, Hun established the Corporation. This entity was founded with a singular mission: to present a lasting solution rooted in nuclear fusion and particle synthesis to the challenges facing humanity.

In 2028, acting on behalf of the Corporation, Hun formally introduced the *Global Exclusive Market Reciprocity Treaty*. This landmark treaty expressed the Corporation's willingness to shoulder the social responsibility that governments and organizations, signatories to the treaty, should bear. It marked the official commencement of the Corporation's provision of residents in the exclusive market area with essentials such as clothing, food, housing, transportation, entertainment, and all necessities for life.

In 2038, in response to the mounting calls for interstellar migration, the Corporation initiated the terraforming of Titan, the moon of Saturn. Affectionately dubbed the *Garden of Eden* by an enthusiastic populace, Titan became a symbol of the Corporation's commitment to expanding human habitation beyond Earth.
......"

Lee was too familiar with all of these, but Hun's exact age remained undisclosed. Stringent information control didn't equate to an absence of accessible information. Underground information dealers existed, yet Lee had never bothered to ascertain Hun's age. Speculation from the limited details in the resume suggested that in 2025, he should have been in his prime, perhaps over thirty years old. Forty years later, he would be at least over seventy. Publicly available data indicated a life expectancy of around 65 years for adult men. Despite this, with the aid of the Corporation's medical technology, Hun's due date loomed close. The realization struck Lee, and he felt a sudden unease. "You mean he... he might die?"

"No one can escape death, especially considering his health isn't too optimistic, and the project of Foundation recently confirmed my suspicions."

"What do you mean?" Lee inquired, puzzled. "What does this have to do with the Foundation? It was just a necessary compromise for the colossal terraforming project on Titan, and perhaps rooted from Shannon Chen's death."

Unconsciously, Lee's attitude towards the High Priestess underwent a subtle shift, evident in his newfound openness.

"Did you not realize that the so-called Foundation is essentially a perfect replica of the present world?" the High Priestess questioned.

Lee, unaware of how the High Priestess obtained such confidential information, assumed she knew everything he did. He replied, "yes, the ultimate goal is to build it into a miniature space city, where humans can survive independently during long interstellar voyages. Isn't this what humans have long pursued?"

Neglecting the question, the High Priestess continued, "when influential individuals sense the end is near, they often reject the reality accepted by ordinary people. To cope, they create or accept lies, transforming them into their perceived reality. China's first emperor replicated mountains and rivers in their tombs, and

Egypt's pharaohs built pyramids."

Lee jumped up in astonishment. "Are you suggesting that the long-lasting Foundation is merely Hun's pyramid? Absurd! It's impossible! Tell me quickly, is this just your conjecture—a baseless conjecture!"

"Priestesses do not make conjectures; I only convey the truth as I know it."

Lee, unable to control his emotions, struggled to convince himself that the High Priestess was merely spouting nonsense. However, thoughts of the sacrificial rituals from his dream, the soulless Pioneers, and the haunting foreign singing voices flooded his mind. He questioned himself. "Was the deserted city in the sky of Titan nothing more than an unfinished tomb? Did he spend his life as a pitiable gravekeeper?"

This torrent of thoughts overwhelmed him, leading to a hysterical outburst. "I don't believe it! I can't believe it! Why me? Impossible, why me?"

Observing Lee's emotional turmoil, the High Priestess left her seat and walked over. She gently grabbed his shoulders and pressed him back into the chair. "He chose you because he doesn't trust anyone else."

"Isn't it because I'm foolish? Because I never asked questions?" Lee roared hoarsely, still struggling to accept the reality.

The High Priestess's hand remained on Lee's shoulder. She leaned down, looked into his eyes, and spoke meaningfully, "no, it's because he wanted it to be you. In his heart, it's not a grave; it's his heaven. He rejected death, believing he would attain eternal life in that sky city—the First Emperor, the Pharaohs—they didn't view their graves as mere resting places, the same."

Lee found comfort in her eyes, stabilizing his mood a bit. However, he couldn't help but complain, "it's not fair!"

"Exactly, it's not fair. Hence, we decided to destroy it. Shatter the impending lie, allowing those once inspired by nothingness to learn to build a new world again."

"Haha! Destroy it! Ha…" Lee laughed manically, while the High Priestess silently returned to her chair without uttering a word.

After a moment, the High Priestess resumed, "it seems you're not ready. You can choose to forget the events of the past two days, just like last time."

"No, I'm ready," Lee's response was decisive. "But I don't

believe what kind of High Priestess you are. Tell me! Who are you? Why do you know so much? Are you and Hun—"

"Yes, we used to know each other. I never intended to hide it. I admired him fervently when I was a girl. It was no big deal. Who could refuse the light as bright and fiery as the sun in those already cold days?"

14. MIA

During the time when Lee engaged with the High Priest, Mia assumed her post at the bridge, standing guard in quiet contemplation. The scene before her seemed stagnant in the tranquil embrace of white light, creating an atmosphere of suspended animation. This unusual silence, while harmonious, also brought about a sense of boredom, leaving Mia with the feeling that the world lacked a certain level of reality.

Occasionally, leaves would drift down from above, breaking the stillness as they descended. The breeze would pass them gently to the flowing water, entangling them in a journey destined for turbulence. Each time this occurred, Mia found herself captivated, carefully observing the unpredictable trajectories of the leaves until they vanished completely from her sight.

In these moments of leaf-watching, Mia's mind wandered when she reflected on her own past. As she followed the descent of a single leaf, her thoughts unraveled like a ball of yarn slipping from her hand, rolling farther and farther away, and it became way more challenging to draw them back again.

For a significant period, Mia considered the moment when she brushed shoulders with Lee in the path from the Consul's courtyard as the origin of her journey.

Before that encounter, the shadow of a young boy had perpetually occupied her heart, acting as her closest confidant. He shared conversations with her, listened to her secrets, and became a companion in her joys and sorrows. For most girls, having their own Prince Charming was a common experience – a fleeting encounter that wouldn't alter the course of their lives. Even if they were to meet him again, recognizing him was unlikely. Yet, Mia's experience made the distinction. With her family's strong genes, she could sense *his* presence with her eyes closed, a feeling that lingered in her heart for an extended period.

Driven by this subtle connection, Mia clashed with her mother and ventured to the decaying city across the ocean, spending three solitary years in a dilapidated college. It was a city with characteristics that made it least appealing for the young people of the time—decaying, degrading, and persistently in a state of decline. What drove her was the unforgettable fact that their first meeting unfolded there in a light fog-enveloped promontory long ago. Enchanted, she roamed through deteriorating streets, attempting to catch *his* essence, feeling unpredictable signals in the ethereal time and space. The torment of alternating hope and despair accompanied her throughout this futile pursuit. The sudden death of her mother compelled her to end the search and return to Shallow Harbor. Surprisingly, she then sensed a looming aura, unmistakably *his*. At first, that feeling was just a spark, subtly reminding her of the imminent arrival of this person. However, subsequent crossing shoulders with him in the courtyard ignited a wildfire of emotions in her heart, making her restless and sleepless, yearning for an immediate encounter.

Aware of *his* presence as a guest at her uncle's, Mia hesitated to approach her uncle directly due to their strained relationship. He, referred to as a smiling bodhisattva, maintained an amiable façade with her, considering his current position and the luxurious mansion inherited from her mother. However, Mia sensed the hidden sinful thoughts beneath the surface.

Then, the grand party arrived as if destined. She meticulously applied makeup, secured her long hair, donned formal attire, and prepared for the eagerly anticipated reunion with the most poised posture, only to face the bitter reality of *his* complete lack of recollection.

He didn't remember her at all, which wasn't surprising; who would recall a fleeting episode from childhood? Yet, she still held onto the image of *him* as the boy who had been with her day and night in her heart. She had hoped that when they finally spoke face to face, she could witness *his* sudden joy. However, to her dismay, *he* knew nothing about her and had no recollection of their shared past.

The loss felt like cold rain, extinguishing the enthusiasm in her heart and revealing the illusion she had chased—an illusion that theoretically should not exist in the shaman's genes.

As a riot swept through Shallow Harbor not long after, Mia wasn't surprised at all, having foreseen the inevitable through her encounter with Lady Snow in the court. Yet, it wasn't the impending events that struck her most at that moment; it was the profound sadness, humiliation, and hopelessness mirrored in Lady Snow's eyes. Shamans inherently possess a heightened ability to empathize, but without proper training, this gift can become a double-edged sword. When Mia felt *watched* by Lady Snow, it was as if she had entered Lady Snow's own world, and endured the horrific atrocities inflicted by her monstrous father after her mother's death. The weight of these experiences nearly brought Mia to the brink of collapse.

On the day she returned from Chyi's home, she sought refuge in her studio, sobbing and trembling, oblivious to the billowing smoke and the relentless gunfire from the outside world until Chyi appeared, breaking down the door and forcibly pulling her away.

It wasn't until later that Mia grasped the true catalyst altering the course of her life—a force akin to the breeze tearing down leaves from their branches. That wasn't the reunion with Lee, but the profound gaze shared with Lady Snow that held the transformative power.

In retrospect, Mia recalled a pivotal moment when General Chu, the leader of the Scavengers, granted her and Shiaojun Chyi freedom under the condition of joining the Organization. Without a moment's hesitation, Mia embraced this opportunity. In her view, figures like General Chu held the potential to provide a modicum of solace for Lady Snow's tragedy.

In the end, with Chyi's assistance, she escaped to the other side.

Immediately, she sensed *his* presence again—not too far, not too close. How could she release the anticipation built up in her heart over several years? In the days spent resting at Chyi's home, there wasn't a moment when she didn't yearn for *his* arrival.

The awaited evening finally came, just as Chyi escorted her back. As the sun dipped, casting a scarlet hue across the sky, a strong sensation overwhelmed her. *He* was finally here, seemingly within arm's reach, prompting her instinctive search, yet in that very moment, *he* quietly vanished.

Was this enough to drive her to leave the place and live in seclusion with Madame Shaw in Edinburgh, Scotland, for several years?

At least, at the time, she believed it was.

The encounter with Madame Shaw in Edinburgh felt like a twist of fate, setting the stage for their subsequent meeting in advance.

"Sharmin, as a shaman, you should have a shaman's proper name. What about Mia?" Madame Shaw, though lacking shamanic lineage, possessed a deep understanding of shamanic training. At a glance, she detected the potent genes hidden in Mia's blood. "The Haelion family is already very famous, but I didn't expect you to have the lineage of Persian Magus!"

With Madame Shaw's guidance, Mia's telepathy, mind control, and empathy skills flourished. She inevitably garnered the attention of the Organization. After several conversations and teleportation with the High Priestess, Mia ascended to the rank of Priestess, astonishingly becoming the High Priestess's tacit heir.

Throughout this journey, Mia kept everything about the Organization concealed from Madame Shaw. She never revealed that, from their initial meeting, she felt a maternal connection between Madame Shaw and *him*. The substitution effect of that blood connection played a significant role, at least initially. It bridged the gap between the boy in her heart and the reality of him, simultaneously creating a peculiar relationship between Mia and Madame Shaw. They resembled a master and apprentice, mother and daughter, and more intriguingly, a couple.

Several years later, when the High Priestess assigned her the almost impossible task, Mia's heart remained undisturbed. She listened attentively and calmly, unaffected even as the name was repeated multiple times. It no longer sparked any imagination or turmoil within her. In response, she smiled with a sense of relief, feeling more at ease than ever before.

"Request authorization."
"Authorization is granted."

Mia vividly recalled that scene. She leaped lightly out of the cabin, avoiding direct eye contact with Lee on the screen above the connecting corridor. Instead, she turned her face sideways, loosened her long hair, shook it gently, and tied it up again.

It was her first mission, and upon landing, she was assigned to the Prometheus, responsible for supplying daily provisions to the Foundation. There was no need for speculation; she knew he arranged it deliberately.

"Welcome to the Foundation!"

She could hear him masking his surprise, attempting to welcome her with ceremonial formality.

"What a City of Sky!" She looked around, feigning nonchalance.

This routine became a sort of ritual between them. Every few days, the Prometheus loaded with supplies would depart from Titan to connect with the Foundation suspended in outer space. During these moments, he would wait in advance in the central control area. She would smile at him through the screen, everything proceeding cautiously and slowly as planned. Then, unexpectedly, he appeared one day in the shuttle cabin.

"Mia, I need to go to the ground!" He called her Mia. As she pondered the implications, he slipped into the cockpit and sat in a seat in the back, just a step away from her. Resting his chin in his hand, he stared at the side of her face. Sensing it immediately, she looked back quickly, then turned away in an instant. In that brief exchange, she caught the panic flashing in his eyes and the countless vicissitudes etched into his face by the years.

A sudden sadness overwhelmed her, prompting her to close her eyes, preventing tears from flowing. Simultaneously, an inexplicable fire ignited in the heart of the almost wasteland, without warning.

After touching down on the *Comfort Zone* on the surface of Titan, she observed him striding into the icy expanse, dissipating into the distance like a wisp of ethereal mist.

In the vast sky, a faint bright star twinkled—the distant sun.

His silhouette stretched long, cast by the dim light, appearing cold and desolate.

She eventually caught up, prompting him to halt and face her.

"I'm sorry..." He struggled to remove the protective shield from his spacesuit, his breath turning into instant hoarfrost as he gasped for air.

Though his words were muffled, she sensed his sincerity. Removing her own protective shield, she approached, brushing frost from his face with her hand and sealing his lips with hers.

"There... there was... a methane lake. Now... now it's gone. I truly hope... you've also... seen it. It was... magnificent, ..., a view that I will never forget," he gasped, his words faltering due to the lack of oxygen.

Until now, Mia couldn't convince herself that the encounter at the remains of a methane lake was a carefully designed opportunity, crafted to gain Lee's trust in the most natural and discreet manner. Ever since then, her plans had unraveled like wild horses set free, losing their direction entirely.

"Mia—"

The retrospection was abruptly halted; she didn't realize when Lee had positioned himself in front of her, his complexion pallid.

"I want to get out of this place, now!" He pleaded weakly.

An indescribable melancholy welled up within Mia. She assisted him in settling on a rock by the bridge, offering solace, "you're not in good shape now; it's better to go back and rest."

"Enough, I want to go home."

"Home?"

"Yes, home. My home in San Francisco."

"Are you okay? Still struggling with what the High Priestess told you. You accepted it last time; you can do it this time too."

Mia was a bit taken aback; Lee's reaction was evidently more intense than she anticipated. Yet, she persisted in comforting him, sensing an ominous premonition. Besides the factual information she had shared with Lee last time, she felt the High Priestess must have divulged something else to him.

"If you're not comfortable in Avalon, we can go elsewhere— Brittany or anywhere you wish. But I can't let you return to San Francisco; it's too risky!"

"Don't worry, they still need me. And besides, I have to go back eventually."

Mia remained silent for a while before sighing and conceding. "Alright, I'll take you to gather your belongings. Then, we'll board one of Lady Kim's ships—it's slower but safe enough."

Observing Lee standing motionless, Mia nudged him, "are you planning to wear this?"

Lee glanced at the robe on his body, finally breaking into a sheepish smile.

Back at their place, Lee freshened up with a shower and changed into the clothes Mia had laid out for him. Breakfast was ready on the table, and Mia helped arrange his ride – a fishing ship leaving once a day, still an hour before departure.

"Despite Avalon's fancy tech, it's not entirely self-sufficient. We trade with Northern California, mostly seafood for necessities," Mia explained while packing Lee's bag. She made sure to include a pistol and earnestly advised, "stay safe!"

In this moment, Lee felt a twinge of sadness. He pulled Mia into a hug, sealing their farewell with a kiss. Mia didn't resist, but her response lacked excessive enthusiasm.

As Lee left Avalon, he observed the outside world just awakening. Morning mists draped the sea, and an unfamiliar red tint painted the eastern sky.

15. TRAP

The ship, moving at a slow pace, reached the Golden Gate Bridge as noon approached. The dissipating fog unveiled the silhouette of San Francisco, and soon the boat docked at the Bay Street pier, a mere half-hour walks from Lee's house.

As Lee walked along, his steps were deliberate, and his thoughts echoed with doubts about whether he had once again made a wrong choice. When he passed the corner near Russian Hill, a sudden unease crept over him—an unmistakable feeling that he was being trailed. Startled, he turned abruptly, only to find a mysterious figure vanish in an instant. This prompted him to heighten his vigilance. Swiftly unloading his backpack, he retrieved the pistol Mia had provided, securing it in his pocket. Hastening his slow pace, he dared not linger, acutely aware of the pressing urgency.

After reaching home, Lee noticed the door open and bloodstains still tainting the hallway. Despite the unsettling sight, he didn't dare to pause for a closer look. Instead, he entered the house and sought refuge in the storage room under the stairs. As anticipated, within a few minutes, he heard someone entering— soft, careful footsteps. Peering through the thin crack in the door, he identified a tall, slender figure in a black overcoat, surveying the surroundings and reaching into his pocket.

Without hesitation, Lee, gripping the gun in his hand, burst out, "don't move!"

The man, visibly surprised, promptly tossed the gun he had just retrieved to the ground and rushed toward Lee in defense. "Hey, Mr. Lee, I'm not your enemy!"

Lee couldn't afford to be lax. Freeing one hand, he grabbed a roll of packing tape from the storage room, closed the distance in a few strides, and wound the tall man into a living mummy until he stood subdued. Only then did Lee pick up the pistol from the ground, push the man onto the couch, and secure the door.

"Mr. Lee, I'm on your side. Mr. Warren sent me to ensure your safety, but the other side outnumbered us that night, and I was helpless!"

Warren, Dave's last name, rang a bell, but Lee couldn't trust easily. He pressed the gun against the man's head, demanding sharply, "who sent those people that night? Who killed Sophia?"

The man trembled, pleading desperately, "don't—don't! I'm innocent, I don't know who they were. I've informed Mr. Warren; he can find out. The person who died has nothing to do with me! I—"

"Knock knock…" Right then, someone banged on the door.

Lee's heart skipped a beat. He quickly rolled up the *mummy*, stuffed it in the storage room, locked the door, and tiptoed over to the living room, peeking through the peephole.

A woman stood outside—Talma, the same guide who had been driving him days ago.

Lee sighed in relief, stashed the gun behind his back, and cracked the door open, wanting to get rid of her fast. "Why the comeback? Weren't those credits enough? I don't exactly have a treasure trove here!"

"Hey, Mr. Lee, you've got me all wrong. I'm here for something else. Something fantastic!"

Afraid Lee might slam the door on her, she leaned in, right shoulder against the frame, left hand fumbling behind her like she was searching for something.

Lee jumped, yanked out his gun, and aimed it at her head.

The girl, totally caught off guard, stumbled back, dropping whatever she was holding. "And you? Ran into a bunch of characters like you—acting all loyal but low-key eyeing some bitcoins. This time, it's a game-changer. The deal is a cool one grand…"

Relieved that it wasn't a weapon, Lee brushed off her words. Still feeling a bit off, he went out to help her pick up the fallen piece—a blown-up color photo, a rare find in this era.

Talma snatched it back, saying, "if it's not your jam, no worries, tons of others are all over it!"

With the *mummy* still in the head, Lee was on the verge of dismissing her when a realization struck. "Wait—" he shouted, grabbing the photo again. He recognized the person – Danny, as depicted by Ethelinda.

"Geez, you're a real headache! One grand! Those aren't just points, they're bitcoins! If it wasn't a fat stack, I wouldn't even bother. I get it, you're living the good life, but trust me, there'll be times when those bitcoins will be a lifesaver!"

"You know him?" Lee asked coldly.

"If I do, why bother finding you? It was an old client, who just hit the jackpot, and out of the blue remembered his younger brother who headed your country ages ago. That's when he cooked up this deal, hoping my connections can help figure out a way to bring him back."

Lee talked to himself, "Danny's kin in Northern California?"

"No way, you actually know him! Hit the jackpot!"

"Where does your client live? Take me there, now!"

Surprising Talma, Lee turned back, grabbed his backpack, and securely locked the door.

Talma's *vehicle* was parked on a desolate patch on the Russian Hill, and Lee identified it right away—it was one of the specialized drones meant for transporting passengers from the landing platform of space planes in the bay.

"I strongly suspected you guys tampered with it! What surprises me is that nobody reported it."

Talma overheard Lee's muttering, her face registering surprise. "You serious, or is this, like, some kind of joke?"

Lee caught on but not entirely. "What was I joking about?"

Hearing that, Talma grinned again, "alright, guess you're really new to this, so let me fill you in. Whether it's here or on your turf, savvy folks know it's not exactly a joyride to go that far on a rocket. Still, when the chance pops up, they're down for the trip, you know? Why? Profit, my friend. Wanna guess what they're tossing my way for this deal? Less than two hundred! You guys snag the lion's share, and who'd bother reporting it, right? Pretty dumb."

Lee snorted in response. "Their bosses aren't as clueless as you think!"

"Hah!" Talma's tone started with disdain. "You're really not as sharp as I thought. If you don't turn a blind eye, who'd willingly take on this kind of grunt trip?"

"Shut up!" Lee retorted; his frustration evident.

Talma had no option but to begrudgingly climb into the driverless vehicle. As Lee approached, she couldn't resist expressing a hint of irritation, "finally I can speak... Destination, Mendocino, 1000 Main Street."

"Mendocino..." Lee still had a vague recollection of this place, which seemed to be a small town near the Pacific Ocean. Perhaps during a New Year's Eve or Christmas celebration, his family had spent their holidays there, a time when his mother was still with them, and he had just started to walk. In the endless meadow by the sea, the family would playfully chase one another. Lee could still recall the distant sound of waves, the sunset casting a golden hue over the sea, creating an atmosphere filled with joy.

"Wait." Lee suddenly returned to reality. He couldn't even remember Sharmin Haelion! How could he retain memories from his toddler years? Something must have been amiss lately. Memories from the past were flooding back, driven by an inexplicable urge with a mystical power that transformed his view of events he had long avoided. Partings were no longer steeped in sorrow, loneliness emanated strength, and fear seemed to evaporate. However, amidst this transformation, the truth remained elusive. Lee found himself grappling with the uncertainty of it all.

The small aircraft inched its way northward along the coastline. Overloaded and buffeted by the harsh wind hit, it trembled persistently, as if teetering on the verge of falling apart. Fortunately, the journey was relatively short, and they eventually began to descend, landing unsteadily on the lawn in front of a spacious mansion by the sea.

Lee leaped out of the cabin, rolled his shoulders to relieve the tension, and scanned his surroundings.

Talma, taking on the role of a genuine guide this time, eagerly started explaining as soon as her feet touched the ground, "this place is like a fortress, surrounded by mountains on three sides and the sea on the other. It's got a rare stability in this era, drawing in loads of wealthy dudes looking to lay low. But man, living here is not budget friendly, and even the clothes are straight from those floating cities, and let me tell you, they're not cheap!"

Lee disagreed, grunting, "humph, might as well move to a floating city then!"

"Hah! Move to a Floating City?" Talma chuckled. "It's not that simple, man. You know. Each floating city has its own boss, its own set of rules, and most of them don't care about money. Take Aurora City, the closest one from here—every time it takes in a new resident, everyone else living there has to agree unanimously. One person's 'no' can ruin it! Plus, slots are limited. At the end of each year, those lucky enough to make the list get a shot to present, but convincing all those people? Oh, you can't even imagine how hard it is. But if you're interested, I've got a way. A gal pal of mine is an expert at this. In just a few years, she's sent in a bunch of folks! Truth be told, life in Aurora City might not be worse than yours—"

"Let's go inside!" Lee impatiently interrupted.

The house, while not new, boasted rich decorations, featuring an exceptionally wide veranda and marble steps leading up to it. As Lee scanned for the doorbell, Talma took the initiative and knocked with a *knock*.

"Hey Mr. Nikolas, it's Talma. You made the right call. The info you wanted? We're making some progress."

After a prolonged silence, Talma grew a bit frustrated, muttering, "likely heading out for a mountain hunt."

Unable to resist the insistent pull of curiosity, Lee grabbed the doorknob and twisted it. Surprisingly, the door opened easily.

Leaning in, he found himself in a dim short corridor, greeted by a potent scent of gunpowder that caught him off guard. "Oh no!"

"Mr. Lee, I've been waiting for you for a while!" Before Lee could retreat, a familiar voice froze him in place.

"Zhukov?" Lee's question hung in the air as the man materialized at the end of the corridor.

"Mr. Lee, come in and let's talk. I don't understand some of the clues I just found, and I'd like to ask you for advice."

Lee was completely stunned, but he could only walk forward with a stiff expression. Talma, on the other hand, followed him closely, feeling at a loss.

At the end of the short corridor was a spacious and bright living room, with three tall full-length windows framed a view of the sea. Zhukov picked a chair and sat down by the window, gesturing for Lee to take a seat too. Lee, noticing armed soldiers on the other end of the room and fresh bloodstains on the white carpet, obediently took a seat opposite Zhukov. Talma attempted to follow, but Zhukov blocked her with a disdainful gesture, issuing an order to the soldiers with a look of disgust, "take her down first!"

Two soldiers promptly approached, seizing Talma from either side and dragging her out of the door amidst her desperate screams.

Lee, though lacking confidence, forced himself to ask with anger, "Zhukov, what's up your sleeve?"

Zhukov responded deliberately, "oh, Mr. Lee, no secrets up my sleeve! The real mystery is all yours…"

"You've been monitoring me all the time?"

"Okay, let me tell you the truth, Mr. Lee. Since the first investigation report came out, we have confirmed that what happened at the Foundation was an illicit invasion. Someone pretended to be a Pioneer, infiltrated, and planned sabotage. According to the information we currently have, the sabotage was supposed to be an attempt, but the saboteur hijacked a transport ship and escaped. Her name—we later believed—was Mia." Zhukov paused, his eyes fixed on Lee, observing the subtle changes that flashed across his face. Only after being satisfied did Zhukov continue, "initially, we speculated about the possibility of your connection with Mia. Of course, due to your alleged amnesia, we found no evidence to confirm this suspicion. However, the events of the night before, when a mysterious woman—whom we judged to be Mia—sneaked into your home in San Francisco, the discovery of the tunnels, and your mysterious disappearance, almost led me to conclude that you have been complicit all along, from the Foundation to what you've done here in San Francisco!"

"None of that makes sense. I only found myself caught up in all this without any clear reason or understanding," Lee defended.

Uncertain if Zhukov approved of Lee's seemingly less assertive defense, he adjusted his tone, "surprisingly, you returned to your San Francisco home, contradicting my assumption that you had completely escaped—you know, Boss was furious after I lost you. Luckily, we detected your new target—this remote town—and made some unexpected discoveries, almost compelling me to reconsider my previous conclusions."

"Unexpected discoveries?"

"Very unexpected!" Zhukov immediately took out a few enlarged old photos from the coffee table next to him, handing them to Lee. "Examine them closely. If your visit has nothing to do with Mia, we need to rewrite this story, and it's giving me a headache!"

Lee quickly glanced at the photos, finding them similar to those in Talma's possession. As expected, each photo featured Danny, alone or with others. Curiosity struck: Was Zhukov also investigating Shannon Chen's old case, or was he involved in shooting down the flying car in Abandoned Harbor?

"Who are these people? I have no idea!" Lee tossed the photos back to Zhukov.

Zhukov picked one photo, pressed it onto the table, and dragged Lee over. Pointing at a figure, he said, "look closely, who is this person?"

Lee approached with reluctance. The photo depicted Danny with a group of individuals in what seemed to be a living room. Zhukov directed Lee's attention to a figure in the background reaching for a vase on the table, apparently oblivious to being captured in the scene. Despite the obscured angle, Lee easily recognized him, prompting a shocked exclamation. "Dave?"

Zhukov, unsatisfied with Lee's reaction, said, "isn't your response a bit slow?"

Lee, growing impatient, asked rhetorically, "Zhukov, what do you mean?"

"If you're involved in secret activities for Dave, I don't care. But our boss needs an explanation!"

Lee realized Zhukov's misconception, relieved but maintaining a stern expression. "You're jumping to conclusions! Let me tell you, I was more surprised than you are seeing Dave in this photo! If you want the details, fine, I'll explain. But don't blame me later for involving you!"

Lee quickly decided to fabricate a story. The unresolved case had already disrupted his peace, so why not involve more people to complicate things? This way, he could divert their attention from

Mia. So, he tapped on Danny's image in the photo and spoke deliberately, "this guy's name is Danny. Over a decade ago, he signed a contract with a biochemical company, *Great Evolution* or something, up in Northern California. They treated his terminal illness in a clinical trial, causing severe mutations—immunity to sickness, injuries, death by natural causes, and a lack of dreams. And the head of this biochemical company—now I think—was Dave."

Zhukov looked stunned as Lee continued, "this case cost Shannon Chen his life. He had seen this mutated Danny once just before his unfortunate fate. I couldn't find any information on either Danny or *Great Evolution*, suspecting all data has been destroyed. But who would expect someone still preserved old photos!"

Zhukov stammered, "the woman who approached you that night, was it also for this?"

Lee, realizing Zhukov was successfully tricked now, smiled. "Exactly. She's from the floating city at sea, promising to help me find some remaining data. Luckily, a tunnel from my house leads to the Hyperloop—my father dug it during the war. We followed it to the coast of L.A., where their people were waiting."

Zhukov became speechless. After a pause, he muttered, "how should I explain this to the Old Man?"

"Tell the truth. Tell him …" Lee suggested, "Yiming Lee felt the unexpected incident involving his former superior, Shannon Chen, was too suspicious. Therefore, he had been secretly investigating. Unexpectedly, the clues led to his current boss, Dave. Feeling uncertain about how to handle the situation, he had no choice but to confess to the investigative bureau."

"That sounds good. That's good!" Zhukov approved. "Mr. Lee, wait a sec, I'll arrange it."

As Zhukov left the room, soldiers remained. Lee turned to the window, quietly wiping cold sweat. The reminders of Zhukov's cruelty—the blood on the carpet, Sophia's death—served as a grim testament to what he could do.

"Disband!" With a swift command, Zhukov's demeanor shifted back to his usual confidence. He approached Lee, giving him a reassuring pat on the shoulder. "Okay, the Old Man wants to take charge of this personally. You're coming back with us."

"When?"
"Right now."
"Now?"
"Yes, immediately."
Lee had no choice but to trail behind Zhukov as they exited through the back door. Before them stretched a vast meadow, dominated by the imposing presence of the colossal spacecraft, the renowned Warship "Khan." Fueled by a potent nuclear fusion ion engine, it could traverse the globe in under half an hour.

Boarding the warship with Zhukov, Lee observed through the porthole as the scattered soldiers congregated at the gangway. As he settled into his seat, a sudden realization struck him. "Where's Talma?"

"Don't worry, she's been taken care of."

Lee shuddered at the revelation that another innocent life had been sacrificed on account of his actions. He couldn't deny that he had unwittingly plunged into a perilous situation.

16. CASTLE

In the kitchen, Lyu was meticulously preparing dinner, unwilling to compromise on the details even though only she and Temur remained in the house. Taking extra caution, she diced the potatoes and fried them in butter until they achieved a tempting golden brown, so that extended exposure in the soup might not lead to their disintegration. Meanwhile, the tomatoes in the pot had simmered to a delicate consistency, releasing an enticing aroma of beef, celery, and lemon that wafted through the air.

Life revealed its newfound charm in these moments, prompting Lyu to marvel at its possibilities. The years of enduring the harsh realities of a dark existence had nearly extinguished her capacity for imagination. However, since relocating to Lee's apartment, it felt as if she had stepped into a long-forgotten dream. The exact moment when she had kindled her love for dreaming eluded her memory. In the bygone days, no matter how dire the circumstances, she could always find solace in the realms of sleep. Those dreams served as a portal, transporting her back to a time when family gathered around a table adorned with silver candlesticks and bouquets, seemingly untouched by the hardship of life. The fleeting despair upon waking was the minimal toll she paid for these ephemeral escapes. Wiping away tears that trickled in secret, she begrudgingly accepted the harsh reality that awaited her.

Now, however, this dream felt prolonged, simultaneously bringing joy and unease. She recognized the paradox that the longer and more blissful a dream, the more acute the pain upon awakening. Fortunately, most of the time, such contemplations were fleeting, and by choosing not to dwell on them, she could stave off the unsettling apprehension that lingered in the corners of her mind.

"Bang dang!"

The sound of a rough knock echoed through the living room, signaling Temur's return. Despite Lyu's repeated attempts to convince him to abandon his bad habits, he remained obstinate.

"Sister, they found some of the information you wanted. It was a long time ago, they said. It seems that since when, that person—what's his name?"

"Saeed Hosseini."

"Right, Saeed Hosseini. Everything about the guy has been hard-destructed. Yes, hard destruction. I don't know what they mean by what they told me."

Lyu comprehended the gravity of the situation. Her father had mentioned to her that certain information would undergo "hard destruction" if its potential harm was deemed severe enough to spiral out of control. This implied that, in the future, even her father and Hun wouldn't be able to retrieve this information. However, Saeed Hosseini was merely a scientist engaged in pure astronomical research. Lyu pondered, questioning the rationale behind pushing the information about him to the point of hard destruction.

Lyu's curiosity disrupted her peace of mind, making it impossible to continue cooking. Hastily, she poured diced potatoes and shredded cabbage into the soup pot, closed the lid, rubbed her hand on her apron, and hurriedly made her way to Temur.

"They also griped about how these things were super risky and swore they'd never touch them again!"

Lyu responded with a casual *um*, took the information card from Temur's hand, opened a terminal, and exported all the available information.

After scrutinizing the information, Lyu couldn't find anything particularly noteworthy. The collection consisted of Saeed's publications on Sirius research, spanning over a decade. The recurring hypothesis posited by Saeed was that Sirius was originally a three-star system, transformed into its current double-star state due to a supernova explosion in the distant past. Saeed suggested the presence of either a neutron star or a black hole concealed within the aftermath of the explosion. However, this hypothesis lacked substantial evidence. Saeed's sole supporting detail was a myth prevalent among the ancient Dogon tribes. According to the myth, the tribes survived the Great Star Outbreak by sacrificing maidens as guided by their gods, a cruel scene depicted in Lee's painting.

Lyu felt a sense of exhaustion and disheartenment. She questioned the driving force behind her persistence in studying such a question, unable to provide herself with a convincing answer. Perhaps it was the unsettling painting on the wall that deeply troubled Lee, and since she possessed some knowledge about the depicted scene, she felt compelled to solve the puzzle for him. Even aware that Lee might not appreciate all her efforts, she found it difficult to find peace of mind if she did nothing.

That night, Lyu lay in bed, tossing and turning, unable to find sleep.

The thoughts, firmly confined in the past, were suddenly set free on that quiet night. The elusive essence of the vanished youth lingered amidst the ruins, irresistibly drawing her to explore those forgotten corners.

She admitted that when she first saw Lee's photo from Temur, a surprising joy had welled up within her. In her younger years, this tall and handsome young man, a frequent guest at her house, had briefly captivated her. However, being born into a prominent family, she couldn't allow herself to be enchanted by a man; it was more fitting for a man to fall for her. During school, despite her using a pseudonym, the imposing bodyguards surrounding her hinted at her unusual identity. This led her peers to either vigilantly keep their distance or deliberately flatter and annoy her.

Consequently, she had no contact with peers of different gender during a time when her heart was just in the bloom of romance. This circumstance gradually fostered in her a mysterious fondness for older men resembling her father. She knew she wouldn't fall in love with any of them, but she enjoyed the flirtatious glint in their eyes when they were provoked. Lee, however, was different. Despite her apparent enthusiasm, he remained indifferent, a natural melancholy etched between his eyebrows, occasionally tinged with a hint of shyness on his face. Strangely, it was this very indifference that deeply attracted her.

As time passed, things changed, and Lyu never anticipated reuniting with Lee under such desperate circumstances. At that moment, she keenly realized her own depleted self, devoid of any remaining charm. Faced with the man she had once fallen for, her heart brimmed with indescribable self-doubt.

"Quack," the sudden sound of the door opening echoed through the living room, followed by hushed footsteps, startling Lyu. She clutched the coverlet tightly, her heart pounding. After a moment's contemplation, she resolved to leave the bed. Tiptoeing to the door, she cautiously opened it a crack, and bravely peeked outside.

"Pang," the lights flickered to life, and she recognized the familiar voice.

"Gia, what time is it?"

"It's 3:41 a.m. on March 1st, dear Lee."

Lyu breathed a sigh of relief, her tense heart easing. She draped a coat over her cold shoulders and approached the living room. "You're back?"

Despite her preparations, Lyu's sudden appearance startled Lee.

"Lyur?"

"I can't sleep." Lyu noticed the distress on Lee's face and whispered, "it must have scared you."

"It's fine." Lee replied in a subdued voice, heading to the kitchen. As he emerged, he carried a half-full glass.

Taking a substantial sip, he settled on the sofa. After a brief uneasy silence, he spoke to Lyu with a solemn expression, "I can now confirm that your father did not kill himself. He must have been aware of an important secret hidden in high ranks of the Corporation, so he suffered misfortune."

The revelation shocked Lyu. She hurriedly asked, "what secrets? What secrets could endanger my dad?"

Lee hesitated slightly before replying, "I don't know all the details yet, but your previous guess was correct. He must have recognized the mutation that occurred with Dan after their meeting, and figured out who was behind it, and…"

Lee paused, a look of helplessness on his face.

Lyu began to sob, and an air of heaviness settled in the room. After a while, Lee continued with a grave tone, "I am sorry. And one thing I've got to know for sure is that you, and even Temur, might have been put into a very dangerous situation. You're no longer safe here. You two must leave immediately after dawn, find a safe place to hide, go to Ethelinda's!"

These unexpected words made Lyu's body tremble violently. Standing silently before Lee for seconds, she didn't utter a word. Suddenly, she stepped forward, seized the brandy glass Lee had placed on the table, gulped down most of its contents in one go, and without looking back, ran into the bedroom, not bothering to close the door, collapsing on the bed in tears.

Indeed, she had long grasped the reality that no matter how sweet a dream was, there would always come a moment of abrupt awakening.

Lee considered offering words of comfort but found himself glued to the sofa, unable to get up for a long time. Exhaustion weighed heavily on him.

This time, Zhukov escorted him back, and initially, Lee doubted if he could make it home. Along the way, memories surfaced of Pioneers enduring similar ordeals—trapped since landing. Resorting to any means, they only managed to extract the elusive name "Mia" from them. Though Lee had once escaped this predicament, he lacked the confidence to evade it a second time, especially given that returning was a direct order from Hun.

However, upon landing, Zhukov not only spared him embarrassment but also arranged for a flying car to take him home. Lee questioned in surprise, "is everything settled?"

Zhukov, patting his head as if remembering, replied, "oh, almost forgot... it was indeed a dire day. The Old Man wants to see you tomorrow, so be ready!"

"Huh?" Lee exclaimed, bewildered.

Zhukov cautioned, "stay alert for information and prepare to go to the Castle!"

Muttering softly, Lee repeated, "castle..."

The flying car ascended slowly, disappearing into the night's haze. In the far east, a faint glimmer of white light heralded the approaching dawn.

Lee had never visited the Castle, and he had no expectation that he ever would. The Castle, known as Hun's exclusive domain, was rumored to stand on an atoll island secluded far from the mainland.

Both the island and the encompassing waters were under his private ownership, barring even the Corporation from setting foot on its grounds. To deter unwanted access, a no-fly zone was enforced over the island. Any aircraft disregarding warnings risked being swiftly neutralized by high-energy laser cannons deployed on geostationary satellites.

Throughout recent years, Hun had maintained seclusion, seldom making public appearances. He operated from the confines of the Castle, orchestrating the Corporation's activities from a distance. Even within the Corporation, only a select few had the privilege of encountering him in the Castle.

So, what exactly does such a meeting mean? Lee had no clue.

The strong desire to sleep hung over Lee like a dark cloud on the eve of a storm, but he couldn't fall asleep, leaving him deeply puzzled. Attempting to rise and pour another glass of Brandy, he discovered his body unresponsive, a unique exhaustion coursing through him—one he had never felt before, the kind that gripped people when they were approaching the end. This realization sent a shiver through his heart, prompting him to inflate his chest in an attempt to shake off the weariness. As he struggled to move once more, the defiance of his limbs led him to bite down hard on his tongue. The ensuing pain jolted him awake, only to find that dawn had arrived unnoticed.

The door to Lyu's room remained ajar. Moving cautiously, he called out, "Lyur!"

Silence prevailed. The room stood empty, the bed neatly made.

"Lee, don't forget about the meeting with Doctor Hun. The shuttle arrives at six o'clock, and you still have forty minutes!" Gia reminded eagerly.

On the rooftop, a sleek flying car awaited him.

As Lee approached, the hatches on both sides unfolded slowly, offering a generous welcome. This momentary display of hospitality eased the anxiety and tension in Lee's heart. He straightened his back and ran his fingers through his messy hair.

"Requesting authentication... fingerprints, iris, DNA, identity confirmed: Lee, internal number 2932200. Security checks in progress…"

Suddenly, various probes of different styles extended out of nowhere, thoroughly scanning Lee and leaving him defenseless. The anxiety that had briefly dissipated now surged back into his heart.

"Security check passed, ready for take-off. Estimated time to arrive at the destination is 90 minutes."

The flying car ascended swiftly, transforming into a bright spot that silently disappeared into the sky.

In the heart of the jungle, amidst the island's embrace, the Castle stood.

Upon laying eyes on it, Lee found himself fixated on a singular question: Why was it named a Castle? It bore no resemblance to the conventional image of a castle—no towers, no moats. Furthermore, it deviated from the archetypal concept of a castle, lacking the features of both traditional East Asian castles and medieval structures. Instead, it assumed the form of a pyramid. If one were to stretch the definition to include a pyramid as a *castle*, then it might qualify as one.

A faint ache crept into Lee's head, and he came to realize that he wasn't genuinely contemplating the question. The current tension gripping his nerves was a product of obsessive thinking fueled by overwhelming stress.

Now, he found himself at the base of this peculiar *castle*.

After landing, the flying car vanished without providing any guidance, and Lee, driven solely by his instincts, followed a path that led him here, to the foot of the Castle.

Perhaps it was the Castle's will.

Lee recalled the moment he stepped out of the hatch, he caught sight of the conspicuous gable protruding above the jungle, gleaming in the sunlight from a distance. Coincidentally, a winding path lay before him, leading into the dense, lush green jungle.

Go to the Castle.

It felt as natural as teenagers returning home from school: entering, navigating the living room, climbing stairs, and slipping into their room.

Its exterior was smooth and flawless, crystal clear, forming a colossal mirror: palm trees swaying in the gentle breeze, lush broadleaf forests, the expansive blue sky, occasional drifting clouds... Everything in the vicinity appeared to be perfectly mirrored on its surface.

A few suspended steps remained between him and the structure, and the clear, pleasant sound of flowing water emanated from below. As he ascended, he eventually caught sight of a mirrored reflection of himself on the outer wall. However, there was no apparent entrance to be found.

Examining his mirrored reflection, he felt perturbed by the tired and distracted appearance.

Abruptly, the mirror image disappeared, revealing an opening in its place.

"Welcome!"

A gentle female voice echoed from the entrance, and he felt a warmth, walking in with a faint sense of anticipation.

17. DOCTOR

The interior space was remarkably expansive; Lee intuited it constituted nearly the entire castle, yet it remained vacant. Milky hues enveloped everything, from the floor to the ceiling, a solitary staircase ascending to the upper level, and two sets of sofas with a coffee table at the center, appearing eerily empty, resembling distant toys. Scanning the surroundings, Lee's eyes encountered abundant greenery, the verdant flow nearly cascading in. It became apparent that the building's four walls were entirely transparent from the inside.

"Finally, you're here, and I feel happy!"

Lee was stunned.

Hun's voice seemed different from what Lee usually heard, but it wasn't the sound itself that astonished him. It was the greeting. Despite having experienced memory disturbance for some time, he clung to the belief that on the day he encountered the High Priestess in Avalon, she uttered the same words, with an eerily similar tone.

"Sir. Mr. Hun..." As soon as he spoke, he panicked. It was only then that he realized he had never thought about how to address this highest-ranking figure.

Now, he could only stand there like a child who had made a mistake, stiff and respectful, watching Hun descend the stairs step by step. He seemed steady and full of energy, but Lee still noticed the efforts he put in to maintain this posture, such as the excessive calmness and the frozen expression that appeared from time to time during the march, all indicating his extreme concern about his image in the eyes of the others. When individuals were overly focused on their image, that often signaled something wrong with them. Lee then considered that it might be precisely for this reason that Hun chose to remain secluded on this isolated island and neglected meeting anyone.

The High Priestess was not wrong, Lee pondered.

"Just call me Doctor." Hun took a seat on one of the couches and extended his hand, gesturing to the other.

"Relax, sit! It's been a long time since I've had a guest." His hand lingered until Lee respectfully sat down.

"Mr. Lee, do you need something to drink? Tea or coffee?"

Lee heard the gentle female voice that had welcomed him, but he couldn't locate its source. He shook his head and looked at the doctor, saying, "no, thank you!"

"I'm a little disappointed that you look so nervous. Relax, I'll allow you to ask a question first."

Hun's words made Lee feel a bit ashamed. He lowered his head, pondered for a while, and finally gathered the courage to speak, "I want to know, why did you summon me this time? What's the special reason?"

Hun responded casually, "I guess that's not really what you want to ask, is it?" Seeing Lee faltering, he continued, "I want to assure you that this time I summoned you because I simply hope to alleviate the confusion in your heart as much as possible."

"Then... What—" Lee's tone became urgent. "What is the real purpose of building the Foundation, after all?"

Hun remained as calm as ever and answered softly, "to perpetuate human civilization."

"That's from the official statement—" Lee muttered.

"I don't know what lies those people fabricated to convince you, but I have only one answer for you—for the sake of human civilization," Hun said.

Lee was startled, realizing that the Doctor had a far greater understanding of him than he had imagined.

Hun continued, "your generation... Though I'm uncertain if

you've had the opportunity to delve into Asimov. Speaking of which, um... the idea of a unified ideology wasn't my goal, and the actual implementation was likely to be disorderly. However, to ensure the continued existence of this world, it became a necessity... Asimov, the writer, painted a picture of a world teetering on the brink of destruction in his works. A perceptive individual within that world foresaw its impending demise. Instead of attempting to avert the looming catastrophe, this person opted to proactively prepare for the emergence of a new world. Thus, beyond the confines of the current world, he laid the groundwork for a new one in advance, calling it *Foundation*."

Of course, Lee wouldn't be familiar with Asimov. Although his father had preserved a collection of physical books, he harbored disdain for sentimental attachment to the bygone era of the previous generation and never bothered to glance at them.

"So, did they just let the original world be destroyed?" Lee asked.

"It was inevitable."

Hun appeared pleased that Lee had posed the question, and he continued, "they must have told you that the current world was fragile and vulnerable, and that's true. Because it is fragile, we have to carefully maintain it, and because it is vulnerable, we cannot let people know this fact. Our mission is to build the prototype of a new world before the current one collapses, so that the spark of civilization can continue. I guess you've been to those floating cities. What makes them different? Wasn't their purpose of existing the same? I never deny their existence—that's why they still exist. I hope in the not-too-distant future, we can prove that compared to them, the Foundation is the ultimate and only winning solution."

"But how do you even convince yourself? The Foundation is far away from the earth, and there's nothing there."

"Just because there's nothing there, anything becomes possible; 'all existence springs from nonexistence,' you know?"

"I don't understand; I've spent so many years there, and the only feeling is... that, it's like a tomb." Lee deliberately threw out the words.

Hun's tone now carried a hint of irritation. "Do you comprehend the true origin of the world's deterioration? Perhaps not entirely. The root cause lies within humanity itself—something you might be starting to understand recently. It's not merely my perspective; even Aurora, in a somewhat ironic turn, explored similar paths through a citizenship referendum. The Central Christian State's attempt to redefine God is essentially another endeavor to alter human nature. However, they all overlook a fundamental truth: As long as people can communicate without isolation, negative aspects of human nature tend to proliferate like contagious viruses."

"So, you established your Foundation far away from Earth, intending to personally decide the chosen ones of the isolated world?"

"I'm not seeking to decide; rather, I aim to shape. Elizabeth and her team have achieved significant advancements. While the Pioneers aren't flawless, they're progressing toward perfection. Shannon Chen's Titan project laid the groundwork for the Foundation. However, his goal was too impractical to be acknowledged, as it risked transforming a new world into a more degenerate version of Earth—"

Upon hearing this, Lee could no longer hold back. He posed the burning question, "did Shannon Chen truly take his own life?"

The question caused a sudden shift in Hun's demeanor, his expression turning grim. However, he maintained composure, staying silent for a moment before speaking earnestly, "Lee, the purpose of summoning you this time is to reveal certain truths. The reality might not be aligned with public presentation, but I won't tolerate baseless speculations. You know, this time you've been accused of dereliction of duty, and Zhukov strongly suspected you were conspiring with the invader—I simply dismissed it. On the other hand, Dave has grown impatient, yet, despite my approval of the new commander he recommended, I still sought to affirm the trust between us."

"Trust?"

"If it weren't for trust, how could I have handed the Foundation—the result of years of painstaking management—over to you for more than a decade without questioning?"

Lee suddenly noticed a strange glint in Hun's eyes, but he couldn't decipher it. Undeterred, he pressed on, "so, what's the truth then? Are you backing Dave's biochemical transformation research, turning humans into the walking dead? Chen died after finding the truth; am I headed down the same path?"

Hun defended, "no, Shannon and you are completely different.

He was much more cunning than you. When I rejected his plan, he couldn't suppress his ambition. He tried to put me in checkmate and ended up reaping what he sowed." After a brief pause, he continued, "our goal isn't turning humans into the walking dead; it's about helping them adapt to the demands of interstellar travel, making them stronger and more resilient, even perpetual!"

Lee felt shocked, despite receiving the expected answer. Unable to contain himself, he blurted out, "so, the true goal is for you to achieve immortality, right?"

Hun fell silent, looking a bit weary. He gently closed his eyes and said, "for the new world, we all need to achieve immortality."

"Have you achieved it?" Lee pressed. "At least, I don't see any anomalies in you." Pausing, he added, "you look even older than I imagined."

These words spilled from Lee's lips unprepared, and he expected Hun to be furious. Instead, Hun remained calm, saying nothing.

Suddenly, he stood up, approached Lee, patted him on the shoulder, and said slowly, "I'm asking you to go with the new commander and return to the Foundation together. There, I hope our mutual trust can be proven."

After saying this, Hun's face showed traces of exhaustion. He slowly stretched out his right hand and said, "Lee, trust your own judgment and follow reason."

Lee accepted Hun's extended hand, feeling the warmth.

"See you soon," Hun said meaningfully, then focused on maintaining his majestic descending posture as he walked up the steps.

Before Hun disappeared, Lee asked abruptly, "Doctor, do you still dream?"

Perplexed, Hun didn't answer.

"People don't dream after Dave's treatment," Lee remarked as he exited.

After leaving the Castle, Lee felt as if the trajectory of his fate had become an unstoppable bullet, hurtling towards a predetermined destination beyond his control.

As soon as he touched down, a series of messages flooded in from Dave. The first informed him about the transition arrangements with the new Foundation commander, followed by a pre-scheduled meeting agenda. The final message conveyed that the new commander would be paying him a visit that very day.

Amidst this deluge of conflicting information, Lee found a short, stout, and bald man with a friendly face come to his doorstep. Introducing himself as Liam Mohammadi, he explained that Dave had arranged for them to get acquainted in private.

Lee reclined on the sofa, putting his feet up and casually sipping from a freshly filled glass.

"Have a seat, make yourself comfortable." He gestured to Liam. The latter, feeling a bit cramped on the distant single sofa, struggled to find words. His eyes landed on the large painting.

"Interesting painting. Are you into Dogon culture?" Liam tried to initiate a conversation.

"How do you know it's Dogon?"

Caught off guard, Liam stammered, "I... uh... guessed. Probably not Dogon at all, right?"

Lee remained indifferent, closing his eyes. Not rudeness, but sheer exhaustion kept him from responding.

"Mr. Lee, Mr. Lee..." Liam tentatively called, raising his voice when met with silence. "You seem tired. I'll visit another day."

As Liam stood up to leave, he reminded, "Mr. Lee, don't forget to let Mr. Warren know that I stopped by!"

Left alone, Lee felt too fatigued to move, drifting into a deep sleep.

Over the years, whenever he was confronted with a harsh reality he found hard to accept, drowsiness became his body's refuge from anxiety—an attempt to escape dangers through slumber. In this state, he could retreat to his old dreams, feeling as if he were nestled in an escape pod suspended from a colossal ship, tuning out the waves as he closed his eyes.

It was reminiscent of the early days on Titan when he arrived, seeking solace beneath the surface, sipping Brandy to find warmth after its prolonged absence. His aversion wasn't to the objective coldness—the indoor climate system maintained a minimum of 25 degrees Celsius, his rule—but rather to the surroundings: snowfields, icebergs, sand dunes, remnants of methane lakes, the distant, desolate sun, and the looming giant moon beyond the clouds. All these elements cast an irresistible chill.

Consequently, he rarely ventured outdoors, preferring to stay in front of surveillance screens, observing Pioneers inspect superpowered laser arrays, drones clouding the dusky sky, and autonomous robots traversing neighboring gigafactories. The once silent ice fields transformed into lively hubs, triggering memories of a southern city he once knew.

Seclusion had never been Lee's intention; as a child, he enjoyed bustling metropolises and crowded places. He never envisioned spending his life on this uninhabited ice world—it wasn't part of his plan. The issue lay in his lack of serious life planning. In his eyes, the concept of either/or was absurd, making choices seemed foolish, given the absence of objective judgment for past decisions. The Corporation's sudden shift in strategy to build the Foundation stirred considerable commotion, nearly sparking a crisis. Lee, however, remained indifferent. When he learned the Foundation would be established in space, he casually hummed, "that might be a good thing." Even when Shannon Chen risked discussing the conspiracy behind it through a private channel, Lee remained nonchalant and evasive. It wasn't until Chen's unfortunate incident that he felt a twinge of remorse, though regret remained a fleeting emotion he chose not to delve into.

The new Foundation resembled a floating city in the sky, and Lee often stood in front of the expansive porthole in his headquarters, gazing out at the vast starry expanse. Behind him, holographic projections continually switched among scenes, with Eve, the AI host of the Foundation, introducing him to the newly arrived Pioneers. Uninterested, he occasionally turned around, idly toying with the ring in his hand. Then, in a particular moment, an unmistakably familiar figure swiftly passed by. His initial reaction was disbelief, and he thought it must be an error. When he asked Eve to replay the scene, what he witnessed left him breathless.

"Sharmin..." He uttered the name with a shudder, opening his eyes.

By now, the projection had vanished, the porthole was gone, and the living room lay in darkness, casting the few rays of sunset that had slipped through the shutters in a dazzling light.

18. FOUNDATION

After more than three months since the meeting between Lee and Hun at the Castle, the Himalaya Spaceship made another successful arrival at the Foundation and docked with it. During this time, Lee had fully regained his memory, and it was challenging for him to reconcile the once-disheartened middle-aged man—dismissed due to an accident, immersed in gloom, and seeking solace in past memories—with his present self.

As he gazed through the porthole into the vastness of deep space, the most magnificent and grandiose project in human history unfolded before him. Memories of vibrant activities played out vividly in his mind, almost as if they had happened just yesterday. Gratitude filled him for emerging from the boundless nightmares, allowing him to reassess the reality in front of him and reclaim control of the helm of his life amidst the surging waves.

He recalled the time when the accident was fresh, and he had turned to Mia, pleading for the wiping of his memory. In that critical moment, there was no room for hesitation in his heart. The prospect of a direct escape back to Earth didn't seem as idyllic as Mia painted it. After all, she remained a woman, and her choices were probably influenced by cherished ideals.

He clearly remembered the shock on Mia's face. "But, what if… if these memories of yours never return? I mean, in case—since I haven't had a chance to experiment with many similar operations."

"If I can't recall anything, then you'll treat it as if we've never met."

At that moment, He met Mia's gaze with concern, and then nodded, signaling her to proceed.

He noticed as Mia's eyes closed, she turned her head away.

Lee had long sensed the guilt harbored by Mia in her heart, and he was willing to let this guilt persist. In doing so, he might gain a trace of desired tranquility in his own heart. Moreover, this guilt had its reasons. He recalled on that night when Mia first confessed her true identity and the mission she bore, he couldn't clearly determine whether it was a natural expression of emotions after their sincere connection or if it originated from some long-conceived motive—a question he didn't bother to ask at the time. The idea of returning the Foundation to all of humanity carried a sense of justice, and, at least in that moment, he yearned for the fantasy of achieving great success and then secluding himself with Mia in some unnamed corner of the Earth.

That was what Mia told him on that night. "When it's over, we'll go to Brittany." Then, she swept her long hair to the back of her head and looked at Lee with an innocent gaze.

"Good, Brittany."

While Lee knew nothing about the place, he had a sense that it held promise, evoking a poetic notion of "Drifting away in a boat, uncertain of the destination."

Gradually, Lee found himself deeply drawn into it.

On the day of the final task, he navigated the biometric verification successfully, inputted the host key, initiated the module upgrade, and established a secure connection with the service node Mia had provided. The host recognized the integrity and legitimacy of the data. However, at this crucial juncture, a sharp alarm abruptly pierced the air, and the host forcibly suspended the upgrade process: "Severe Warning! Potential self-destruct motives detected in the upgrade data. If you proceed, Self-Destruction will be activated in 120 Earth days, please confirm!"

Lee stared in disbelief, turning to Mia with a shocked expression. "Eve's software implanted a protective net at the lower level. It can detect any potential destructive motives. She won't be wrong! What's going on?"

Faced with the interrogation, Mia froze, unable to provide an answer. Eventually, Lee chose to believe in Mia's innocence.

Wiping sweat from his forehead, he uttered weakly, "abort the upgrade."

"Confirming upgrade cancellation. Alarm deactivated!"

Before they could even breathe a sigh of relief, several Pioneers, alerted by the sound, rushed into the control room, approaching them step by step.

"Stay where you are!" Lee's voice pierced through the tension, commanding them to halt.

However, instead of immediately retreating as usual, those people behaved like a pack of predators surrounding their prey. At times, they stood still, and at other times, they advanced slowly.

Observing this, Mia swiftly reached for a special headset, placing it on her head. Confronting the encroaching individuals, she closed her eyes with deliberate calmness.

In silence, the Pioneers collapsed to the ground, their awareness erased.

"They will never know what has happened," Mia, still catching her breath, reassured Lee. Detecting his lingering suspicion, she admitted, "I forcibly erased this segment of their memory, though traces may remain."

Offering a feeble explanation, Mia mentioned, "the service node was sent by the High Priestess to fulfill her enduring vision—that is, for humanity to collectively own the Foundation."

Lee chose to believe Mia; he was willing to trust her, regardless of her actions or words. So, he promptly fabricated a lie that would be difficult for anyone to believe.

"Maybe someone tampered with it."

Having finally spoken the words that lingered in his heart for years above the ruins near the methane lake, he grew indifferent of unraveling the events that followed. Despite their strangeness and lack of logic, he focused solely on the present, investing all his energy in cherishing moments with Mia. He knew well that unless there was a mole within the higher-ups of the Corporation, Mia would not have a service node capable of successfully connecting to Eve, in fact, Mia herself would not have appeared in front of him.

Yet, what did that matter? She was here, and he was content.

Now, Lee's memory about the accident was crystal clear. It

took some time for him to gradually calm down. Then, he ushered Mia into the Foundation's internal launch tube, unwilling to waste a second as they swiftly shuttled to the docking bay where the Prometheus silently awaited.

"This supply ship is equipped with the latest light nuclear ion engine. It can take you back to Earth even without the solar sail, and there's enough supplies on board, at least for a year!"

"What about you?"

Lee bowed his head and spoke softly, "I—I won't go back with you..." Then, as if a sudden realization struck him, he urgently inquired, "or—can the erased memories be restored?"

"It can be done, as long as I leave behind enough reliable clues. Why do you ask?"

"Erase my memories too. Let me feel like nothing ever happened... It's the safest way."

"This—isn't it." Mia hesitated for a moment but eventually agreed. "Okay. But is there something that has been lingering in your heart, something you can't forget?"

Now, Lee knew that the clue Mia left behind was the starfish, but he still had no recollection of ever mentioning this to her.

The gate opened, drawing Lee's mind back to the reality.

A total of two hundred Pioneers gathered in the transfer hub after a successful disembark, marking the largest landing operation to date. Normally, such a grand operation would be heavily publicized, widely announced, but strangely, there was no public information released from preparation to launch. Even Lee himself didn't learn about the number of people boarding until the moment of launch.

By that time, vaguely recalling what had happened at the Foundation, Lee was anxiously concerned about two things.

Firstly, the day after Liam personally visited, during the formal handover meeting at headquarters, Dave strongly demanded that he hand over the upgrade key to Eve. This request was quite suspicious. Lee's key was given by Chen, and naturally Liam's key should have been provided by Dave. However, it was evident that Dave did not have the key, indicating that, regarding Liam taking over as the Foundation commander, Hun did not give substantial approval.

Secondly, shortly before departure, someone from the

Organization approached him, bringing a new service node. What surprised him was that the person was Chyi. On that day, Chyi unusually spoke very little and refused to answer any questions from Lee.

"The High Priestess sent me."
"How can I trust you?"
"You don't need to trust me!"
Indeed, whether to believe or not was entirely up to Lee.

In contrast, Liam was in high spirits during the long trip. As Lee didn't feel much camaraderie with this person, he deliberately avoided him throughout the entire journey. However, Liam always went to great lengths to strike up a conversation with him, perhaps because the journey was too long and lonely.

"Mr. Lee, it's time to disembark!" Suddenly, the guy appeared behind him, giving him a pat on the back like an old friend.

At this moment, Lee could still endure the discomfort in his heart and maintain courtesy with this person, but when he requested to take over the commander's residence in the name of the new commander after landing, he categorically refused. Although he believed that Liam wouldn't dare to act recklessly, he understood that this trip was no longer as leisurely as it used to be. On the other hand, this strengthened his determination. Whether it was the "takeover" mentioned by Mia or the "destruction" mentioned by the High Priestess in Avalon, Lee was willing to accept it.

As Lee disembarked from the spaceship onto the Foundation, he was immediately struck by the profound silence. In response, he couldn't resist muttering, "a tomb."

"What? This place will become a paradise—"

Surprisingly, Liam interjected, taking control of the conversation. He pointed at the starry sky, gesturing around and saying, "over there, and there, those're where tombs will be!"

"You are fortunate to be the elect of the Foundation; it is your supreme honor!" Early the next morning, Liam couldn't wait to assemble the Pioneers for a briefing.

Lee was still in the midst of a dream when he was awakened by Eve, who transmitted a holographic image of the scene to him.

"Turn it off, turn it off!" Lee impatiently gave the order.

"Sorry, according to the newly granted terms yesterday, Mr. Mohamadi currently holds the highest authority. All Foundation personnel must participate in the Pioneers' landing ceremony as per Mr. Mohamadi's request."

Lee chuckled. He couldn't figure out whether Liam was genuinely foolish or pretending to be foolish. The Pioneers had been shaped by the Mind Division using special methods, making it impossible for others to predict their behavior. What difference could there be between a *briefing* and talking to a brick wall?

"Selfless! Ruthless! Fearless!"

The crowd began chanting slogans, and Lee couldn't help but glance at them with a stern look. They were fervent, with the same posture and expression, making him feel a bit nauseated. He immediately turned his head away. At that moment, the corner of his eye caught something unusual: Someone was clearly crouching in a corner, lost in thought.

This was unusual. The Mind Division referred to such situations as "deviations"—when a Pioneer exhibited behavior markedly different from the group.

Intrigued, Lee zoomed in, magnifying the crouching person several times.

"Oh my God!"

Once he clearly saw the person's face, he involuntarily took a sharp breath and exclaimed. Without a second thought, he rushed out, darting into the nearest teleportation tube and giving the command, "square!"

"Cherish the glory before you; the future belongs to us!"

When Lee arrived at the square, Liam had just finished his speech. He adjusted his collar, feeling satisfied with his meticulous preparation over the past few days.

After a few seconds of silence, the crowd suddenly dispersed in a tumultuous manner. The scene resembled dropping a drop of hot water into an ant nest—chaotic yet organized. However, this created a lot of trouble for Lee, as his field of vision was now filled with people moving around. They all had similar expressions and postures, making it impossible for him to focus on the inconspicuous figure in the distant corner.

In the blink of an eye, the square became empty. The artificial light projected from the enormous dome gradually weakened, and eventually, the surroundings became as dark and desolate as a night on Earth.

Lee was unwilling to give up, persistently searching every corner. At this moment, a ghostly figure unknowingly swayed behind him.

"Yiming, we meet again!"

Startled, Lee abruptly turned around. "Doctor? How did you—"

"I said I hoped our mutual trust could be proven."

"But... I don't understand..."

"You should understand. When the people around you are meticulously preparing to plot against you, you need to be careful with every step."

In the past, Lee would have found it unbelievable to hear such words from Hun's mouth. However, now he completely understood the fear that the powerful leader had accumulated through the natural aging process, and he even felt sympathy for it.

"But... it is impossible for your to be here without alarming someone!"

"You mean Elizabeth, right? Well, I owe her one. If she could sneakily send Mia up, why couldn't she do the same for me?"

"What? Mia was sent by Elizabeth?"

"I'm disappointed in your judgment. Did you even ask her when Mia first revealed the plot? Don't lie; it's impossible that you didn't know."

Confronted with the doctor's reproach, Lee found himself speechless and had no intention of defending himself. Since he first heard Mia's name, his focus had been solely on identifying her, without considering why she appeared millions of miles away. While he did suspect the Organization's infiltration into the Corporation, he never imagined it would involve someone as high-ranking as Elizabeth. *So, the entire Mind Division, including those Pioneers, were creations of the Organization?* He asked himself.

"But do you still trust her, trust her creations?" Lee asked, alluding to the Pioneers.

"Of course. Why not? Look at the achievements she has made, look at those people. As chosen ones of the New World, they are perfect! I want to ask you, now that you know the true identity of the so-called High Priestess, will you still trust her?" The doctor asked with profound meaning.

These words finally stirred up Lee. He retorted loudly, "impossible! She can't be the High Priestess. I've met her myself; I know what the High Priestess looks like!"

"Of course, she is the High Priestess. Zhukov gathered concrete evidence just before our departure. I wish it weren't true. Over the years, I relied on her so much; she's one of the few who truly understands my intentions—"

"Then where is she now?" Worry crept into Lee as he trembled while asking.

"Don't worry. I didn't hurt her, and I won't go that far, at least not to that extent."

At this moment, the doctor raised his head slightly, fixed his gaze on Lee, and spoke slowly, word by word, "now, all of this is no longer relevant. For many years, I have been holding high authority and tried to control everything, but in reality, it didn't matter much. I've come to accept fate and do what needs to be done. Power is no longer significant to me; if they want to fight for it, let them. However, the mission I told you about last time, the mission to create a new world, I will not give up on that, even if eternal life is unattainable. We can still fulfill it, don't you think?"

Lee remained unmoved by these seemingly sincere words, finding them less persuasive than those from the High Priestess, although neither held meaning for him. He responded, "so, you want to be here with these Pioneers? Demonstrating your superiority during your last moments?"

"Yiming, make the choices you believe are right. That's my only purpose for this trip. I want to witness it myself!"

With those words spoken, he turned away at a slow pace, gradually vanishing into the darkness. He walked with a tired and weary gait, morphing into an ordinary elderly man. Perhaps, at this moment, he no longer felt the need to maintain the composure and steadiness he once wanted others to see. That's what Lee thought.

"By the way, I still dream."

Dr. Hun's last words echoed in the darkness.

19. CONFESSION

Lee dragged heavy steps back to his residence, only to find an unexpected scene awaiting him: a person sitting serenely by the window, unmoving, as if lost in contemplation of the vast starry sky outside.

"Beautiful! Perfect! Mr. Lee, to tell you the truth, I never dreamed in my life that I would have the opportunity to watch the starry sky from such an angle!"

Startled by the intrusion, Lee recognized the figure as Liam and couldn't suppress his anger. "Liam, you dare to—Get out! Leave my room immediately!"

Liam rose from the wicker chair with an air of peculiar indifference, making it challenging to discern if it was his natural demeanor or a deliberate facade.

"Ah, Mr. Lee, let's not escalate your anger! Since you weren't here, and the door was unlocked, I thought it best to come in and wait," he said.

Even under Lee's stern reprimand, Liam maintained his politeness, speaking in a gentle, docile tone. "Am I not also pressed for time? Mr. Lee, after all this time, it's about time for us to initiate the handover—I mean, the upgrade key of Eve. Among the tasks assigned by Mr. Warren, this one takes top priority. Once the handover is completed, you can return to Earth immediately and relieve yourself of this burden."

Only then did Lee grasp that his hidden boss hadn't given up. Despite this, he saw no reason to yield to Liam.

Dismissing him with disdain, Lee retorted, "that's impossible! Go fetch your boss for the handover!"

At this, Liam's facade cracked, revealing a hint of displeasure. As Lee approached with condescending scrutiny, the displeasure transformed into a fierce expression.

"Lee, I have no choice! I must stay!"

Muttering to himself, Liam's hand trembled as it reached into his pocket, pulling out a small pistol, aiming it at Lee and loading a bullet awkwardly. "Ka—"

"Wait... what the hell are you doing? You mad?"

Lee couldn't have anticipated that Liam would resort to violence. In response, he instinctively took a few steps back, raised his hands, and signaled cautiously for Liam not to move.

"Mr. Lee, I've said it. I can't help it. Cooperate. Take me to the host. I need to personally verify the key. I have to stay. It's my only chance at survival!"

As Liam's hand shook, the gun's muzzle wavered. Forced to comply, Lee found himself escorted into a teleportation chamber. The journey to the main control room took a mere half-minute, yet when he emerged, he was drenched with sweat as if submerged in water. With a gun pressed against the back of his head, he approached the console of Eve step by step, feeling like a condemned prisoner.

Witnessing the imminent success of the mission, Liam grew increasingly excited. He began striking Lee's head with the gun's muzzle, urging impatiently. "Hurry! Hurry!"

Lee, lacking any special training, felt his nerves on edge, and Liam's erratic behavior pushed him beyond control. Finally, in a desperate move, he slammed his head into Liam.

"Bang!"

Following a sharp sound, Lee felt a burning heat on his face, his ears ringing in the aftermath. Instinctively, he reached for his cheek, finding warmth and stickiness on his hand. Simultaneously, he confronted the contorted visage of Liam, the gun's barrel quivering once more.

"Bang!"

Another sharp crack echoed, leaving Lee momentarily disoriented about the location of the gunshot. He stood petrified, motionless, anticipating his own descent. Unexpectedly, Liam howled, crumpling to the ground, the gun slipping from his grasp, and blood oozing from his shoulder.

"Help! Help me… I don't want to die…" Liam clutched his wounded shoulder, moaning in pain.

Lee snapped back to reality, spotting Doctor Hun in the shadows of the control room. He holstered his gun and approached slowly.

Surprised to see Doctor Hun, Lee exclaimed, "Doctor?"

Meantime, Liam's cries intensified. "Help me!" he pleaded, turning desperate eyes toward Hun. "Doctor, it's you. Save me, please! I'm valuable… Only I know the true purpose of the Foundation. Only I know Dave's secret—a secret beyond life itself…"

Lee recognized Liam's ramblings as the desperate plea of a dying man and swiftly ordered, "Eve, send the medical robots immediately!"

"Wait!" Hun halted the command.

"Doctor, are you really Doctor Hun? Do you know Saeed? No, you probably don't know. Dave won't tell anyone. Yes, he was hard destructed long ago, but he… he didn't do what he claimed. He… he didn't disclose any harmful information. His hard destruction is because he discovered the secret, the secret of Sirius!"

"Saeed?" Lee exclaimed. "Saeed Hosseini?"

"Yes, that's me. I'm still alive. Dave secretly kept me because I'm still useful. He wants to hoard this secret for himself…"

Liam's pained expression and labored breathing prompted Doctor Hun to crouch beside him. Gently caressing Liam's bloodied hand, Doctor Hun spoke softly, "keep talking. You won't die. Share the secrets with me, and I'll save you. I can still grant what you want."

Liam's eyes gleamed with intensity as he struggled to articulate, "the world is about to be destroyed, truly! Long ago… For tens of thousands of years, there was a Supernova eruption, leaving behind… a neutron star. Right, Sirius is not a binary star system; it went unnoticed until I… I discovered it. Not just discovered it, but

I crunched the numbers... precise calculations. Then, I... I reached a conclusion... The most crucial revelation in human history... I plotted the trajectory of Sirius D... Yes, D... The fourth star... The companion to the neutron star... and It's a black hole."

"Black hole? Did you say the companion star to Sirius's third star is a black hole?"

"Haha... Oh, yes... In astronomical calculations, I excel. I figured it out... It's a black hole! More importantly... I worked out its trajectory!"

Liam's excitement grew, breath quickening.

"It escaped! You know? The eruption set it free! And it's headed our way... toward our solar system... It's approaching us! Hahah... Hah!" Liam suddenly burst into laughter. "It's moving at an incredible speed! Unbelievably fast!"

"What?" Lee and Doctor Hun exclaimed simultaneously.

Liam reveled in their strong reactions, closed his eyes, bit his lip, and continued, "understand? Soon... People will notice Neptune's orbit shifting... It might have happened already, and now you grasp the idea, right? The Foundation is the sole... Only it can evade, escape this catastrophe... All else... Nothing will survive... All will be torn apart... and obliterated... The black hole will annihilate everything! But, but we'll survive, Doctor, won't we? We'll endure here in the Foundation. Let's initiate acceleration immediately! Give me the key; we need to do it."

"Do you believe this nonsense?" Doctor Hun glanced at Lee and threw him the question.

"I think it's better to call for medical assistance and revive him," Lee replied uneasily.

"Bang!" Doctor Hun fired a shot, the sound reverberating as the bullet struck Liam's head.

"I've received a message from Zhukov regarding your boss, Dave. Let's go!" Doctor Hun, covering his nose with a disgusted look, exited the control room.

Lee felt as if he were glued to the floor, unable to move for a long moment.

"Come with me. There's something you need to know," Doctor Hun commanded.

Zhukov's message came through the holographic projection, revealing an old face with a haggard expression. Lee recognized the face as his boss, Dave, who appeared drastically changed from months ago. Dave wasn't in his usual luxurious office; instead, the surroundings were dimly lit with monotonous furnishings, and the only recognizable element was a small table in front of him. A shadow moved to the center of the projection, and once the scene stabilized, Lee identified the person as Zhukov.

As Zhukov slowly retreated, Dave, visibly frustrated, began speaking, "I concede, Doctor, but winning isn't a certainty for you. Things have come to this point. All secrets are no longer secrets. Do you comprehend that everything will ultimately come to an end? This must be your deepest fear. Death profoundly terrifies you; otherwise, you wouldn't have sought me out. You found the right person. In this world, only I can alter its course. Only I can halt the aging of your flesh. So, the Foundation is nothing without me! Before the apocalypse arrives, only I should choose its citizens! As for you, Doctor, your Pioneers are nothing more than a joke! It is the immortal warriors that are indispensable in interstellar travel, not slaves at the mercy of others! Those walking corpses, hmm... they can't even compare to a robot servant! I understand your intent completely. You perpetually feel superior, unwilling to command any species stronger and smarter than you. Unfortunately, your aspirations fell through, and I haven't dared to modify a single cell of yours. You've probably sensed it with your old wisdom. As you often claim to be unique in this world, who would dare to make you anything less than yourself?"

At this moment, a peculiar smile crept onto Dave's face, causing the doctor's expression to quickly stiffen, and several green tendons bulged on his forehead. If Dave had noticed the change, he might have felt satisfied, but he remained in the interrogation room from over an hour ago, continuing, "have you observed that your body is deteriorating day by day? Yes, this is the most natural process. As for the Foundation, without me, at best, it's merely your super-luxurious tomb."

Doctor Hun shouted, interrupted the projection, and staggered backward, almost falling, but fortunately, Lee promptly supported him, holding his arm and helping him to sit on a chair.

"Tell Zhukov to handle it properly!" The doctor weakly ordered.

"Yiming, I always believed the world couldn't do without me now, and it wouldn't go without me in the future." Doctor Hun's feeble voice gave Lee an ominous feeling.

"I was all wrong! In truth, I already knew. How could he deceive me? How?" Hun transformed into someone entirely different, resembling an ordinary old man nearing his limits. His gaze wandered into the distance as he continued, "remember when you asked if I dream? I do, especially lately. Lee Nan appears in my dreams—why do I keep dreaming about her?"

In that moment, he fumbled in his pocket, extracting a ring. Trembling, he attempted to hand it to Lee, but it slipped through his frail grasp, clattering to the floor. Reacting swiftly, Lee stepped forward, preventing it from rolling too far. As he grabbed the ring in his hand, he was surprised to recognize its uncanny resemblance to the one he owns.

"This ring, I'll give it to you. You're still the commander here. You have the highest authority now; do as you wish!"

Lee intended to return the ring, but upon hearing this, his hand froze mid-air. He glanced at the old man before him, sensing moisture in the corners of his eyes. It was a scene hauntingly familiar—many years ago, in a San Francisco hospital, he stood in a similar position facing his dying father.

"Do you know? There are only two rings like this in the world. The metal used to make them is unique—the first new substance I obtained after the success of the particle synthesis experiment. It's the heaviest known element within the stable island. I named it 'Naninium.'"

Tears welled up in Lee's eyes. He stepped forward, knelt down in front of Doctor Hun, and held his hands.

"Yiming, I should have let you read Asimov's book. It's all my fault. If you read it, you'll know about a character, *the Mule*. He conquered the universe but led a miserable and lonely life…"

Seeing the sadness on Lee's face, Doctor Hun smiled. "Don't be sad. Death isn't the end; it's just one point among many in your entire life. I regret trying to extend the line while neglecting the brilliance of each point."

Gently holding Lee's hand, Doctor Hun whispered, "I'm tired. It's time for a rest."

Lee released his hand and exited slowly.

After closing the door, a sudden "bang" startled him. Surprisingly, his emotions didn't undergo intense upheaval. Instead, an unusual calmness settled over him at that moment.

EPILOGUE

The scorching sun of midsummer mercilessly roasted the pitiful metal carriage, transforming it into a huge furnace. Lyu sat on a long bench near the window, feeling restless and irritable due to the heat. She stretched her neck, running her fingers through her long hair, hoping for a touch of breeze to pass through and alleviate the annoying stickiness clinging to her body. Having just taken a shower, she remained damp. However, the refreshing coolness lasted only a few minutes before being engulfed by a continuous stream of sweat. Being immersed in water all the time was impractical, akin to having an illness. She didn't want to copy Ethelinda either, lying on the floor all messy with her clothes barely covering anything.

Suddenly, a rare cool breeze swept through, causing Lyu to involuntarily loosen her shirt, welcoming the refreshing coolness. Simultaneously, the sky darkened, and in the distance, vast dark clouds approached, accompanied by flashes of lightning and rumbling thunder.

"It's finally raining!" Lyu raised her eyebrows, urging Ethelinda, "Ethie! Ethie! It's raining! Get the laundry!" Ethelinda, still half-asleep, hardly mumbled a response.

Lyu sighed, stepped over her and grabbed the doorknob, jumping down to retrieve the laundry, which was hanging on the rope and dancing with the wind. As raindrops began to fall, Lyu felt relieved, tossing the laundry towards Ethelinda.

Suddenly, a figure in the mix of rain and mist caught her attention.

"Temur!" Lyu exclaimed, grabbing an umbrella and jumping out into the pouring rain. When she returned, both of them were drenched. Lyu handed clothes to Temur, urging him to change.

Temur unloaded his backpack with one hand, handed it to his sister, took the clothes with the other, and turned, slipping into the bathroom facing the car door.

The backpack's weight raised suspicions in Lyu's heart. She voiced her concern, "Temur, you didn't go back there again, did you?"

Since the day they left Lee's apartment, she had repeatedly instructed him not to go there casually. However, at this moment, she hoped he would answer *yes*. She could scold him again, but she could also take the opportunity to ask if he had seen him in person.

The sound of rushing water from the bathroom came, and Temur, still washing, replied, "I did go there, but please don't scold me. I didn't take anything from his home!"

Lyu doubted it and opened the rain soaked backpack, only to find several old notebooks inside. In this era, it was rare for people to come across paper and pens. The unusual nature of these items sparked Lyu's curiosity, prompting her to pick one up and gently rub it in her hands.

"Temur, what's inside the bag?" She asked.

"I don't know. I found it on this trip. Originally, they were in a box in the hallway," Temur said, changing his clothes and handing a note to Lyu. He added, "here, this is a note for him. It says it's from his dearest person. Sister, there are some things I feel you should know about Lee Yiming. I feel that he is not as good as you think."

Lyu's heart tightened as she opened the rain-soaked note, revealing blurry yet delicately written words:

Yiming,

It is now the appropriate moment for you to know the truth, and for me to convey the apologies that have lingered in my heart for numerous years.

The one who loves you most,

Lyu felt a pang in her nose, holding back tears.

She sat back on the bench, took a deep breath, and began to read one notebook after another. They exuded the unique antique scent of passing time, silently pulling Lyu's thoughts into another world.

June 15, 2059, Overcast Turning to Showers

Never did I expect to hear about Elisa's departure from Mia's lips.

Though I had sensed it coming, preparing myself mentally for this moment, it turns out I merely deluded myself into thinking I was ready. This isn't the first time I've felt utterly defeated, but unlike the previous instance, I find myself devoid of the faith and strength needed for another battle.

It was my love for Elisa that allowed me to climb out of the abyss of despair, and now that Elisa is gone, with whom shall I share my gaze?

Of course, there's still the love for Yiming, but ironically, I can't forget that half of his existence comes from him!

...

February 15, 2059, Sunny

Today, I finally saw Yiming, the one who tugs at my heartstrings.

I couldn't engage in a conversation with him like kin, and our meeting lacked any warmth, leaving me with profound pain and regret. His countenance still carries a shadow that lingers in my heart to some extent. I hope I persuaded him, or perhaps Mia did.

In my heart, the satisfaction revenge could bring has never captivated me as it does now. The meticulously planned scheme of several years is on the verge of success, and the prospect of its realization fills me with joy!

Elisa vehemently opposed this journey, yet she did not intervene. Over these many years, we've lived amidst constant quarrels, cold wars, and reconciliations. Surprisingly, rather than driving us apart, these struggles have brought us closer.

The next time I meet her, I might find myself acting coy, apologizing to her.

....

January 1, 2059, Sunny

Another new year begins.

I don't believe I can quickly escape the shadows of defeat.

Abandoning the idea of destroying the Foundation is out of the question. Aside from resorting to this method, how else can I make his cold heart feel even a hint of remorse other than letting his life-long efforts crumble before him?

......

December 31, 2058, Cloudy

Received news of Yiming's safe landing.

The suspended anxiety lifted, yet the hatred resurfaced with renewed intensity.

......

September 10, 2058, Overcast

Received a message from Elisa this morning: Mission failed!

......

February 19, 2058, Sunny

Early in the morning, Elisa informed me that the starship carrying a new batch of Pioneers had set sail.

Elisa confessed to me that she never revealed to Mia that the true purpose was to destroy the Foundation. The mission she conveyed to Mia sounded much nobler: not only to reclaim the Foundation for all of humanity but also to successfully and peacefully subvert the Commander of the Foundation and bring him back to Earth. She explained to me that this was a political necessity; she had to ensure that all the followers involved in this mission felt they had a noble motive.

Many times, I may not agree with Elisa's methods, but deep down, I understand that they have been the key to her continuous success over these years.

February 14, 2058, Sunny

Today marked the most exhilarating moment of my life. After brunch, Mia bid me farewell, expressing her intention to embark on a journey. I gently touched her hand and kissed her cheek. As I gazed into her tear-filled eyes, guilt washed over me. I almost felt the urge to explain to her that the entire mission entrusted to her by the High Priestess was a meticulously planned scheme of mine over the past few years.

Many of the lies were not deliberate. If I hadn't intended to conceal my relationship with Elisa when we first met, then all subsequent lies would have ceased to exist.

In my heart, I prayed for her, blessed her. I envisioned her safe return, bringing Yiming with her. I pictured the four of us finding a place to seclude, a new journey in my life.

……

January 12, 2057, Overcast

Elisa told me that yesterday she conveyed her mission to Mia for the first time. Mia's calm demeanor left her highly satisfied.

……

December 3, 2056, Overcast

I had Mia accompany me on a mountain climb, and all the way, she held my hand as we walked in silence.

Several times, I couldn't resist the urge to take off the wig I wore on my head—Mia was unaware that it was a gift from Elisa, meant to shield my brainwaves. Since Elisa noticed Mia's rapidly advancing abilities, she worried that Mia might delve into my inner thoughts. Moreover, I faintly sensed a hint of jealousy from Elisa towards Mia.

However, if Mia couldn't feel my brainwaves at all, wouldn't she become suspicious?

Every time I look at Mia, she exudes innocence and purity, with occasional traces of sadness on her face. If I inquire, she would simply smile lightly, saying it's nothing. If her nature is truly this pure, then even if she senses I'm hiding something, she may not want to ask too much!

......

January 1, 2053, Overcast

How many New Years have I spent in Edinburgh? I've lost count.

Elisa is still absent, but she had someone deliver a gift to me.

......

June 15, 2052, Sunny

It's been several months since I heard from Elisa. The unease accompanies my longing, making it difficult for me to sleep through the night.

Mia must have sensed something; she always initiated conversations with me and even helped me style my hair today. Seeing her young and delicate face in the mirror, I couldn't help but admire her, saying, "Mia, you're really beautiful." Her cheeks flushed with embarrassment as she shyly replied, "Madam Shaw, you define what beauty is. You must have captured many hearts when you were young!"

At that moment, I almost pulled her into a tight embrace.

......

April 23, 2052, Rain Showers

Had a brief conversation with Elisa this morning. She informed me that significant events had unfolded within the Corporation. The Old Man had become increasingly distrustful, not putting faith in anyone. The mission on Saturn's moon Titan was unexpectedly halted by him, and the entire top echelon was in turmoil. She mentioned that she would have to reduce contact with me in the short term.

So, what about Yiming? Will he return safely?

......

September 3, 2049, Sunny

Having lived with Mia for a few months, I find myself gradually growing fond of this girl. She brings back the long-lost feeling of being a mother in my heart.

Mia has been keeping from me the fact that she joined the Druids a while ago. Let her continue to preserve this secret. If she were to discover my relationship with Elisa, it's hard to say if she could accept it.

......

July 1, 2049, Cloudy

Sharmin's extraordinary talent is astonishing. Elisa attempted brief telepathic exercises with her and believes her aptitude surpasses all the priestesses she has encountered, including herself. Elisa is determined to nurture Sharmin, stating that she will become a formidable asset for us.

Sharmin seems to have been aware of her exceptional intuition beyond ordinary people for quite some time. When I explained to her that the blood flowing in her veins carries the lineage of Magus, she showed no surprise. Instead, she happily accepted the name I carefully chose for her.

I named her Mia.

......

May 8, 2049, Sunny

Elisa brought news about Sharmin. It turns out she is the only daughter of Lady Haelion, who once ruled over Shallow Harbor. Unfortunately, Shallow Harbor now lies in ruins, explaining her constant sorrow. Every time I think about it, my sympathy and compassion overwhelm me.

The good news is that Sharmin actually joined the local Druid organization when escaping Shallow Harbor. So, Elisa could establish direct contact with her without needing my assistance.

May 3, 2049, Rain Showers

Had a lengthy conversation with Elisa. I brought up Sharmin, and she expressed interest in incorporating her into the organization. I suggested arranging a meeting between them, but Elisa disagreed, opting to have her subordinates gather information first.

Elisa's caution reminded me that I'm indeed not as prudent in such matters as she is.

......

April 20, 2049, Sunny

I found a tenant, a girl of striking beauty. Her demeanor is gentle, yet her expression carries a hint of sorrow.

The moment I saw her, my intuition told me that the blood flowing in this girl, with eyes like emeralds, was extraordinary.

Her name is Sharmin Haelion, and her lineage traces back to a renowned shamanic family. Can she read my thoughts? It's hard to say, but there is always an elusive warmth in her gaze when she looks at me.

......

January 3, 2049, Overcast

During my conversation with Elisa, I mentioned my loneliness, and she suggested finding a tenant. This suggestion angered me, and the conversation ended on an unpleasant note.

Upon reflection, I don't find it to be a bad idea, so why couldn't I control my emotions at that moment?

......

January 1, 2049, Overcast

New Year.

Elisa has finally gained recognition within the Corporation. However, with this recognition, the chances of meeting her have become increasingly scarce. This New Year, I find myself celebrating alone.

I understand in the onslaught of time, my appearance has already shattered, and my body grows increasingly frail. A bout of flu in early winter left me bedridden, and if it weren't for Elisa arriving in time, I'm unsure if I, this little old lady, could have weathered through.

I begin to reminisce about Shaw Lin. Memories invariably return to that winter night long ago, when the icy river water stiffened my limbs, blurred my consciousness, and only allowed him to laboriously drag me back to the shore. Upon learning of my six-month pregnancy, he couldn't help but reproach me. Yet, seeing my tears, he encouraged me to carry the child, expressing his willingness to help raise him. So, have I never truly loved him? But why do tears well up in my eyes when his face comes to mind?

I also find myself missing the San Francisco Bay—missing the thick fog, missing the blazing sun. I despise Boston's harsh winters and summers and am not truly fond of Edinburgh's unpredictable weather. After all these years, I've come to realize that the climate of the San Francisco Bay, where I briefly lived for a few years, is my favorite.

December 24, 2048, Overcast

During the day, I retrieved the meticulously crafted ring from the jewelry shop. It looks identical to the one I left for Yiming, with the same pattern engraved on the outer surface, but this time, it's made of platinum—how could I possibly obtain that peculiar metal from before?

This is intended to be the New Year's gift I plan to give to Elisa.

……

May 2, 2048, Sunny

Elisa sent me the information about Lee Yiming early in the morning. She believes my speculation was correct—this Lee Yiming indeed hails from Northern California. He recently obtained a Ph.D. from Berkeley, his family resides in San Francisco, and his father's name is Shaw Lin.

It's been a while since I last cried, but today the tears just won't stop flowing. Elisa asked if I wanted to move in with her. I appreciate her kindness, but she doesn't understand—my sorrow comes from the past, and the wounds of the past are not something that can be healed in the future.

May 1, 2048, Sunny

I can hardly believe what I saw in the news today!

Yiming! He's being dispatched to Titan! But when did he join the Corporation? Elisa never mentioned it to me!

He is truly my Yiming! That handsome face! Those eyes that always held a hint of shyness!

Could it be him? Could it be that he found him? Could it be that he's grooming him?

No, this is a reality I cannot accept. He has already taken everything from me, and I cannot let him take away my Yiming!

……

March 1, 2045, Cloudy

Elisa is going to work for the Corporation, reigniting hope in my heart.

She asked me to move with her, and I didn't immediately agree. I know she is reluctant to leave me alone in Edinburgh.

I have never told her that in this lifetime, I probably will never have the courage to approach that city. I will never forget how I was heartlessly abandoned, how much humiliation I endured, and the depths of despair I experienced there.

If it weren't for Shaw Lin, I might have died in the river long ago. He is a good person, but what I owe him, I'm afraid, can only be fully repaid in the next life.

......

April 15, 2040, Overcast

Elisa is an outstanding pragmatist, and this is why I have so much confidence in my revenge plan. She has founded a company dedicated to mind control, and I understand her intentions. Those who closely monitor the activities of the Corporation can sense that their ability to control collective consciousness has long reached its limits.

......

January 1, 2040, Overcast, turning to light rain

Another New Year.

During dinner, Elisa mentioned her new plan. She said she had decided to infiltrate the Corporation from within. I am a bit worried about her safety, but she said this could pave a new path towards the ultimate goal.

......

September 9, 2037, Overcast

The mission failed. In reality, we should have anticipated it. How could we have obtained his whereabouts so easily?

......

July 11, 2035, Cloudy

Today, the Druid Order was officially disbanded. Elisa told me that this is exactly what we wanted. The government's action undoubtedly fueled the fire, and the citizens who were initially neutral have almost all shifted towards our side. She has been planning to establish an underground resistance organization for a long time, and now is the best time.

......

March 3, 2032, Sunny

In the evening, Elisa and I went mountain climbing. At the top, we happened to catch the sunset, a breathtaking sight.

Elisa embraced me and kissed me.

"I have a plan—" I took the opportunity to bring up the revenge plan that had been brewing in my heart for a long time. I didn't tell her that my target was a specific person. Instead, I made her believe that my intention was to save this world on the brink of collapse.

After hearing it, she held me even tighter.

......

April 2, 2031, Cloudy

I saw on the news that France officially joined the "Exclusive Market," leaving only Brittany and a few small free states on the Scandinavian Peninsula as barely independent in the entire continent.

I don't know how long Scotland can hold out. If Scotland falls, I will leave, go to Northern Europe, or even return to North America.

I watched his live broadcast speech in the French Parliament, passionate and eloquent. A young woman who had never faced adversity happened to encounter him in his prime; how could she not be captivated? So, I gradually realized that this was not my fault at all.

I have always had thoughts of revenge, but never as intense as now, and never felt it so real. I won't overestimate my strength, but Elisa will definitely do everything she can to help me. She has already earned the love and admiration of the Druid followers, who secretly regard her as a priestess. She will surely use her power to assist me.

......

August 15, 2026, Overcast

Elisa bought a house at the foot of the hill, and you can see the sea with just a turn outside. This reminded me of the days when Shaw Lin and I moved to San Francisco. We lived in an apartment at the corner of Lombard Street, where you could also see the sea with just a turn. I would stand quietly in the street, holding little Yiming who couldn't walk yet, daydreaming in the sea breeze.

With the house, it feels like settling down. Elisa wanted to give me a pseudonym; she picked several, but I wasn't satisfied. Finally, I told her, "just call me Madam Shaw."

I was originally Madam Shaw, in the past and now. Shaw Lin was kind to me, and I shouldn't forget him.

......

July 3, 2026, Sunny

Northern California has declared independence, establishing a new republic.

These days, I've been contemplating whether I should go back to San Francisco to see Yiming before leaving. Elisa didn't mind, but she asked me to keep my distance and just take a few glimpses. Taking a few glimpses would be fine. Counting the years, he's already eight!

July 2, 2026, Sunny

The situation is becoming dire.
Elisa and I decided to openly acknowledge our relationship several years ago—back when liberalism was thriving, and we took pride in it. Now it's different; there are almost daily instances of extrajudicial punishment in Boston.

Elisa has chosen to leave the Americas because she's concerned for my safety. So, she asked me to pick a place I'd like to go. I blurted out, "Edinburgh!"

When I was very young, I watched an animated film called "The Illusionist," and it left an indelible impression on me. Since then, Edinburgh has been a place that captivates my soul and dreams.

……

March 20, 2020, Overcast

Now, I'm hiding in a narrow apartment in Boston, feeling extremely depressed. The stay-at-home order hasn't ended, and the pandemic outlook is grim, making it hard for me not to doubt if my choices were wrong.

For several nights in a row, I dreamt of Yiming, dreaming of him being taken away in an ambulance, and of him crying loudly while Shaw Lin looked helpless. If it were just a few days later, I might have made a completely different decision, and Yiming's life wouldn't have changed because of it. However, whether that would be good or bad, who can know?

I could have lived my whole life with Shaw Lin, but I could never love him. Elisa is different; every time I smell her fragrance, I tremble, she bewitches me, makes me sacrifice, and also makes me fear.

Am I really destined to repeat the mistakes of the past?

March 15, 2020, Overcast

Finally, Elisa helped me settle into an apartment, with the Charles River outside the window, and the distant cries of seagulls in the early morning. The weather on the East Coast is cold, and Boston still shows no signs of spring, making my mood even more gloomy.

Massachusetts just issued a stay-at-home order, but due to the nature of Elisa's work, she's becoming more absent from home!

The Moleskine notebook I ordered from Amazon has arrived, even though it was delayed for several days due to the pandemic. At least my enthusiasm for journaling hasn't waned.

That's good; I'll use it to record the brand new life I'm about to embrace!

These notebooks were filled with miscellaneous details, each with a different style – some were finely bound in genuine leather, some were made of cardstock with loose pages, and some were even hand-bound. Looking at the dates, the timespan covered three to four decades.

Lyu flipped through one after another, reading every word that mentioned "Yiming." She hoped to piece together this chaotic series of fragments into a complete story. When she finally put down the last one, the post-rain sunshine happened to slide in through the window. In a daze, she felt as if the rain had lasted for a century.

POSTSCRIPT

At the outset of writing, I didn't realize that the first task was to tell a story clearly. After a wild outburst of impulsive expression, I found myself unable to continue suddenly. The already written chapters were disjointed and incoherent.

The reason I could continue later was that in April, Douban initiated a writing competition. Without much thought, I signed up, hoping to ride the wave of online traffic. Writing alone without readership wouldn't provide the necessary feedback for improvement.

The actual effect was quite ironic. In an era dominated by social media influencers, it is unprecedentedly difficult to get the voice of an ordinary individual heard. So, until now, I miss the BBS era when everyone had an equal opportunity to voice their opinions.

However, there were positive factors as well, such as the requirement for regular updates that finally forced me to complete it.

The subsequent time was mainly spent on revisions, with the core still aiming to tell this story well.

There are two lines of character relationships in the story. One involves Lee Yiming, Sharmin (Mia), and Chen Lyu, openly portrayed. The other line involves characters like Hun, Lee Nan (Madam Shaw), and Lin Shaw, hidden in the background. Lee received the most attention in terms of words, but he is not the person I want to focus on. He is ordinary and lacks personality, much like the most common people around us: selfish, without commitment, indecisive. However, if he happens to be handsome and with a striking appearance, he can easily win the hearts of women. And if, by chance, he is thrown into the crossroads of changing the world, he may still make some remarkable decisions.

I believe the true protagonists of the story should be Mia and Madam Shaw. Their delicate and pure hearts are what I strive to show readers.

Lin Shaw, January 1, 2021.

Made in United States
Orlando, FL
20 March 2024